THE AU PAIR

There's No Returning Home
AYON READS

AYON PUBLISHING

CONTENTS

Chapter 1

ENOUGH IS ENOUGH

"You worthless sack of shit!" "Don't walk away when I am talking to you!" I yanked the door open and stormed out of the apartment. She cursed my name as I ran up the three flights of rustic wooden stairs to my haven on the seventh floor. "Come back down here!" "I am still speaking to you!"

I ignored her yells as I stumbled my way to the front door of my room. Out of breath and with tears in my eyes I pulled the heavy iron key from my pocket and I unlocked the door. *Click, clack, click clack* the old metal door screeched as I opened it.

"You'll pay for walking out on me!" She wailed. Her voice was distant now, but I still looked behind me to make sure she had not followed me. She hadn't, so I hurriedly stepped inside my room.

Wasting no time, I slammed and bolted the door behind me causing the mirror on it to shake violently. Crap. I ran over to stabilize it, and as I did that I caught a glimpse of my own reflection. I felt disgusted.

Was this really how I looked now? Had the Dax family caused me so much hurt, pain and fear that my physical self had changed? Yes, they had. I looked awful. The happy and outgoing guy from just months ago was gone.

My tanned skin had become an ashy pale white, and that was because I worked so many hours that my only free time was at night. My body fat had all but disappeared, and I was at least ten pounds underweight.

Even my bright smile had slightly shifted since one of the kids had broken my retainers, and my golden hair was turning darker because I never saw the sun. This was not me. Tears filled my eyes, and I lost it. I let everything out.

I cried till my eyes were dry, and until my shirt was soaked. This was no way to live. Enough was enough. I was done living in fear and harassment. I was done taking orders from the Daxes. They would not get another ounce of my blood or sweat from me. Their punching bag was leaving.

Never again would I give them the satisfaction of treating me like a prisoner. No, I shouldn't say like a prisoner because at least inmates had rights. Something that the Daxes took from me. To them I was nothing but a mere peasant.

A peasant who cleaned everything from the toilets to the hairy clogged drains. A peasant who got nothing but table scraps to eat. A peasant who was fucken fed up with it all. It is truly unbelievable that I had suffered over four months with them without completely losing it until today.

Anyone in their right mind would have left this awful family right away, but the truth is, I couldn't. I was their slave. They had taken my passport away from me, but even if they hadn't, I was still confined to them. Not by ropes or chains per say, but by the irony of life.

I did not have enough funds to go back home. I had spent every single dime I had on my ticket to this hell hole. Which sadly left me with a tough predicament. Stay with the Daxes and have a roof over my head and scraps of food to eat, or live in the streets and beg for food. Not an easy choice.

Moreover, as much as I would have wished to ask my own family for money or help, I couldn't. Unfortunately, we always lived paycheck to paycheck, and the last thing I wanted to do was worry my loved ones regarding my situation. It was my fault that I got into this mess, not theirs.

Plus, as pathetic as this sounds, I guess my pride also contributed to me not leaving. I did not want to be seen as a disappointment by coming back before my gap year was over. Being viewed as a failure by those that I care for was a big no no, especially after all it took on my part to convince my familia that going to Europe was a good idea.

It came as a big shock to everyone when I announced that I would be taking a gap year abroad. Everyone assumed I would go straight into university after graduation since I was a top honor roll student. My family and friends told me that it was not a good idea to take a gap year, but I was headstrong on going to France.

"I'll grow as a person, and come back stronger than ever." That was the same phrase I would repeat to anyone who tried to convince me to go to college, or to get a job locally instead. I regret uttering that sentence every day of my life now.

I had been terribly wrong, and because of that I've been suffering in silence for months. If I had listened and gone to school, maybe then I would have grown as a person. Sadly, I eagerly chose to go Europe to become an au pair for the Dax family instead.

I was so excited by the idea of becoming an au pair. I read all the articles of how it was the perfect job for anyone looking for a new cultural experience. It seemed so exciting. You go to a foreign country. You live with a host family, and they pay for your meals plus board, and even for a language school.

All you have to do in return is work five hours a day for your host family. Doing things like light housework, cooking and some child-care like babysitting. Nothing to it, and you are even guaranteed one full day off a week, plus a little bit of pocket money.

To put it simple you do your share of the work as if you were part of the family. You teach them your mother tongue and they teach you theirs. A true cultural experience.

I really believed I had found something unique. The adventurous side of me was thrilled, but man, how wrong had I been. Getting kicked and slapped by kids on a daily basis while adults yell at you is not a good feeling.

I should have known this was "too perfect." Instead of getting a culture experience and gaining a new family I got literal hell. I became a slave of the Daxes. I was severely abused verbally and physically by them. I learned to fear, and for the first time of my life I lost the sense of who I was. I became a victim of the Daxes.

In just four short months my world had been flipped upside down. My dignity had been torn away from me, but that shit was ending now. Today was the day that I would get all of who I was back. The chains have been broken.

That's right I repeated slowly as I gently wiped the last remains of my tears from my face. The hour of weeping is over. My liberation starts now, and there is no time to squander. With a sense of determination, I grabbed my suitcase and tossed it onto my couch bed.

I began to throw all my clothes inside without folding it. I didn't care. I needed to leave immediately. I had to escape my tormentors. The flight that I had booked back home this morning was in 4 hours, and I did not want her coming into my room while I was still here.

I was sure she had called her husband after I stormed out of their apartment. I had maybe 45 minutes tops to vamoose before he came into my room with the locksmith, and I did not want to be here when he arrived.

He was worse than she was. He thrived over making others feel like dirt. If she was a monster then he was the devil, and I am certain she would make our argument look like an all out war of the dead.

We had argued over my passport. I had not been in possession of my own documentation for over four months! The Daxes had tricked me into handing them my passport on the very first day of my arrival.

That said, what really sucked was how easily they had gotten my passport to begin with, and sadly it was me who had given it to them right before I even stepped into their house. I was so gullible then.

I remember ringing their doorbell on my first day, and before I even set my luggage down they told me, "We need your passport for immigration reasons, but we'll give it back in a few days." I recall thinking it was strange that they would ask for my passport before they even greeted me, but I decided to give them the benefit of the doubt.

I wanted to trust them. I wanted to believe that we were going to be a true family. I mean that is what the au pair program is, you get a "new family," so I gave them my document without second guessing anything.

Regrettably I soon learned that I had made the wrong choice. Shortly after stepping foot in their house the youngest kid punched me in the gut, and threw a glass bowl at my forehead. Luckily it didn't shatter, but part of my pride did as the parents laughed and laughed.

I wanted to ask for my passport back at the very moment, but as pathetic as this sounds I wanted them to like me, so I didn't. Instead I made a promise to myself that I would give it a week before I made any rash decisions.

Fast forward to the end of seven awful days, the only thing I got back from the Daxes were yells of humiliation and more bruises from the youngest child. Needless to say, by the end of the week I knew it was time to not only ask for my document back but also to have a serious conversation with the Daxes on how I was being treated.

Moreover, I also needed to have a talk with them on why they hadn't registered me for my language classes that were supposed to be starting that very next day. Ironically, even with all these things going against me I still held onto hope that I could fix things with them.

Truthfully speaking, I was quite optimistic that a sincere and simple conversation would make everything better. I really thought that maybe our "misunderstandings" had been a cultural difference. Sadly, looking back, at that point I was still so naive. The worst was yet to come.

I vividly remember going down the stairs and knocking on their door like it was just yesterday. Juliette, the host mom answered the door, and instead of saying hi, she said, "Why the hell are you here so early?" I remember being taken aback, and without thinking I blurted out, I need my passport, and the money for the language courses.

She stared at me in total silence for about five seconds, and I knew immediately that my life had changed forever. She got a cruel twisted look on her oval shaped face. Her beady eyes got even smaller and she started to laugh. A laughter that was meant to hurt and to not give joy.

"Hahaha," she cackled as her black bob bounced up and down on her shoulders. She looked scary, but then she got serious. Her ghostly white face turned bright red, and I swear her beady eyes grew an inch.

Reflecting back on it now, that was the moment that she revealed who she truly was. The words that she uttered next will forever be with me.

"Wait, you thought I would waste money on a language school for a dumb backward hick like you?" "You are not worth it." "In fact you do not even have the worth to speak our beautiful French language." "It would sound like an animal trying to speak."

She then gave me the evilest smile that I had ever seen in my life, and said, "You are not getting your passport back until your contract of one year ends." "You are our pet now." "Oh, and if you think that you can go to the authorities and ask for your passport back, well think again."

"They won't believe that a classy family like us would ever take the passport of some trash like you." "Hahaha, and as punishment for lying they would probably void your passport, and ensure that you never get one again in your scum life." I had no words to express what I felt at that moment other than fear and anger.

I was thousands of miles away from home with no money and I was alone. All I could do was keep my mouth shut because at the end of the day Juliette was right. Before coming to France I had researched everything that I could about au pairs, and unfortunately while not common, some au pairs had had their passports also taken.

They were only returned back to them after their contract was up. Of course, they were forced to work as servants. Woefully, none were ever believed, so why would I be any different?

It was that realization that showed me how fucked up the world truly was, but it was also that understanding that allowed me to make one simple vow to myself. I would do all in my ability to get my passport back before I ever stayed a year with the Dax family.

Having said that, soon after that conversation things got worse. I took humiliation after humiliation. I had to not only wash their toilets, but their friends' toilets. I cooked not only for them, but their friends. I was not allowed to speak unless spoken to.

I was called every name in the book, from *pute, to connard*. I was even forced to clean their underwear by hand. Once I asked why I could not just use the washing machine, and Alexandre the host dad grabbed a pair of dirty underwear and tossed them at my face and said, "You see how those smell, that's why!"

It was awful, but I persevered, and kept my faith without ever worrying anyone back at home. In fact, I never once told my family what was happening. I made it seem like I was living my dream. They were happy for me and their happiness gave me the strength to stay strong up until that fateful day where I discovered where my passport was being hidden.

Chapter 2

THE PASSPORT TO FREEDOM

I was quietly scrubbing the floor tiles with a toothbrush one morning when I overheard Juliette, my hypocrite host mother talking to her friend over the phone. They were laughing about how she had snagged the perfect servant from the USA. "Yeah, he can't go home because he has no money!" "His family is dirt poor too." "It is too perfect."

"He can't even complain to immigration here in France because we are giving him food and board, so it would be his word against ours." "Hahaha!" She was laughing so hard, but I did not react. I just kept listening. She didn't know that I was in the hallway eavesdropping, and that is when I heard where she placed my passport.

She had it in the drawer of her closet. I knew that I could not take my document at that very moment because I still did not have quite enough funds to go home, so I bid my time. Thankfully, after three more weeks of patiently waiting I had enough money saved for my ticket back home!

Oh, but not from the pocket money that the Dax family was supposed to give me, of course they never did that. I was lucky to even have access to their expired food!

I graciously earned the money for my ticket by giving my sweet neighbor private English classes on Sundays. Sunday was my only "free" day because the Daxes had to go to their "charity events." They were gone all day pretending to be "the sweet rich and giving family." If only people knew the truth, but at least that gave me a day off. Which, in turn, allowed me to work six hours each Sunday with my grateful neighbor. All I had to do was talk English with her.

Funny enough, we grew quite close during these four months, yet I never told her how the Daxes were using me like a toy. She is well into her late eighties, and I did not want to worry her.

She already had enough on her plate. Her health was slowly deteriorating. Fortunately, since we lived right next to each other, it was easy for me to quickly stop by and check in on her before going back to my place. *Hrmph*, "my place," if you can call it that.

In reality I lived in a tiny room, but I was extremely grateful for it. Candidly speaking, that was the only thing the Dax family did right as members of the au pair program. They gave me a decent place to stay.

I had a private chambre de bonne, or "little room" on the seventh floor of the building they co-owned with the other tenants. My place was not much to look at, but it was cozy enough. Nonamusingly, in medieval times it was where most servants lived, but nowadays they are considered "student rooms;" or in my case a servant room still.

There are always one or two chambre de bonnes on the last floor of most buildings in Paris. They tend to be super small, and the ceilings are quite low, but I didn't mind that.

At least I had my own personal space, away from the Daxes. In retrospect they probably only gave it to me because they did not want someone who wasn't at "their level" living with them, but that didn't matter to me now.

What mattered now was for me to finish packing. I quickly grabbed the last pair of jeans from my cabinets and tossed them into the suitcase. Wasting no time, I zipped the old black suitcase up, and then I was finished.

My heart was beating rapidly, and with a flickering hand I reached into my pocket and pulled out my passport. I stared at it in disbelief. I HAD MY PASSPORT!

After months of waiting, and over three weeks of preparation, I had gone in for the kill! Not concerned at all that Juliette was there, I had run right past her, and I had entered her room. Without a care in the world I went and grabbed my passport, as she yelled behind me.

That was why she was furious with me right now, but I didn't give two shits because not only did I have my documentation with me. I also had my ticket home. I was leaving this inferno!

Tears of joy were starting to fill my eyes, but I took a deep breath to calm myself down. I didn't want to cry anymore. I wanted to feel at peace, and enjoy my last moments in my petit room. As strange as it sounds, it was my safe haven from all the hell that I went through.

I remember the first time I came into my room to escape the first major Dax humiliation. I think it was the second week that I was here when it happened. Mylene, the snobby freckled-faced youngest Dax child, had thrown her food all over the floor on purpose, and told me to pick it up.

I had told her no, and that she had to pick it up. Juliette, the host mother slapped me and she threatened to not give me food for a week if I did not listen to her seven year old daughter!

"You will do anything that my daughter asks, you got that?" Like the servant I was, I had to pick up Mylene's food, and to make matters worse the host grandma stood up and threw her food on the floor.

"This is the only thing a piece of shit like you is good for, so pick up our mess now." She had said. Alexandre then started to record me picking up their mess. I almost lost it then. I was close to throwing the spaghetti right at the host grandma's face, but it was Roman, the oldest Dax child who stood up for me.

Unlike his sister, Roman had a kind heart, and the type of aura that makes a person look older than what they are. He was only ten, but when he stood up and moved his wavy hair from his eyes, everyone stopped and listened to him.

"Don't you see what you all are doing?" "This is beyond disrespectful." "Grandma, you should know better than to belittle someone!" It was so embarrassing having a ten year old defend me, but what could I do other than go to my room and cry.

It was only there that I felt safe and I guess it was because I knew the Daxes absolutely hated the idea of coming up here. This little room was too tacky for their taste. It was anything but fancy, and all it had inside its beige-colored walls were a couch bed, a large mirror and a tiny desk.

Nothing more, but to me it was perfect, and surprisingly it had a hidden gem. The one secret this servant's room had was the incredible view from the window. That view was amazing, and I wanted one last look before leaving this nightmare behind.

I gently put my suitcase by my door and headed toward the window. I pulled down the frame and pushed the window open. The view was breathtaking. I could see all of central Paris. The beautiful tan buildings with the iconic gray rooftops.

The busy streets with millions of people wearing every piece of fashion imaginable. The sights of the cafes and monuments like *the Pantheon* and *Notre Dame*. It was a terrific view, but it was time to say bye to it all.

I delicately closed the window, and put my passport safely inside my pocket. I placed my backpack over my shoulder, and I pulled my suitcase next to me. I was all set, and ready to go. I could barely contain my glee. My family will be in for the shock of their lives!

No one back home knew that I was coming. What's more, I was not expected to be back home until my year was up. Which unfortunately meant that my arrival will lead to countless questions. Questions that quite frankly I wasn't ready to answer, and honestly speaking, questions and subjects that I wouldn't be able to talk about for the next couple of months.

Luckily, since Christmas was just three weeks away I could make up an excuse of how I had come back home for the holidays. That would keep people at bay with any unwanted inquiries, and that would give me time to find the perfect excuse as to why I was coming back home permanently.

I already had a couple of ideas that I think could work. As simple as this sounds, after Christmas I would simply say that I missed everyone, and that I was ready to start college now. Hopefully my family and friends would support me without thinking too much of it, and then I could peacefully get my life back; without having to relive the horrors of my au pair experience.

I could then start school at the local community college as soon as January, and I could get a part time job somewhere. Yep, in fact that is what I will do and say! *Phew*, feeling better about what lay ahead, I breathed a sigh of relief. A warmth of security passed through my body.

For the first time in four months I had a plan to better my future. No more setbacks and abuse. All I had to do now was get to the airport. It was time to go.

With sweaty and trembling hands I opened up the *Uber* app and searched for a driver to take me to the *Charles de Gaulle Airport*. I entered the address and waited. Man, the ubers are so pricey, but it is what it is. I just wouldn't be able to afford any food for the day, but it was okay.

I ordered the driver. *Your driver is on their way. They will be here in 7 minutes.* Perfect. I opened the door to my room, and I placed my key on the couch bed. My armpits started to sweat. It was time to go and that meant heading out of the building. I would have to pass the Daxes' apartment.

I felt my heart jumping from my chest. Sweat was dripping from my forehead, but I had to do it. I closed the door behind me, and passed my sweet neighbor's room. I hated to be leaving without saying goodbye, but I did not have time.

Instead I slid a handwritten letter under her door, and then I awkwardly grabbed my heavy suitcase and went down the first flight of stairs to the sixth floor of the building. My heart then stopped. "I am telling you Alexandre, he ran into our room and went into the closet." "He got his passport."

"He entered our room without permission!" "He is trying to leave without finishing his contract." "Never in all the fine history of the Dax family has a servant done this." "What are you going to do about it Alexandre?"

"I will beat some sense into him, Juliette." "If he thinks he can get away from us that easily then he has no clue what we have in store for him." "We are a family of power and influence and there is no way that a hick like Max will tarnish our name."

"He should be happy to have been given the opportunity of servicing us." "What if he accuses you of beating him, Alexandre?" "Well we will just say that he stole from us, won't we Juliette?" "That sounds like a plan to me."

"After I am through with him he will not be able to walk after this, and we will force him to stay till his contract is over." "He thinks he has rights?" "He has no rights." "No one messes with the Daxes."

"He has a duty to serve us for another seven months and I will make sure he does it." "I knew you would solve this sweetie, now go beat that sense into him." "He has no idea what inferno awaits him for doing this to us." Alexandre grunted, as I tried to keep myself together.

I felt like I would suffocate. I couldn't breathe. My blood ran ice cold. I knew that this had just become a life or death situation. This family was so prideful that they would never let anyone get an upper hand over them.

I mean, for crying out loud, they were saying this openly where anyone could hear them. They didn't care. They were wealthy and powerful enough to do what they wanted. Damnit! How in the world was I going to get out of here without being seen by them?

Think Max, think. What should I do? The wooden floor started creaking as Alexandre made his way up the stairs to my room. I had about two seconds before he would see me. I had no choice and took my chance.

I swung my luggage and it met Alexandre right on his squared jaw as he was coming up the stairs. He fell backward and landed on his butt on the previous step. "You bitch!" "You'll pay for that!" He said as he massaged his bruised face. I ignored him, and I swiftly ran past him as I clutched my suitcase next to my body.

"Get him Juliette, he hit me!" She quickly came up the steps and tried reaching for me, but stumbled on her own feet. She fell right on her back. I effortlessly dodged past her, and she began to yell. "You won't get away!"

Well see about that I screamed back at her as I flew down to the first floor. Wasting no time I pulled the massive wooden-front door of the building open and I jumped outside.

Where was my *Uber*? I ran into the street and looked in all directions. Voila! I found the white *BMW* and waved the driver down. "You are going to *CDG*, correct?" Yes sir. "Okay, let me put your baggage in the trunk."

The driver got my bags, and I got into the back seat of the car. Ten seconds later we were on our way to the airport. Without a second to spare because as I turned my head back toward the building, I saw Alexandre and Juliette coming out of the front door turning their heads in all directions. They were looking for me, but it was too late.

Chapter 3
THE AIRPORT

"Are you heading back home, or going on vacation?" The uber driver looked at me through the rearview mirror with a smile. I am going home. "Did you have a good time in France?"

Yes, I responded dryly. The driver's cheeks slightly reddened. I felt bad not engaging in conversation, but I had too much on my mind. "Are you sad to be leaving?" No, I am not. He turned his head and gave me a sly stare.

I wanted him to stop talking to me because I was freaking out inside. I avoided his stare, and he took the hint. I did not want to be rude, but the truth is, I was scared out of my mind. I was fearful that the Daxes would come follow me in their car.

I was also terrified that they would call the police on me. After hearing their conversation on the staircase, that was their only option to keep me, but would they do it? Would they really say that I stole something from them?

I guess the real question is, would they risk me exposing their secrets to the police? In my time with the Daxes I learned quite a few things about them. I learned that a lot of their money comes from illegal deals and not their actual empire, but does that really matter?

Alexandre had said it perfectly, "It's his word against ours." I felt my back begin to sweat. My breathing was getting heavier. I needed some air. This was getting to be too much for me. "Sir, did you hear me?" Huh, what?

"I said, we are almost at the airport." I jerked my head in surprise. I had been so lost in my own thoughts that I hadn't noticed that we were arriving at the airport. Woah, where did the time go?

The driver pulled into the international departures terminal, and slowly parked in the ten minute drop off section. "We are here." "I will get your luggage out." Thank you so much, I told the uber driver as he took my luggage out of the trunk. "It is my pleasure." "And sir, may I add, whatever is bothering you, just know you will be able to get through it."

I felt goosebumps begin to form on my arms after hearing the driver say that. Something in the way he said it made me feel uneasy. It felt like a premonition of what was to come. In all honesty it spooked me a bit, but I smiled back at him and said, thank you. He nodded his head and drove off.

I gently rubbed my forehead to try to shake the creepy feeling away. After all, I was only one flight away from taking my life back. It was time to be happy, so I took a deep breath and smiled while I made my way to the entrance of the airport.

Sadly, my smile did not last long because as soon as I passed the automatic doors of the *Charles De Gaulle Airport* I became a bit dazed. The place was beyond packed, and it did not help that there were colorful Christmas decorations everywhere, causing me to be blinded by the lights.

What's more, the foul stench of armpits caused by having so many people stuck in one area was making me nauseous. It smelled like rotten onions. I felt like I needed to vomit, but instead I swallowed the feeling back down.

The last thing I wanted to do was ruin someone's day by having my throw up all over them. Instead, I tried to think of nice smells like a buttery croissant to calm my stomach as I began to squeeze by everyone in an effort to make my way over to my airline.

Thankfully, after a gruesome ten minute struggle I made it to the airline area, but to my bad luck the line to drop off baggage was huge. I did not want to wait in this queue, but I had no choice. I started to feel agitated, and it did not help that I was sweating like a steam-fryer.

Okay, breathe Max, after this you can sit down and wait for your flight to board, I told myself silently. I took several deep breaths and my stomach started to unknot. *The line to see the flight agent will be at least another thirty minutes*, an airport employee announced.

Oh man. The longer I waited, the more time I had to overthink about the Daxes. I really hoped that that wicked family would just forget about me and let me be. I never did anything bad to them.

I was always their perfect servant, who not only took their kids to school, but also some of their friends' kids. Why couldn't they just leave me alone? Maybe they would? Maybe they would just see that I wasn't worth the stress, and just, *Excuse me sir, you're next.*

I turned my head in surprise. The lady next to me was pointing at the counter. I guess time flew quicker when I overthought. Which is not a good thing, but at least it was finally my turn to drop my luggage off.

Passport please. I gave my passport to the gate agent. She smiled her bright-white smile at me as she moved her long brown hair out of her face. *How long were you in France for?* I was here for four and a half months.

Oh that is nice. Where were you staying? In central Paris. *Wow, I love central Paris, you are so lucky.* Yea, I guess. *What was the purpose of your trip?* I was an au pair.

An au pair for only four and a half months? Don't they usually stay a full year? Why was she asking me so many questions? She was making me nervous. *I was an au pair in London before I started working here.* Wow, that is really awesome. I smiled at her blankly.

You can place your luggage on the scale. I placed my luggage on the scale and she printed out my boarding pass. She handed me my passport, and said, *Have a safe flight.* I smiled at her, and started to walk towards customs.

My legs suddenly felt like a thousand pounds. This was the make it or break it moment for me. If the Daxes had called the police on me then it would be at the border control that I would be stopped. There was only one way to find out.

I quietly walked over to the customs station. My stomach was in knots as I weaved my way through the line to await my turn. Each minute that passed felt like an eternity, but I did my best to calm my nerves by thinking of positive things like spending Christmas with my family and being free again.

Those thoughts helped ease my mind, and finally after twenty minutes of trying to keep myself together, it was my turn. The custom's officer signaled for me to come, and with a racing heart I made my way to the cubicle. I waited patiently for the officer's instructions.

Passport please. I handed him my passport. I felt my heart thumping in my throat. He opened my document and looked for my "student" visa. He found it and took one quick look at me, and then stamped it. Five seconds later I had my passport back in my hands.

I felt the blood rush back into my extremities, and with all the happiness in the world I crossed the customs area and made my way to the security side. Fortunately, I only had my backpack with me, so I quickly passed security with no issues. Then I was through.

I was on my way to my terminal! The Dax family had not called the police on me. The nightmare was nearly over. I was going home! I could barely contain my glee as I made my way over to *Terminal E.*

I started to smile at everyone that I passed! They probably thought I was some sort of weirdo, but who cares! My four and a half months of torture were almost finished, and as embarrassing as this sounds as I reached *Gate 33E* I did a small twirl.

I felt like I was on top of the world, but I calmed my giddiness down a bit. I had to get serious again. My plane was boarding in twenty-five minutes. It was time to go and freshen up for my eleven hour flight, so I headed across the hall to the restroom.

Which for some strange reason was quite fancy. It was one of those restrooms with two identical sides. Each side had about ten urinals with three large buffet style sinks, and five stalls. It also not only looked clean, but it smelled fresh.

Well, that is a nice surprise. Here I was thinking I was going to freshen up in a dirty airport bathroom. Things are going my way, I thought to myself as I walked over to the sink nearest to the back of the bathroom. Once there I placed my backpack on the part of the counter that wasn't wet.

I then started to wash my hands. The warmth of the water made me feel secure. I couldn't help but grin stupidly. In fact I was smiling so much that I did not notice when a group of men came into the restroom until they were right next to me.

I felt a little embarrassed because they saw me smiling at myself, but who cares. I was returning to my casa, and besides they are strangers so who gives a damn what they think. I started to giggle at my own nonsense while I washed my face.

"Hey, you are not French, right?" The man nearest to me asked in a thick French accent. I glanced over at him. He was about six feet tall and based on his crow's feet he looked to be around forty years old. He had pale skin and dark hair.

I felt nervous being next to him, but I did not want to be rude so I responded to his question. No, I am not French. What gave it away? He smiled at me. "Well first of all you don't have the look." "You look poor." What did you say? Had I heard him right?

"You heard me." "You look more like an animal than anything." I glared at him with hate in my eyes. I was in shock. My rage was bubbling inside of me. I was about to tell him off, but decided against it. I did not need this.

I was just twenty minutes away from getting my life back, and I did not want to be involved in any issues that might prevent that. Instead I grabbed my backpack and walked around him.

"Where do you think you're going?" The man blocked my path. "I was not done talking to you." I tried to shuffle past him, but he pushed me. I reacted on instinct and swung my backpack over his head.

He was quick and blocked it, and before I could retaliate again the three other men that were in the restroom came charging toward me. They apprehended me and took me inside a person with disabilities stall. I tried to run out, but they threw me down. I landed with a bang as my shoulder slightly hit the wall.

Why are you doing this to me? I yelled in my broken French. They mocked my French and they slammed me into the floor. Some of the air was knocked out of me. I tried to get a better look of what was happening. I was confused and terrified.

They formed a circle around me, and I immediately started kicking the air. My foot hit one of the guys on the chin. He cursed in frustration. I yelled for help, but it was no use. I did not hear anyone in the restroom. I knew they had locked the bathroom doors. I was alone.

I tried to stand up again and I felt a hard kick on the side of my stomach. I started to punch the air, and I felt myself hit someone on the face. I was greeted back with a blow to the side of my head. Everything went dark instantly.

Crr, Crr, Crr, I woke up to the crunching sound of wheels turning on gravel. I tried to move my hands but they were tied. I painfully opened my swollen eyes, and saw that I was in a garage. It looked like an airport parking garage. It was gray and smelled like engine oil. What was happening?

Suddenly, I felt the pressure of someone's hands on my back and then I realized. I was on a wheelchair, and I was quite possibly being wheeled into someone's car. I desperately tried to move my hands and legs, but they were in restraints.

I attempted to wiggle my head to the side to see who was wheeling me, but the pain on my neck was intense. Everything went dark once again, and I do not know how long I was out for, but when I woke up it was completely dark.

I tried to scan the area that I was in, but it was pointless. It was as dark as a moonless night. I was scared. My hands and feet were still tied. I had been kidnapped, and in my heart I knew it was the Daxes who had ordered this kidnapping.

There was no way that they would have let me go that easily. I should have known. At one of their dinner parties where I was their waiter I remember once overhearing one of their conversations. Juliette had made a joke about how no one does them wrong without paying a price.

At the time it sounded like nothing but a simple joke to me, a cruel jest, but a jest nonetheless. Everyone had laughed, but now I knew that they were not joking. They had been dead serious.

Their influence and power knew no bounds, and now I feared for my life. My God, please help me. Please do not let them kill me, I pleaded out loud. Please, help me escape this place. I have so much to live for, and so much to do. I cannot leave my family like this.

"You can cry to God all that you want, but he will not help you." My breathing stopped. It was Alexandre. There was no mistaking his low pitched voice and heavy French accent. "Do you think we were going to let you humiliate us without any sort of consequences?" Why are you doing this to me?

"Look what you did to us!" He shouted. "My kids grew fond of you." "Roman looked up to you, and you decided to leave without saying bye?" "How dare you!" "Mylene even started to like you!"

"You probably just came to France for only one reason, and that was to gain influence from our name to launch your career!" What? What, career? What are you talking about? "Don't play stupid with me, Max." "You are nothing but a user, and a thief!"

I never once used your family, and I never stole anything from you guys! "Yes, you did!" "You entered our closet without permission to steal your passport that belonged to us!" "Did you really think that we were going to steal your pathetic identity?"

My passport belongs to me, and not to you Daxes! You guys said I would have it back in a couple of days, and you only used it as a weapon against me! "That's the issue with you vermin." "You are all idiots, and do not understand how life works." "Just like hogs, if we don't hold something against you, you filths won't work!"

Do you not hear how crazy you sound? I was a slave in your home! I came to France to find a new family by being an au pair. I did not come to launch any career through your family's name. I didn't even know your family had a wine empire. You are the ones who treated me horribly. "We treated you the way you needed to be treated."

If you wanted a slave, why didn't you hire one! I am not a serf. I am just an innocent student who simply wanted a new cultural experience, and your family ruined that. "No, you are the one who ruined everything by being you!"

"We had hopes for you, but when we saw you, we knew you were not worth it." "Juliette and I realized that all you were worth was being a servant to us." "Look at you." "You are nothing but a nasty mestizo." "You are not pure blood like us."

This couldn't be true. This had to be a dream. This family had treated me like dirt because of my origins? I could barely contain my rage. My eyes started to get blurry, and with all the strength that I had left, I shouted at him. WHY DIDN"T YOU JUST LET ME LEAVE THE FIRST DAY THAT YOU DAXES SAW ME?

"We didn't get rid of you because you are young and strong." "Even though you are not worthy of us, you do speak English and you can clean, so why get rid of a good slave like you?" I told you I'm not a fucken slave!

"Oh, but you are, and since you did try to leave us before your year was up, you must be punished." "If you thought your life was hell before, then you are in for a ride." "For starters you will not have access to any means of communication anymore!"

You can't do that! You think my family and friends won't come looking for me the second that I go one day without talking to them? They will go through hell and back for me.

"I know they will." "You mestizos are a nuisance to our world." "You multiply and reproduce like animals, but just like animals you are all stupid." "You will simply send your parents an audio telling them about the wonderful day you had today, and then we will figure out the rest later."

He began laughing again. "Your life is in the palm of our hands." "Get ready to suffer more than you have ever suffered before." I had to be hallucinating. I just had to. People could not be this cruel, could they?

"And if you are inclined to tell your family and friends back home what you are living through, I will not only kill you, but I will kill them." There it was. My fate had been sealed. My life was in the Daxes' hands.

"The worst thing you could have done in your miserable life was hitting me with your bag." "You'll see how nice your life was when you get to where you are going." "I bet you are scared now, aren't you?"

I did not answer him. There was no point in engaging with him, yet he still rambled on. "You won't be in Paris anymore." "You are our property now." "The only way that you will ever be free again is by doing everything that is required of you, but that shouldn't be an issue."

"I know that you are good at doing what you're asked of, so if you continue to follow our rules and promise to be a good slave then we will release you at your one year mark." "You see we aren't that bad." He mockingly glanced at me like I was trash.

I felt like my body was being penetrated by his glare. Then he came closer to me. Out of instinct my body bolted up. I managed to stand up even though my hands and feet were tied.

He came face to face with me and said, "I will have fun with you." "Maybe you will become one of my better servants." "You listen to everything I say, and I will make sure to get Juliette off of your back."

Chapter 4

THE COUNTRYSIDE

My body filled with goosebumps. His warm breath sent shivers down my spine. What was he implying? It couldn't be what I was thinking, could it? Whaatt, what doo youu mean? I asked him, not meaning to stutter. I didn't want to give him the satisfaction that I was terrified. "Well, well, well Max." The hair on the back of my neck stood up. I wouldn't be getting an answer now.

It was Juliette. I recognized her high pitched voice even before I made out her face as she came in through a dimly lit doorway. "Here you are, and all tied up I see." Her voice was beaming with joy. "It is a pity that you decided to betray us." She was grinning from ear to ear. Her fake veneers were practically glowing in the dark.

"I am sure Alexandre has caught you up with your new work placement." She glared at me with her beady eyes and laughed out loud. "To think I was growing fond of you too." "You listened and did everything I asked for." "I was quite shocked when you went into our room without permission, but I guess that is why one should never trust people like you."

People like me? Juliette, you are no better than I am. "Hahaha, I am definitely better than you are Max." "You are just a piece of shit." Her words infuriated me. I was tired of the belittling, but I held my tongue and stayed quiet.

She was looking for a fight, and I was not going to give her one at that moment. Especially since I was at their mercy. "Cat got your tongue, or did you learn your place again?" I pathetically nodded my head in agreement. "Good, I knew you would come to your senses." Her voice sounded triumphant.

"Well, Alexandre now that Max understands who the bosses are, we better hurry back to Paris before the kids have dinner without us." "Oui, ma chérie." "Go start the car, but let me have one last word with Max." Juliette agreed, and walked away leaving me alone with Alexandre.

"You see, I can easily get her off your back, but remember what I told you, Max." Once again, I nodded pitifully. He started to laugh. "Good, now don't try anything stupid." "See you tomorrow," he said as he walked away from the room. Slamming the door behind him with a bang.

The room shook in response causing me to stumble to the floor, but I quickly got back up. Even though I was beyond hurt I would not sit around and do nothing. I immediately began to pull at the ropes on my wrists.

My shoulders burned as I tried to get my hands free, but little by little the knots started to loosen. I then began to bite into the rope. The taste of the thread was bitter, and the texture was burning my lips. I did not care, and I continued to tear chunks off of the rope.

I tugged and pulled it in every direction, and as I was freeing myself I heard a voice. It was a soft voice. It sounded like a young woman, maybe my age. "Max, I am here to explain what will happen now." She had a heavy accent. She sounded like she was from somewhere in Asia. She began to get closer to me.

Get away from me! I yelled at her as I finally freed my hands from their imprisonment. I grabbed the rope that I had just untied from my hands, and began to swing it at her like a whip. I am getting away from this jail!

"Please, I am not here to hurt you, Max." "Listen, you must come with me or else they will punish you." I do not care what they do! I was just kidnapped and I know damn well that the first 48 hours are the most crucial hours. I am getting out of here. "You must listen to me." "If you don't, the guards of the compound will hurt you."

I heard every word that this woman was saying, but I did not care. I was too busy untying the ropes from my legs. "Listen to me please." No! I yelled as I painfully jolted to the door.

Fortunately, she had left it partially open, so I kicked it fully wide. Instantaneously, I was blinded by the bright flights of the hallway, but I didn't care. With all the pain in my body, I ran into the hallway like a dazed mouse in a trap. Unfortunately, within two seconds I saw them.

The same group of men that had beaten me merciselly were standing outside just a few feet away from me. I quickly tried to run back the other way, but one of them pulled my arm so hard that I thought it would come out of its socket.

Intuitively, I turned my head to look at the person who had pulled me. It was the man who had originally offended me in the bathroom. He glared at me with amusement in his eyes, and then slapped me hard on the face.

I felt warm blood in my mouth. My eyes got watery and my nose felt itchy. This was too much. I was dead tired of this abuse, so I swung at him. To my demise I missed, and I was punched in the face.

I fell to the floor, and that is when the woman came running behind me. "I am so sorry Jean." "He is confused." "Please, I will take him up to his room and explain his job." Jean looked at the woman and nodded.

She knelt beside me and helped me to my feet. This time I did not try to run. I simply went with her, completely defeated. My head was pounding with every step that I took. "Hang in there with me, Max."

She was encouraging me. How did she know my name? I was going in and out of consciousness again. I stumbled a bit, and I had to stop walking. "Do not stop now Max." "Just a little further." The woman glared at me again with sympathetic eyes, and then led me into a new room.

It was an enormous living room that was almost empty. It had wooden floors and a big piano right in the middle. There were two leather couches, and a deer's head on the wall. It felt chilling walking through it.

"This is the main living room of the Daxes countryside house." Their countryside house? Where are we? "I'll explain everything once we get you all cleaned up, okay?" Okay, I managed to mumble.

"By the way, my name is Kaoly." "I am from Vietnam." "I am also an au pair like you Max." I'm not an au pair! I am not here under my own will, Kaoly. The Daxes have kidnapped me!

Please, help me. "Max, I will help you, but first let's get to the room to get you all fixed up." "We are almost there." "It will be okay," she encourangily said as she grabbed my hand and moved me forward. I didn't resist. Something in her voice made me trust her.

"We just need to get through this hallway, and then we are there." I looked straight ahead. The hallway was huge. It was easily over seventy feet in length. It had picture frames hung in all directions. I glanced at some of the frames that were hung at the beginning of the hallway. They looked old.

They were black and white. In fact I think the first couple of pictures were actual paintings. The paintings had people wearing old style clothing. They reminded me of the clothing that people would wear during the 1700s or so. The women had long puffy dresses and the men had leather tuxedos.

"The first picture is of the Dax family that started their mighty wine empire." "This hallway is a homage to the Dax legacy." What a legacy. "The last few pictures are of the Daxes that you know, and that picture right there is of a young Alexandre Dax."

"He is the current heir to their empire." I followed Kaoly's gaze as she pointed to the picture frame of the sinister Dax patriarch. It made my skin crawl. He was probably eighteen in the photo, and he was sitting on the back of two people.

The people were dirty and wore bandanas. They had to be the grape pickers since they were in a field of grapes. Both of them had frowns on their faces, but not Alexandre. He was carrying a bundle of grapes, and he was smiling from ear to ear.

I felt disgusted and looked away from the frame. "We just need to turn left up here." I followed Kaoly until we reached a door that was seemingly hidden from view. "Let me unlock it."

She pulled out a small key and unlocked the door." "Be careful, we will climb down two flights of stairs, okay?" Okay, I quietly whispered as Kaoly pushed the door open. A dim yellow light came on, and we started climbing down the stairs.

I carefully descended down the first couple of steps. They were hard to see because they were dark gray. Dark gray like walls in the room. It creeped me out. In fact, this room looked like a prison.

Not only that, but it felt like a cell too. As I gently tapped on one of the walls I could feel that it was pure concrete and metal. I was sure that no noise was able to penetrate these walls. This wasn't good.

I couldn't do this. I wouldn't be one of those people who stupidly went down to their own doom. I decided to run back up the stairs. I was getting out of here. Dead or alive, but on my terms. I will get out of here.

I ran up two stairs at a time until I reached the door. "STOP, Max!" "If you leave now, not only will they kill you, but they will also go after your entire family and friends." "Everyone that you care for will be dealt with."

"The Daxes will slowly torture them, and tell you all about it!" Kaoly's statement made me stop dead in my tracks. She was yelling, and out of breath, causing her voice to become hoarse and hard. It made me stop reaching for the door.

Did she really believe that they would go that far? I knew that Alexandre had said he would, but would they really kill my friends and family? I wasn't too sure before, but hearing Kaoly's certainty of it made me see the reality of it.

"Come back down, Max." Going against my intuition, I took one deep breath, and walked back down the stairs. "Thank you, Max, and now look, this will be your room for the next six months."

No it will not, I silently thought to myself. "You will come here every day from 10:00 pm to 5:00 am." "That is our rest time." "Feel free to make yourself at home."

I walked around the place. It was a large room with four sets of bunk beds and solid white carpet. The carpet was spotless. To the left of the bunkbeds was a door that was partially open.

I could see that it was a bathroom. Kaoly met my gaze. "You can wash up and take the rest of the day for yourself, but tomorrow we must be up at 4:30 am to be ready for work at 5:00 am." Kaoly, is there any way that I can take tomorrow off just to heal?

Kaoly looked at me and walked closer to me. "Max, you either work, or you get killed." "This isn't a game anymore." "Once you get sent here you truly lose all your rights." Why are you here then? What did you do? Were you their old au pair?

Kaoly's eyebrows got closer together as her look intensified. "I was never the au pair of your host family, but I was the au pair for Sophie Dax." Who is that? "Alexandre Dax's sister." Oh, okay, but what do you mean, were? "After a month of living with Sophie Dax I could not take it any longer."

"Max, she did not have kids." "She lied and said Mylene and Roman were her kids." "She wanted a slave." "She was awful, so after four weeks of living with her I knew that I had to leave."

"As a matter of fact, I wasted no time and left that same day that I came to the conclusion." How did you do it? "I discreetly left in the night, but that didn't help." "One minute I remember leaving, and the next thing I remember is waking up in the same location that you woke up in."

"I have been here for ten months now, and I really want you to understand that this is life or death." "There is no in between." "Max, I have been through hell and back, but I have learned to do what is required of me." "I learned to survive, and you will too."

Kaoly, will you always be Sophie's slave? "No, thankfully my contract is up next month, and I am being set free." How can you be so sure that she will set you free? "My visa will expire, and I have to have a meeting with the immigration office in France." Will you expose the Daxes then? "There is no way that I will do such a thing."

"Max, these people are very powerful." "If you make one wrong move not only will you get hurt, but so will your family and anyone else you care about." "When my time is over I will do everything I can to forget about this nightmare."

Kaoly stared at me with tears in her eyes. Her voice quivered as she spoke. I could see her body tense up as she talked to me. Something terrible must have happened to her. There was no doubt about that.

"Anyway, I still have some work to do, so I have to go." "You will probably be asleep by the time I come back, so I will see you tomorrow morning." "Please try to get some rest," and with that she was gone, and I was finally alone.

I felt scared, and I was angry. On top of that my entire body hurt, especially my face. I gently touched it. Oh my gosh, it felt beyond swollen. How did I even look? I had to see. I slowly walked toward the restroom, and I pushed the door open. The lights turned on automatically.

I made my way over to the small sink that had a faded iron-crusted mirror hanging over it. I stared at myself. My left eye was completely shut. It was as swollen as an apple. The right side of my face was purple from where I had been punched. My lips were twice their size, and my nose was covered in dried up blood.

To worsen my situation, my body was bruised from my chest to my feet. I had open gashes on my arms and legs. My entire stomach was dark purple. My ribs were black from bruising. How was I still standing?

I mean, I felt my pain, but the way I looked was criminal. I should not be able to stand, let alone walk, but I was. This gave me a little sense of renowned faith. I was stronger than I thought.

I would find a way out of this, but first I had to shower. I needed to wash my wounds, so with that I painfully began to remove my clothes, and I headed to the tiny shower in the corner of the restroom.

I turned the faucet handle and let the ice cold water drip over my body. There was no warm water. Shockingly enough the cold water made me feel better. It sprung me back into rational thinking. The clouds fogging my brain were gone now, and I knew one thing. I would escape this place, regardless of what Kaoly and Alexandre told me.

Not only would I escape, but I would also warn my family of what was happening. My family knew how to defend themselves, and they could hide if they had to. Yes, I would not stay here for seven more months. There was no way. I would do all that I could do to survive, and not just survive. I would also expose this family to the world.

Feeling a tad better, and much more motivated I turned the water off after a five minute shower. I carefully rinsed myself dry, making sure to not make any opened wounds bleed, and then I grabbed my dirty clothes. Unfortunately, I did not have any spare clothes. Oh well, I changed and I headed to one of the empty bunk beds.

I chose the bed furthest from the entrance of the room, and got in. The sheets were surprisingly soft. They felt like marshmallows on my bruised skin. The pillow was not as soft, but still silky. I placed my head down, and the next thing I remember was being woken up.

"Max, Max it is 4:50 am and it is time to get the day started." Kaoly was calling my name, but I was only able to open one eye. My left eye was so swollen that I could not open it. On top of that my body felt like it had been hit by a truck going 100 miles an hour.

"I know it is hard, but you have to get up." With all the strength that I could muster I got my beaten up body up. It was time to start the slave work for the day. "You have about two minutes to get washed up." What just two minutes? "Yes, it took me fifteen minutes to wake you."

I'm sorry. "It's okay, but please hurry." I quickly headed for the bathroom. The automatic lights made my swollen left eye open slightly. I did not want to see myself in the mirror, so I hurriedly washed up, and met Kaoly by the door. I am ready, Kaoly.

"Okay, so for today we must get the house ready for a special dinner that Sophie Dax will host." "We must leave the house spotless." Okay let's do it. Kaoly smiled at me, but her smile had no glow to it. It was as if it were mechanical. What had happened to this poor girl?

"Max, are you alright?" Huh? Yeah, sorry I was kind of daydreaming. "It is okay." "Follow me." I followed Kaoly up the stairs and out of the hallway of Daxes to another corridor that led to a large open lodge.

"You will take care of the bar area." "All the supplies that you need to clean are in the small closet behind the pool table." Okay, I got it.

"I'll be back to check up on you during our break at 7." "See you then." With that Kaoly left me to clean the massive bar.

The room was probably the size of a real *Denny's* dining place. It was impressive, and the walls were colored cream. It had one long island table that had ten seats. The bartender area had easily over one thousand kinds of drinks hanging on the walls.

There was a decently sized pool table on the far edge of the room. Also, there were two well sized TVs in the bar. Each tv had four leather couches below it, and in front of the couches was a small table. The tables had a deck of cards and a wooden chessboard that matched the floor.

Which was bare except for the carpeted area where the couches were in. It was a nice bar, but the one thing that made this room amazing were the giant windows that let all the natural lighting in. The enormous windows took the entirety of the right wall.

They were almost crystal clear except for the smudges near the rim of the window. I guess I will start cleaning there. I headed to the cleaning supply closet, and I pulled out the French version of Windex, *Monsieur Propre*, and I went to work.

Surprisingly, I welcomed the quietness and calmness that came from cleaning. I had no one rushing me. Plus the gentle wiping of the windows helped distract my mind from the hell that I was living in. Peculiarly, I was so distracted that I got startled when I saw a strange lady enter the room.

In a heavy French accent she said, "You must be Max." "I can see why they kept you at the apartment in Paris." "You are beaten up, but still I can see that you are a young attractive guy, but you are not pure." "You can easily fool the common folks, but not us elites, you are mixed blood."

She stared me down like I was a piece of meat. "I have been informed about the hell you gave my brother Alexandre yesterday." "Just so you know if you try to pull that shit on me I will not hesitate to discipline you right away."

She came closer to me and stared to stare at the windows. "You are doing a good job." "Make sure this entire bar area is spotless because if it isn't you already know the consequences." She smirked and left, leaving me with a bitter taste.

She had given me several backhanded compliments, and to be frank I really didn't care. If the Daxes thought that they could offend me by making fun of my culture then they really were stupid.

Hmm, I guess they're looks match their personality. I quietly joked to myself as I pulled a broom out of the supply closet, and I continued cleaning. Soon enough the entire bar area was spotless. Perfect, and it was only 6:45 am.

That left me with over fifteen minutes of down time before Kaoly came back, so with that I went over and sat next to the window to enjoy the sun's rays coming in. The rays felt good on my swollen face, and they made me feel relaxed.

Almost to the point where I dozed off, but Kaoly walked in before I did. "Max, it is time that we have our breakfast." Okay, how far is the kitchen from here? "We are not going to the kitchen." "Unfortunately, we must eat outside."

"There is a small refrigerator there where our food is located. I didn't even react to what Kaoly said. I expected it. I simply followed her and we had our breakfast. It was water with stale old croissants and jam. At least the bread tasted decently.

"Max, next we must clean the guests' rooms." Let's go, follow me." I followed Kaoly to the second floor, which was the guest floor. She showed me which rooms to clean and then left to do her work.

With my cleaning supplies in my hands I started to clean the first of the three rooms. Again, I was cleaning things that were already clean. Which was a good thing for my healing body, but it was becoming boring and repetitive.

Instead of it calming me down, it was now making me think of my hell again. I was starting to feel agitated until I reached the third room.

The third room was quite small. It had one bed and a tiny restroom. I remade the bed. I cleaned the spotless toilet and sink, and then I started to wipe down the wooden floor. I scrubbed it gently with a wood polisher.

It smelled nice, but regrettably I added too much polisher to the floor. There were parts of the tile that were a tad too wet, especially near the rim of the bed, but that was an easy fix.

I pulled out a towel to gently dry that area, and as I dried the area a loose thread of the towel got stuck on one of the tiles. I carefully tried to remove it, but to my luck the tile of the floor came off. It simply yanked off like a puzzle piece.

Crap, I rushed to put it back into its spot, and as I was placing it back, I noticed a deep hole in the space where the tile went. It was maybe a foot deep, but this hole was not empty. There was a picture in there.

I froze and stared in complete horror. It was a picture of Kaoly. In this image Kaoly was tied on a bed. Her hands were bound wide open, and so were her legs. She was completely naked. She was crying.

I was shocked. I quickly pulled the picture out of the floor, and saw that there were many more photos underneath. There were countless images of Kaoly tied and bound while crying, and there were pictures of other women and men bound on the same bed. They were all taken in this room. I felt shivers go down my spine. I had to know more.

I rummaged through more photographs, and I found photos of Juliette, Alexandre, Sophie and other people that I did not recognize smoking while laughing as their victims were tied in bed. I felt sick to my stomach. I quickly put the photos back into their place and placed the tile right back in its spot.

My hands were shaking. These people were monsters. No, I shouldn't say people. These things were monsters. I can only imagine the horrible things Kaoly and the others went through. I wondered who the others were? They all looked to be around my age.

They must have been au pairs, nannies or even cleaners that have come and gone with the time. Did they ever make it back home? Were they ever able to readapt to society?

I felt queasy. Just last year I was dreaming about moving to Paris, and now this. I just wish I could call my parents or my best friends, but the Daxes had taken my phone. They probably were texting them as if they were me.

I felt tears creep into my eyes. I felt my heart trying to escape from my chest, and I started to cry. I was hyperventilating. I had to get out now. I had to leave this place. I did not want to end up like poor Kaoly, and the others.

Why is this happening to me? Why, God? What did I do to deserve this? I fell to the floor and laid there. I let my mind go blank and then as if God had answered my cries, I had an epiphany. I knew what I had to do.

I had to take the pictures that I found and go to the *US Embassy* in Paris. I now had actual evidence against the Daxes. I would be able to go home and they would be arrested. There was no way of denying what they did. This was my way out of this hell hole. It was my way of securing my life, and the life of the people that I love the most.

Now I just needed to figure out a way to get back to Paris, and to be honest I needed to know where the hell I was. It would make things easier when I reported the Daxes to the authorities.

Think Max, think. How can I do this? The dinner! Sophie was hosting a dinner tonight, and with luck someone coming to that dinner would be from Paris. I could then sneak into their car when they left! Yes, that is what I will do.

I felt a small wave of hope flush through my body. I ran back to the spot on the floor that contained the pictures and peeled the tile back. I grabbed all the pictures and stuffed them down my pants. This evidence was my ticket home.

Chapter 5

THE PREGNANCY

I had to make sure that I did not lose it, so I fixed the cuff of my jeans into my shoes to ensure no photo would fall off. I took a few test steps and no photos fell from my jeans. Good I thought as I heard a gentle pounding on the door. Kaoly is that you? "Yes, may I come in?" Of course.

Kaoly came in with a smile. "How are you feeling Max?" I am feeling better now, Kaoly. How are you feeling? Her eyes twitched before she spoke. She looked exhausted and depressed, yet she smiled.

"I am doing well." "I am counting the days off until I get to go back home." "One more month." I grinned empathically back at her. I knew she was lying about feeling okay, but I would not pressure her into talking about something that she did not want to, instead I asked her what was next on the schedule.

"Well now we must prepare the food for dinner, so come with me." I accompanied her down the stairs and into the hallway that separated the kitchen to the other areas of the house. There was a large window in that hallway that had a beautiful view of the garden. I looked out the window to get a view of the surroundings that I was in, and then I saw a man that I did not recognize.

Who is that man, Kaoly? "He is the gardener." "He is a nice guy, but does not talk much." "I think he has been here for years now, from what he has told me." I looked at him, and he met my gaze. He had a sad look in his eyes, a soulless stare.

He was around 60 years old. He had tan leathery skin and was bald, but his body looked to be in shape. He nodded his head towards us, acknowledging our presence then walked away. I felt chills go down my spine. Could this man have come here as a young person?

Was he also a slave to the Daxes? Who knows? Maybe I was overanalyzing things. He very well could just be a regular employee of the Daxes, yet the idea of him being a slave to them from such a young age frightened me. Nevertheless, I shook off my bad thoughts and focused my gaze back to Kaoly.

"Okay this is the kitchen Max." "We will spend a lot of time here." I looked around the kitchen. It was enormous. I could have easily spent an entire day trying to figure out where everything was. It was at least the size of a *Jack in the Box.*

There were two sets of three way sinks. There were two giant convection ovens. I counted three normal size refrigerators and four mini ones. There were two stoves each with eight grills on them and there were four microwaves. Wow, this kitchen was a literal restaurant. "I see you are impressed Max." Honestly I am.

"So was I, but now we have to get to cooking." "We are going to make *Marget de Canard with Creme Brulee*." Oh, that sounds delicious. Kaoly stared at me with her eyes wide open. She was surprised that I knew what that food was.

Kaoly, do not forget that I was a slave for the Daxes for almost five months. I have mastered all of their favorite recipes. "Sorry, I forgot about that." Kaoly said. "Okay let's get to work."

We spent nearly two hours in the kitchen baking and cooking, and by the time we finished it was 3:00 p.m. We had worked over ten hours already, with only one small ten minute break. I was getting tired.

"It is time for us to have our afternoon break." Kaoly, you just read my mind, but please tell me it is more than ten minutes? "Yes, this break is fifteen minutes." If this is your humor I do not like it, Kaoly.

She laughed at my sarcasm, but even through her laugh I could see how fatigued and beaten down she was. I was sure she could not take much more. She had that given up look on her face. I felt awful for her, but the only thing I could suggest was for her to take her "fifteen minutes" in the au pair room.

"Oh, I wish I could, but the house is so big that I would spend most of my pause walking to the room." She giggled quietly. "I appreciate you worrying about me, but I'll be fine." "I have survived almost a year of this."

"I can endure one more month." "Besides, you need to take care of yourself." "I'll go get us some water bottles." She headed for the kitchen door, and right as she turned the door knob she fell. Her legs simply gave out. Kaoly! I ran to her. Are you okay?

She was in and out of consciousness. Her eyes fluttered to stay open. I am going to call Sophie to come get some help! "No!" "Max, please do not do that." Why not? They will take you to the hospital!

"No, please Max, do not tell her." "She cannot know that I am feeling unwell." Why not Kaoly? You are sick! I yelled at her in frustration. She glanced at me with tears in her eyes.

"I think I am pregnant." "I have not had my period in 35 days." I felt my body go numb. I knew what had happened, but I had to ask her.

What happened, Kaoly? She looked at me with tears running down her face. "One of the Daxes' friends has been raping me every time he has come to the countryside." "He has come a total of five times here." My heart fell to my feet. I was filled with rage and disgust. I was at a loss for words.

What will you do Kaoly? "I am out of here in one month, so I will do my best to keep from showing." "I am certain that they will kill me if they find out." Do you really think they will kill a pregnant woman? "Of course, they see me as worthless," but Kaoly, how would they explain your death? Especially to your family.

"I am from Vietnam, and they will make up a lie about how I ended up pregnant and ran off with someone." "I have replayed the story in my head countless times." "The authorities will believe them." Can't you contact your parents?

"I don't have a phone, and even if I did, I wouldn't." "I won't put my family at risk." Kaoly maybe you are not pregnant and you are just malnourished? Have you taken a pregnancy test? "No, but I know my body and I feel different."

Kaoly, I am sorry to ask, but will the man that did this to you be at tonight's dinner? She looked at me with tear filled eyes. She turned her head sideways. She didn't answer. I felt like a jerk for asking her that question.

There was an awkward silence, and she stood up and left the room. I felt bad. I would not ask her any more things, unless she wanted to talk about it. Thankfully, she came back to the room ten minutes later looking a bit better.

"Here is your sandwich and water." "Sorry, we only have five minutes to eat, so we must be fast." I nodded my head, and ate as fast as I could. The sandwich tasted like dirt, but I was hungry.

"Are you finished eating?" Yes, I am. "Perfect." "Oh, and Max," yes, Kaoly? Sorry for rushing out like that." "I hate talking about you know what." Kaoly, it is okay, don't apologize, I understand. "Thanks, Max, now come on, we have work to do." I followed Kaoly down the stairs and out the front door of the countryside mansion.

"We have to wait for Sophie." "She should be here any minute with our next task." "If we are lucky she'll be late and we can enjoy this beautiful view of the garden a minute or two longer." "Isn't it beautiful Max?"

I stared out to the front yard. It was gorgeous. The yard itself was massive. There was a pond that flowed through the front gate of the property all the way to the natural river at the back of the house. There were trees in every direction that I turned to. Birds were flying and singing all through the yard.

The grass was dark green even though it was winter, and there were flowers still alive alongside the front hedge next to the gate. It truly looked like paradise, and if I wasn't scared to death and feeling like shit I would have enjoyed it. I took in one deep breath of fresh air and then Sophie made her way towards us.

"Kaoly, I just checked all the rooms, and everything looks spotless, thank you." "Max, good job on your first day, but man you truly look awful." "Look how swollen your eyes are." "I cannot have you looking like that for the dinner party."

"Come with me so I can fix you up." Thanks for the backhanded compliments, I thought silently. "As for you Kaoly, please go get dressed, and meet me at the guest dining room in an hour." "I will, madame." Kaoly rushed back inside the house. Leaving me alone with Sophie.

"Well chop chop, Max." "I don't like to be kept waiting." She snapped her fingers at me like I was some dog. I wanted to grab the pebbles on the floor and throw them at her, but I didn't. I swallowed my pride like so many times before and followed her down the gravel path.

It was hard to keep up with her since she took such long strides. Just like her brother she was quite tall. She was at least six feet, while I was just around five foot ten. "Are you going to keep falling behind or are you going to hurry up?" I did my best to pick up my speed but my injuries were hurting me, and I did not want to drop the photos.

I wish we had just gone inside the house, but instead we had gone through the outside to reach Sophie's room. I did not understand why we did that until we reached her outside door. She opened her door, and it led right into her restroom.

It was obvious that she did want me to see, or be in her room. "Okay sit hear," she told me. I sat down on the whickered styled chair that was in the restroom.

"I need to cover your bruises with some makeup." "You and Kaoly have to cater the dinner, and I do not want the guests to see you in this shape." "They will think that something happened to you."

Well, if they think that then they will be right, wouldn't they?" The words slipped my mouth before I even had time to think of whether I should say them or not. Sophie started to laugh, but then her green eyes quickly darkened.

"Max, you had your chance to serve us at your own free will and you decided to ruin that." "Now you are going to do everything we ask you to do or else." She raised the tone of her voice when she said or else, and then she simply got the make up brush and started to powder my face.

This was the first time in my life that I had ever used makeup. It felt like someone was brushing flour on my mug. It was not a feeling that I liked, and it made my nose twitch. In fact, I was about to sneeze, but Sophie interrupted me.

"If you sneeze near me I guarantee that you will not see the sunlight for one week." I swallowed my sneeze reluctantly. These people really thought that they were Gods. They really saw everyone else as dirt, but their time would come. I will expose them.

"Well Max, I am finished." "You know it is a shame that you are not pure blood." "You are not a bad looking guy, but I digress, go ahead and go get dressed."

"I'm tired of looking at you." I don't have extra clothes for the dinner party. "I know that you idiot!" "The clothes that you will be wearing are on your bed." "Be at the guest dining room by six o'clock."

Okay, I will be there. I hated that I let her call me an idiot, but I had to bite my tongue, for now. I quietly stood up and left her restroom. She shut the door behind me, and I walked back to the front door of the house.

Quickly, I made my way over to the au pair room, and as I passed through the hallway, I looked carefully at the shrine to the Daxes. There were several pictures of them receiving decorated medals by people with the French flag behind them. Something told me that these folks were politicians. That scared me.

If they had ties with politicians then they were super powerful. That was not a good thing. That said, even politicians were not immune to the law, and as long as I had my evidence I was sure that I would be able to take them down. Besides, just like the old saying goes, "A picture is worth a thousand words."

They would get their justice so enough, but now it was time to change and play "the waiter." I quietly reached for the door to the au pair room, but then I remembered that Kaoly may be changing, so I loudly knocked on the porte to give her a heads up that I was coming in. I waited thirty seconds, and then I opened the door to the room.

Surprisingly the chambre was pitch black. That meant Kaoly was not here, which was good. I could change in peace, so I carefully stepped into the room. The automatic lights soon went on as I passed the doorway, and as I started my descent down the stairs a wave of cold air hit my face.

I guess they can't afford a heater in this room, I told myself sarcastically. Oh well, I continued to my bed and laying right on top of it was a tuxedo and shoes.

The tuxedo was navy blue and the shoes were beige. I felt the coat of the tux and it felt like velvet. The shoes were suede. I unfolded the tux and it contained a black vest with a beige tie, and a black dress shirt. It all felt fancy.

Well here goes nothing. I took a deep breath and started to change. I removed my jeans, and carefully I placed the photos on my bed. I then tried on the tight dress pants and they amazingly fit very well. Next I put on the shirt. It felt silky smooth on my skin.

I then tucked my shirt into the pants, and put on my vest. After that, I tied the straps of the vest in place, and then I put my coat on. Lastly, I grabbed the pictures and put them all in the large pocket inside of the coat.

With my pictures safely secured in, I finished tying my shoes and tie. I was all ready, but now it was time to see how I looked. I headed to the restroom for the big reveal, and as soon as I got to the mirror I had to do a double glance because I barely recognized myself. I looked like a fake version of me.

The makeup that Sophie had put on me made me even paler than I already was. All the bruises were covered from my face, and I don't know how she did it, but my eyes did not look swollen anymore. She had even added blush to make my cheeks look rosy and full of life.

To those who saw me tonight, I would look elegant and put together, but in reality I was a slave. The idea made my stomach turn, but in contrast it made me more motivated than ever to escape tonight. I was no one's puppet, and I was no one's fool. I will outsmart these Daxes.

With my smile plastered across my face, I left the au pair room and was greeted by Kaoly right at the edge of the hallway. She was wearing a flowy black dress and red heels with a red bow. She was dressed elegantly, but even with all the makeup she had, her eyes could not conceal that pain that she must be feeling.

"Max, are you ready?" Yes. "Good, we have to go greet the guests now." "You will say hello and ask them if they want their coat to be hung or not." "After we finish all of that we must prepare the table, okay?"

I nodded at Kaoly. We made our way to the guest living-dining room, and boy was it huge. The room was split into two. A living space and a dining space. The living room space was covered with fluffy brown carpet, and the dining room side was covered in luxurious black marble that was so shiny that it reflected back like a mirror.

In both the dining and living room there were four chandeliers. These chandeliers hung pretty high in the ceiling and they were gold in color. I was certain that they were partially covered in real gold.

Unlike in the main living room this one did not have a grand piano. What it did have was a large table that contained different board games, kind of like the tables in the bar. The dining room had shelves of different drinks. From what I could see it was a mixture of alcohol to everyday sodas.

The living room's walls were painted in dark burgundy. It balanced perfectly with the brown fluffy carpet. The dining room's walls were painted in a nude tone. Both sides complemented themselves well.

"The guests are about to enter the property." "I need both of you by the front door of the guest entrance please." "You look like you can pass as one of us," Sophie eyed me down and then left. I ignored her comment and headed to the outside of the guest living room.

As we reached the outside the first car pulled in. Out stepped a man. He looked like your everyday joe. Nothing special about him. Kaoly asked for his coat, but he did not give it to her, so she walked him to the guest living room, and right as she left a second car pulled into the driveway.

I could see that it was filled with people. As soon as they parked, two men and two women got out. One of the men looked to be around sixty years old and the other one was probably somewhere in his mid to late twenties.

Both of the women were in their mid to late twenties as well. They kind of reminded me of the Scooby Doo gang because they were together but they did not seem to fit in with each other. They slowly walked up to the door.

Bonjour, my name is Max, I told them as they got to the front door. The older man gave me a cold stare and said, "Do not talk to us unless you are spoken to." I felt my blood rush to my face.

I felt embarrassed and I stared at them blankly. I did not respond to him because if I did I would have lost it. Thankfully one of the women came over and grabbed his hand and said, "Please, dear do not be like that, he did not know."

The man's cold stare softened as he handed me his coat, and to my surprise his son apologized to me. "I apologized for my father's harsh words." "May you please take our coats for us?" Of course I can. I forced a fake smile and took their coats.

I then led them to the guest room. Please, make yourselves at home. If you need anything just give me a call. "You got it," the son replied. "Don't worry about us, we will be fine," the woman he was with said with a gentleness in her voice.

I headed back to greet the other guests, and a sort of premonition came over me. I had a feeling that those people would be my ticket back to Paris. They did not seem to be as bad as the Daxes, and their car surely was big enough.

They had come in a large *2025 BMW X7*. I could easily hide in there without being seen, and if I got caught maybe the son and the two women would have sympathy for me? Wait, Max, don't get ahead of yourself, I told myself. The first thing I need to do is figure out if they are even from Paris.

How can I know that without asking? Hmm, I pondered. Oh, yes! I could check their coats for any identification! I walked straight to the coats, and prayed to God that something in there would let me know if they were from Paris.

I checked all the pockets of the coats that I hung, and they were all empty. Dammit! My newly found hope was already fading, but wait maybe the coats have an inside pocket like mine. I quickly unbuttoned one of them. Yes, there was a large pocket there. I placed my hand inside and I felt a card!

Please be an id, please be an id. I pulled the card out, and it was an id. It was the older man's id, and he was living in Paris! I felt butterflies flow through me. They were my chance to get out of this prison.

All I had to do now was find their keys. I needed the keys to unlock their door, so I could hide in their car without an alarm going off when the time was right. Easier said than done.

I wondered if they had left their keys anywhere in the coats. I checked every pocket again and there was nothing, but then it hit me. In movies people who have dinner parties tend to leave their keys in a bowl of some sort.

Where would that bowl be? It had to be near the entrance. I swiftly went over by the door and to my delight there was a bowl with keys in it on the table! There were only two sets of keys, and thankfully one of them had a *BMW* logo. I glanced at them to make sure I remembered how they looked. I didn't want to confuse them when all the guests arrived.

Now the question was, when was the perfect time to hide in their car without the Daxes or anyone noticing. It would have to be during a time that everyone was drinking that much I knew, but the issue was whether or not the Daxes would need my services after everyone left. Should I speak to Kaoly about my plan?

No, I could not do that. Even though she is an au pair and a prisoner herself I could not trust her. I knew nothing of her. "Max, can you please help the other guests who just pulled in?" Huh? I jumped in surprise. I had not noticed Kaoly come in. She gave me a wink.

Yes, Kaoly, I am on it. She placed her hand on my shoulders. She knew that I had been day dreaming, but she wanted to prevent me from getting into trouble. Thanks, Kaoly, I whispered to her, and I got straight to work.

I spent the next forty minutes greeting people, and by the time I thought no one else was coming, they came. There was no mistaking that bright red car, even in the darkness. They're *Mercedes* glimmered in the moonlight.

I could see Juliette through the mirror as she applied her lipstick. I could see Alexandre as he changed gears in the car. My stomach tied in knots as they parked. They still had not seen me.

Alexandre got out of the car, and went over to open Juliette's door. How fake I thought. Just a show for the people who could be watching. Juliette fixed her dress as she stepped out of the car, and then they started to walk my way.

They immediately saw me. Juliette had a face full of glee and Alexandre had a "I own you" look on his face. They both smiled, and came over to talk to me.

Chapter 6
THE TRAGIC DINNER PARTY

"Well, well, well who do we have here, Juliette?" "You do not recognize him, Alexandre?" "No, please refresh my memory." "Well, his name is Max." "He used to have the pleasure of working and living with us in Paris, but he threw it all away because he could not handle the responsibility of being an adult."

"Oh yes!" "He is the one who came into our room without permission, and he took something that did not belong to him, didn't he?" "Yes!" "He took a passport that the French immigration told me to take care of until his contract was over." She glared at me with her beady eyes.

"What brings you to this neck of the woods, Max?" Hello Madame Juliette and Monsieur Alexandre, I am here because I disobeyed my host family, and they have placed me in their countryside mansion as part of the cleaning crew.

I truly am sorry for all the harm that I have caused them. I now understand my place. It took every ounce of my body to say that, but they ate it up. Their ego was bigger than their insight.

"Well Max, if you behave maybe we will bring you back." "The kids do really miss you." Juliette said. She then proceeded to caress my head, and she handed me her coat. I took it carefully. Alexandre then came over to me and said, "It really is a shame that you are here, but you know punishments are good to train dogs."

"If you show us that you've learned your lesson you will be back to a much easier work life." He gave me his coat, and as Juliette was entering the front door he quietly whispered, "You do everything I say and I will make sure you eventually get back to the USA, and I mean everything." "If you do not, I will personally make sure your life is a living hell."

He then gave me a wink, and licked his lips while moving his wavy hair from his face. It made my body tense up. Alexandre was acting much differently than he normally did. It scared me. In Paris he always treated me as a worthless piece of shit, but now he was being creepy toward me in a perverted way.

Why the sudden change? Why was he doing this? I wondered, but then I understood. Alexandre Dax was the Dax that I knew the least. In Paris, he was always coming home late from work, and barely had any time off. Any time that I did see him it was with the other Daxes.

I must have never really seen the true Alexandre until now. This realization made my body feel ice cold. I really had to get out of here before something terrible happened to me, especially since his three week Christmas vacation was just about to start.

The more exposure that I had with him, the less safe that I was. This wasn't an ideal thing. Fuck. I felt my armpits start to sweat. This was getting to be too intense again, but I had to calm down.

Breathe, Max, breathe. I will be okay, I told myself. Tonight I will be leaving in that *BMW* one way or another, but first thing first, I had to go help Kaoly set up. Now that the Daxes were here I was sure the party would start.

I rapidly gave my tux a dusting with my hands, and went back inside. I gently closed the door behind me, and as I started to walk toward the guest room I saw bright lights hit the window. It was another car, with more guests. They were late, but I had to go help them. I quickly stepped back outside to greet the new arrivals.

They parked their sport's vehicle at the edge of the yard, and a large man stepped out. He looked to be around sixty-five based on his wrinkles and his receding hairline. He had a big gut, but he was dressed nicely.

He walked over to open the door for a very thin woman who looked quite young at first glance, but at second glance you could see some wrinkles. She was about forty if I had to guess. She looked very elegant and poised, even as she gave the man a slight peck on the cheek.

What a mismatched couple I thought as they grabbed each other's hands and walked to the front entrance of the house. I wouldn't have guessed that they were an item because they look more like friends, but whatever it was none of my business.

I was just happy that they both smiled at me as they gave me their coats. The woman even tipped me ten euros! I was left speechless, but I quickly thanked her. "No need to thank us, and don't worry about taking us to the guest room." "We know where it is at." The woman told me.

I nodded my head and I hung up their coats. They slowly walked into the house. It was time to go help Kaoly, so I reached to close the front door, but then I stopped. This was my chance. It was the perfect time to briskly scope out the *BMV* before I went to help Kaoly setup.

Wasting no time, I hastily made my way back outside and I sped walked to the *BMW.* I looked around it. The windows were not tinted so I could see inside. The car was completely empty, and to my luck the trunk had a grocery sheet! I could pull that over myself and not worry about being seen.

This was terrific. Now I just had to unlock the car. That would put me in a better position for tonight, but the question was, did I have time to unlock the car? Probably not, but I took the risk. I ran back into the house and grabbed the keys from the bowl.

I went to the trunk of the car and manually unlocked it. I did not want to make a noise by using the alarm. I quietly pulled the trunk open, and peeked inside. I could easily fit in here. I felt happy. "Max, are you here?" "Max?"

I almost peed my pants. Kaoly startled me. I quickly closed the trunk. I am over here! I shouted to her. She waved at me as I made my way back to the front entrance. "What were you doing over there, Max?" Oh I was just admiring that *BMW*. It is so fancy. Kaoly rolled her eyes at me and smiled. "Well, come on, let's get the food heated up."

I followed her to the kitchen and we started to warm up the food. "Max, do you know how to set up the table?" Yes, that was one of the first things that the Daxes made sure I nailed. "Okay, so you set up the table, and I will get the food out of the oven." Got it!

I left the kitchen and went to the dining room area. I pulled out all the silverware and started to set everything up. Within five minutes I had almost set up everything. I just needed the napkins. I could not find them, so I walked over to the kitchen to ask Kaoly where they were.

"You look radiant as ever, Kaoly." I stopped walking. Someone was in there with Kaoly. I ducked behind one of the stainless steel cabinets at the entrance of the kitchen and peeked my head out to see who was there. What I saw shocked me to my core.

The last guest, the man who had come with the woman who tipped me, was doing something beyond demonic. He was groping Kaoly. He was touching her breasts as she stood motionlessly. Her face was blank. Her hands were trembling. She looked like she had dissociated her mind from her body.

I felt like throwing up. I wanted to kick his ass, but I knew I had to be smarter. I quietly stood up and backed away into the hallway, and then I called for Kaoly. Hey, Kaoly the forks go on the left side of the plate, right? To my happiness she responded instantly.

"You got it Max." "The forks go on the left side of the plate." As she was responding to me I heard the creep head out of the kitchen. I don't even know why he assumed that Kaoly was alone. I mean he knew that I was there, right? Or maybe he just didn't care.

My blood was boiling. He was probably the one that got Kaoly pregnant. I was starting to see blurry. I was that mad. What did we do to deserve this? All we wanted was to become au pairs and get a new cultural experience. This was wrong!

Kaoly was pregnant, and I was beaten up. Take deep breaths in Max. You can't lose your cool right now. You have to be smart, I told myself. I will get my chance to take action, but now I have to put up with this disgusting shit. I took in another deep breath and went back into the kitchen.

"All done Max?" Yes, I am Kaoly. What about you, and are you feeling okay? "Yes, I am all done, and I never felt better." She said with her almond shaped eyes filled with sorrow. I simply nodded okay. I did not want to pressure her into talking.

"Now we must wait for the Daxes to be ready for us to serve them." Okay that sounds cool, but do we just stand here or can we go sit somewhere?" "Unfortunately, we must stand here, Max." Okay that sounds boring. The least they can do is let us have a board game to play.

Kaoly giggled at my sarcastic joke. "I agree with you." "Look at them, they are all laughing and have a great time." I peered my head through the hallway into the guest room. I couldn't see much, but they sure looked like they were having a good time.

Are they drinking, Kaoly? "You better believe it Max." "By the end of dinner they will be quite drunk." That thought scared me.

"Kaoly, if the guests get too drunk, will they not go home?" "Oh, of course they will go back to their homes." "They do not care if they're drunk." Thank goodness, I silently thought in my head. In order for my plan to work I had to sneak out in the night, even if it meant risking a car accident.

"Max, Sophie has just given me the signal that I was waiting for." Wait, what signal? "She pulled on her ear." What is that supposed to mean? "It means she will excuse everyone to the dining area." "We must get ready." Okay, but what do we do first?

My stomach was hurting from the growing anxiety. I hated being in an area where there were a lot of people, especially not under my own will. "Do not worry, Max." "Just follow my lead." "Do what I do."

Kaoly looked at me with her empty smile. It made me feel a tad better. "Here they come." I glanced over to the living room and all the guests were getting up. There were maybe sixteen people there, not including us. They all looked elegant and wealthy.

Ten out of the sixteen people there were at least over sixty years old. The other 6 were younger. "Right this way Monsieur Dax et Madame Dax." Kaoly moved her head to the chairs she wanted me to sit the Daxes in.

Of course they would be sitting in the front center of the table. "Please take a seat, Monsieur Alexandre, Madame Juliette, and Madame Sophie." I smiled at them as I led them to their seats. I pulled the chairs out and they sat down.

"Very nice to see you so poised Max." "That clothing really makes you look like an entirely different person." "Maybe we will require our next au pair to dress as formally as you are dressed now." Next au pair? I looked Juliette directly in the eyes as she said that.

"Well yes, Roman and Mylene need the babysitting." "I cannot have my babies alone now, can I?" Juliette's acknowledgement of getting another au pair made me lightheaded. I could not bear the fact that someone else would suffer what Kaoly and I have gone through. I could not let this happen, but I could not let Juliette know that I was worried, so I smiled at her.

Alexandre then said, "But you know Max," yes? "Juliette and I have been thinking that after a month of punishment if you behave we will also bring you back to Paris, and we will have two au pairs."

"Both of you will share the room of course." "We are nice people and we know you wanted a Parisian experience, so that is our deal with you." "You do everything we say and we bring you back." "How does that sound?"

I think that sounds, my body froze. I did not dare to look down, but I knew Alexandre was rubbing his hand on my thigh from underneath the table. Juliette could not see because the table cover was obstructing the view. I wanted to scream and shout to the four winds of what was going on, but I couldn't. I had to let it happen so my plan wouldn't be screwed.

"Well, how does that sound, Max?" He repeated with a malicious grin splattered over his face. I think that sounds great, Monsieur Alexandre. I quietly said as I smiled at him and Juliette. They both looked happy at my willingness to be a servant again, so I continued to play the part of an idiot to throw them off of any suspicions that they may have of me.

Again, I want to tell you both how sincerely sorry I am for having disrespected you. I hope you guys have an amazing time tonight, and with that I went back to seat the others.

It took about ten minutes to get everyone seated and served. "Okay now that we are done, time to clean the living room." Oh yay for us. I said sarcastically. Kaoly laughed. "Excuse me, where is the large cooler located?" I turned around.

It was the older man from the *BMW*. "I'll take you, sir." Kaoly left and took the guy to the cooler. Why was he looking for the cooler? Well, who cares. It is not my problem. I waited for two minutes and Kaoly came back.

She handed me a broom and a mop, and we got to work. I swept up all the ashes of the cigarettes that they had smoked. Kaoly reorganized the seats and dusted off the tables. She also took the dirty dishes that they had left in the living room.

By the time we were both done all we heard coming from the dining room was laughter. They were having a good time while

Kaoly and I were suffering. I hated them for it. I even hated those who did not know that we were kidnapped.

They should have suspected that something was off from us. Kaoly looked like a walking zombie and I had bags under my eyes that not even the makeup could hide. Plus I was walking with a limp now.

My body was still hurting so much. I felt like if I sat down I would not be able to get back up, but I had to keep pushing forward. I could not let them win. I was stronger and smarter than they were. I may be poor, but the fact that they have money does not make them any better than me.

"Max, did you hear me?" Oh sorry, what did you say Kaoly? "We are finished cleaning." Good, what do we do now? "Well if this dinner is like all the rest then they will be in the dining-room till at least 9:30 pm." I glanced at the watch on the wall, and it was 8:30 pm. Okay, so are we free now?

"Yes, kind of." If they need us they will bell us." What do you mean by bell us? "I mean what it literally sounds like." "They will shake a bell to call us over." Are you serious? "Yes, so I wouldn't say that we are free because if we are not in that room within ten seconds of that bell being rung, we are in for it."

Okay, Kaoly, then I will just be sitting outside staring at the stars. "Okay, but don't go out too far." Got it. I quietly walked to the door, and right as I was going to open it I was interrupted by the younger guy from the *BMW*.

"Hey Max, sorry I need to go put this in my father's car." "Can you hand me the *BMW* keys?" I reached for the bowl and handed the son his father's keys. "Thanks, don't close the door, I'll be right back."

I held the door open as he went down the stairs with a small cooler in his hand. Why did he have a cooler? Was that the reason why his father went with Kaoly to the freezer? My curiosity emerged.

I watched him carefully as he opened the trunk of the car. My eyes were glued on him as he placed the cooler inside the trunk. He then closed it and locked the car. Damn. This meant I would have to unlock the vehicle again.

"Thanks for leaving the door open for me." "Here are the keys." I took his keys. "I'll walk you back to the dining room." Kaoly told him. "I'll be right back to join you Max."

Okay, I'll be outside Kaoly. Thank God, she left with him. This would give me enough time to unlock the car again, and see what was inside the cooler! My curiosity was at its peak, and as soon as they were out of view I ran back to the car.

I carefully unlocked the trunk, and opened it. Then I removed the grocery binder that was obstructing my complete view of the trunk. My heart stopped. The cooler read "reins," which translates to kidneys in English. This couldn't be true.

Chapter 7

THE ABUSE

Were the old man and his son organ harvesters? I felt my mouth go dry. Things like this surely did not exist. Did they? Was this all a joke? I had to know, now! I reached for the cooler with trembling hands and I opened the lid. I looked inside and to my utter happiness there were no organs. There was simply ice.

I let out a sigh of relief. Unfortunately, I got no relief from it. I still felt uneasy. This was terrifying. There may have been no kidney in the cooler, but the label didn't lie. Did the old man leave the organ in the big cooler? If so the Daxes must be involved too.

This was not good. Fear started to creep all over me, and hearing the howling of the wind rustle the leaves did not make me feel any better. Fuck, it would be my luck that the only way out of the Daxes' home was by leaving with people just as psychotic as them.

This was too much. Sweat started to drip down from my temples. My heart was beating so fast that it felt like it would jump out of my chest. I started to feel panicked. Why didn't I listen to my family and just go to college? Why did I have to go the route that no one went through?

Stop it, Max! I yelled in frustration. Stop blaming yourself. It is Daxes who ruined everything. And fear or no fear I will be in this car by the time it heads back to Paris!

Feeling less terror I closed the lid of the cooler, and I gently pushed the trunk down. I then slowly made my way back to the mansion. I took in one last deep breath before opening the door, and I stepped inside.

I then placed the BMW keys back in the bowl and scanned for Kaoly. She wasn't back yet. She was probably busy with something. I would wait for her outside, so I opened the door and sat back down on the front steps.

I rubbed my temples to relax, and I looked up at the star filled sky. I should have felt peaceful, but I didn't. Even from out here I could hear everyone laughing, and having a good time.

They're laughter annoyed me. Sadly, there was nothing that I could do but sit and wait for Kaoly. Who should have been here by now. It had been at least six minutes since she left. Ugh they probably had her busy with some sort of work! I guess I might as well go and help her before they come get me in trouble.

I slowly stood back up and went back inside the mansion. I was sure she was helping in the guest dining area. I would go there, but first I had to use the restroom. I had to freshen up because the makeup was entering my eyes, causing them to burn. Hmm, where is the nearest bathroom? I pondered. I did not want to go all the way to the au pair room.

Oh yes! The guest area had a restroom at the beginning of the hallway. I will go there. I just had to make sure to not be seen by the guests. The last thing I wanted was to work with make up in my eyes, so I carefully tiptoed to the restroom.

The laughter grew louder as I neared the bathroom, and right as I was about to open the door I noticed that the light was on. Oh great, someone was in there. I guess I'll go wait at the edge of the hall to give them privacy.

I started to turn back, but then I heard whispers coming from the restroom. "No, Jacque, please." "Your wife is in the kitchen." "It would not be right." "Come on Jacque, please sweet baby." "You are only here for another month." "Let me enter your treasure box one last time."

"Please, Jacque, I do not want to do anything." "You really hurt me last time." "I bled for over two days." "That is because you were tight and not ready." "It will not hurt this time." "No, please Florian." "Kaoly, either you do it willingly or I will have to force myself on you." "I will give you till the count of 3."

My blood was boiling. I felt nauseous. Kaoly was getting abused. I had to do something. I had to stop this, but what could I do to not jeopardize myself? "Times up Kaoly." "Take off your dress or I will rip it off."

There was no way that I would let this creature violate Kaoly. I ran to the door and right as I was about to kick it open I saw a light reset switch. Thank you God, I silently thought. I hit the reset button and everything went dark.

I then bolted back to the front door of the guest area, and I crouched down. "What happened to the lights?" "I do not know Sophie, but I will call the groundskeeper to see if he knows what is going on." Juliette stated.

"I think there is a light reset button somewhere near the entrance of the house." Alexandre chimed in. "Let me go see if I can find it." Oh crap. Alexandre was coming my way. I immediately stepped outside. I did not want to be blamed for anything.

Crunch, crunch, crunch, the sound of someone walking on dried leaves made me squeal. "Max, I am sorry." "I didn't mean to scare you." It was Kaoly! She had a smile on her face. Her eyes were filled with joy.

Probably because she had not been taken advantage of today. "Do you know how the lights turned off?" No clue, but I heard Alexandre trying to fix them, so hopefully that means they won't be back on till tomorrow.

Kaoly laughed at my joke, but to my bad luck the lights turned right back on not even ten seconds after making my joke. Oh well, I guess I have the opposite effect on things. "Oh don't say things like that, Max," Kaoly said as she strained her eyes."

"Sorry, for the funny face." "Sudden brightness tends to hurt my eyes." It is okay, Kaoly, I told her with a sly smile. "Have you been out here since I left, Max?" Yes, I needed a little break

My muscles ache, and my head hurts. I am beyond tired. I just want to sleep. She looked at me with pity. I felt bad for partially lying to her. I had not been in here the entire time, but I did feel awful. I should not be complaining to her though. Especially after what she had just gone through.

I wished I could have hugged her, but I did not want to make her feel awkward. Only she could tell me what she went through, and I would not dig it out of her. "You know what Max?" What is that Kaoly?

"The Daxes never stay on the guest side of the house." "They always go back to their part of the mansion." "When the party's over I want you to rest." "I will clean the entire kitchen." But what if they ask for me, Kaoly? "Do not worry; they won't."

"They'll be so drunk that they won't even know left from right." Kaoly, are you sure about that? "Yes," no I mean are you sure that you can handle all the work on your own? "Oh yes, and I don't not want to hear any complaining." "You need to get some rest!"

Tears filled my eyes. This was unbelievable. Kaoly had just given me the opportunity to leave tonight without realizing it. I could now stop stressing about how I would sneak into the *BMW* without being seen by anyone.

I would simply go inside the car right as the party was ending, and that was all. A simple escape plan that was all thanks to Kaoly. I couldn't help but get emotional. Her selflessness to give me a break after everything she went through made the tears fall from my eyes.

I gently wiped them away. "Are you okay, Max?" Yes, I am. I am just so happy that you are doing this for me. I am very grateful for that gesture, Kaoly. It really means a lot. "You are welcome Max, but no more crying okay?" Alright, I whispered softly. "Perfect." "Well, I think they will call the party off in about thirty minutes."

"In the meantime would you like to go stargazing with me by the river?" "It is the one place where I can escape my reality." Say no more, lead the way. I followed Kaoly to the backyard, and as soon as we got there the sound of the nocturnal animals singing filled the night air.

I heard crickets chirping. I heard an owl hooting. I even caught the distant sound of bugs moving around. It all made me feel peaceful. "These sounds beat slaving away over a hot kitchen, don't they?" Oh yes, of course, Kaoly. "Good, now wait till we get to the river and you'll feel true serenity."

"We just have to stay on this path and it will take us directly there." Is the river part of their property? "From what I know they own the part of the river that is right in front of their house." Wow, that's incredible. "Yeah, that's the power of money," Kaoly softly said as we reached the fence that led to the water.

"I hope you are a good climber, Max." Why do you wish that? "Well, we have to hop over this fence to get over to the rivière as the French call it." Why don't we just open the fence? "They keep it locked at all times." Oh, I see, well I am right behind you.

We quickly hopped over the five foot tall fence. It wasn't that hard. There were wooden protrusions that made it easy to climb over. "Do you see those steps over there?" "The ones that go down to the water?" Yeah, I see them.

"Let's take a seat there, and then we can lay flat on our backs on the grass." I followed Kaoly to the steps. They were cold to the touch, but they felt soothing on my bruises. I welcomed the feeling. "Go ahead and lay on your back, Max." I slowly laid on the grass and looked up to the sky.

I was left speechless. The stars shimmered brightly, illuminating the entire sky. It was mesmerizing. "Do you now understand why being near the river is my escape from reality?" Yes, you have the best show in the world from here. "Something like that."

"Max, can I confess something to you?" What, Kaoly? "Those sparkling stars saved me." What do you mean? "I was going to kill myself before I found out I was pregnant, Max." I stood straight up after hearing that. Kaoly, please do not say those things.

"I am serious, Max." "I have been used and abused more times than I can count." "I do not feel like myself anymore." I feel like a body without a soul." "The only thing that stopped me was looking up at the stars, and realizing how tiny each of us are." "They gave me strength." "Strength that kept me going until I got pregnant."

"When I found out that I was pregnant I knew that I had to live for my baby." "Even though this baby was conceived in the most horrendous of ways, I want to keep it." "I believe the stars have given me a reason to live, and a reason to be strong."

I did not know what to say. All I could do was wrap my arms around Kaoly. She needed a hug and I needed to hug someone. We needed the "hugging endorphins" to be released. "It makes me sad that someone as sweet as you is stuck here, Max." Ditto, Kaoly.

"Max, can you promise me one thing?" What is that, Kaoly? I stared at her as she dug into the pocket on the side of her dress. She pulled out a small envelope. "This is the address and names, emails, phone numbers of everyone that is important to me." "If something happens to me, please make sure you let them know."

Nothing is going to happen to you, Kaoly. You are going home in one month. You'll be back in Vietnam. "Can you please just promise me?" It scared me that Kaoly was terrified of getting killed just a month before her departure.

Did she fear for her life? Of course she did. The look of fear cannot be hidden, and it was plastered across her face. I had to say yes, so I did. I promise you Kaoly.

"Perfect." She stood up and headed back toward the gate. "It is time to go." "The party should be over in ten minutes." "You can go back to your room and get some rest."

Are you sure the Daxes will be okay with that? "Yes, like I said, they are probably so drunk they do not even remember who we are." Well then, I guess they should have more parties. Kaoly laughed a little at my lame joke as she led us back to the house.

"Max, you should use the front door of the guest area to enter the house." Why is that Kaoly? "That way the Daxes and their guests don't see you, and you can go straight to the au pair room." You are beyond sweet, Kaoly. "Yeah, well you owe me," she giggled.

"Now I wish you a good night." She opened the back door and went inside the house. I waved bye to her and headed to the front yard with a guilty conscience. I felt bad for not telling her my plan, but I simply trusted no one. Besides when I got out of here, Kaoly would get the justice that she deserved.

I would make sure of it, even if it was the last thing that I did. With that strong motivation in my mind, I made my way to the parked cars. I immediately spotted the *BMW* and jumped for joy. It was time.

I ran to the car, and with my shaking hand I pulled the trunk open. I cautiously crawled inside, and as soon as I touched the carpet I felt an adrenaline rush that sent my head spinning. I was over excited because I had successfully snuck in the vehicle, but I had to calm myself down.

I quietly pulled the door of the trunk back down, and I took some deep breaths. I focused on the cozy soft carpet that the trunk had. It felt squishy like a marshmallow on my hands, and slowly, but surely my adrenaline disappeared. Now it was just a wait and see game.

It took maybe twenty minutes for the man, his son and the two ladies to come back to the car. I heard them say their farewells to the Daxes. My heart was in my throat as I waited for them to open the doors of the *BMW*.

Suddenly, the passenger side of the car opened, and then the driver's side. "Are you sure you want to go all the way back to Paris, dad?" The father responded, "I would rather be at home than at any hotel." "I would rather be in Paris too." "I have a very important meeting that I have to attend." One of the women said. "Well if you guys say so, then let's go."

Please get in already, I prayed as I clung onto the carpet. I felt sweat dripping from my forehead as I felt the weight of people entering the vehicle. Please start the auto, please start.

I closed my eyes waiting to hear the engine go on, but ironically I never did. The car was so modern that it made no noise while turning on. I only knew that we had left because the vehicle started to move forward.

Here we go, I quietly told myself as the *BMW* picked up speed. I held on tight to the carpet as we left the pebbly drive way of the Daxes countryside house. Thankfully, after a few minutes the road became seamless, and we started going faster.

It was apparent that we were on a highway now, but I was not out of the clear just yet. I had to make sure to not be noticed by anyone, which proved to be quite challenging because as soon as we got on the freeway, everyone except the driver and I were snoring.

Which meant that I had to stay as quiet as a mouse. Fortunately, I did just that, and after what felt like an eternity of not moving a single muscle the car slowed down. We slowly pulled into what seemed like a private road.

"I don't think I want to be in a car for three hours ever again!" One of the lady's said. "Yeah me either," the other one responded. "You ladies were asleep the entire ride," the son answered them with a laugh. "Well, so were you," the father jokingly added as they all got out of the car.

"*Hahha*, whatever dad." "Did you have a good time babe?" The son asked one of the girls. "Yes, an amazing time." "What about you sweetie?" The dad asked the other lady." "I had an incredible time."

"Fantastic!" "Can we walk you two gals back to your place?" "Yes!" They both shouted as their footsteps grew more distance from the *BMW*.

Perfect, that gave me some time to do a quick stretch. My legs had fallen asleep hours ago, so I carefully lifted my right leg and stretched it. It felt good to be able to get my blood flowing again.

Unluckily, I had to cut my stretching short because just as fast as they had left the car, the two men were already walking back to the vehicle. *Bang, bang*, they both closed the door as they got in. The car started to move right after. "How much did you make from the kidney?" My heart froze almost immediately when the father spoke.

"I made about 120 thousand euros, dad." "That is not bad at all." "Who did you harvest it from?" "Oh it was just someone that I matched with on *Tinder*."

"Is there any way that she can identify you?" "No, my face was covered on *Tinder*." "People on dating sites are so desperate that they are willing to meet anyone anywhere." "Where is she now?" "I left her tied to a tree, maybe three miles from the Daxes countryside home."

"Juliette will go on a run tomorrow and "find" her." "She will have her hero moment on the news tomorrow, thanks to us." "Oh those Daxes sure love their publicity, but they are good allies, so do not forget that."

"Of course I won't, dad." "Good, and did you deliver the kidney on time to the buyer?" "Yes, I got it to them about thirty minutes early." "Perfect, the quicker the better." "Good job son."

I could not believe my ears. My body was shaking. These people were organ harvesters and the Daxes, at least by association, were in it too. I could only imagine all the pain and suffering that these two pieces of shit had caused.

This was horrific. My body began to feel abnormal. The anger that I felt was not allowing me to see straight. Fear was consuming me, and it made me feel nauseous. I wanted to yell at the top of my lungs, but I couldn't. I started to feel claustrophobic, and tears began to run down my cheeks.

This wasn't good. I knew that I would faint. I tried to calm down, but soon everything went dark. "*Thunk, thunk,*" I gasped for air as the doors closed. I heard footsteps walking away from the car. Indeed, I had fainted from the stress of it all.

This is what my life had come to, but there was still a light at the end of the tunnel. The car was parked, and I was still alive. That meant two things. We were in Paris, and no one had noticed me faint.

Thank you God, I prayed silently. Now I just need to get out of this car. I reached for the trunk handle but stopped dead in my tracks as I heard the footsteps still a little too close to the *BMW.* I froze automatically, daring to not make more noise.

Fortunately, the footsteps grew further away, and within seconds I heard the sound of bolts being unlocked, followed by the squeal of a creaking door being opened and then closed. They had gone into what I hoped was their house.

This was my chance. I carefully peeled the grocery sheet back and lifted my head over the seats. The lights reflecting back in the distance hurt my eyes slightly, so I rubbed them gently and cleared my vision. I could now see the older man and his son through the large house window. They were putting their coats away.

Undoubtedly we had arrived at their home, but sadly it was not in Paris. That much I knew. This house was too big to belong in Paris, and the yard was too massive. This had to be the "banlieue," or the outskirts of the city.

Oh great, I could easily be as far as 20 miles from the actual city. Damn, but hey, at least it was better than being three hours away in a countryside house in the middle of nowhere. This was not going to deter me.

Besides, I was proud of myself. I had escaped the Daxes again, and once these two vile men turned the lights off from their house I would head to the city. Even if that meant running till I got to the nearest bus or metro station.

Yeah, that is what I will do, I muttered to myself, as the lights went off in the house. Perfect timing! Now, I just needed to wait a little while longer to make sure that the lights stayed off.

I'll give them two minutes, I told myself. One second, two seconds, three seconds, one hundred twenty seconds, time to open the trunk. I pressed the button to open the trunk, and I pushed myself to the edge.

I then quickly hopped off, and I walked away from the *BMW*. Wasting no time, I began to look for any sort of gate or door that would help me leave the property. I couldn't see anything, so I headed in the opposite direction of the house. Woefully, I made a terrible mistake. Staring right at me with their canine teeth out were two German Shepherds.

Chapter 8

THE WARRANT & THE DEATH

The dogs started to growl. Their saliva was dripping to the floor. I stared at the dogs, and they stared at me with their big dark eyes. Their bodies were as tense as mine was. We were in a stalemate, but the dogs were having none of that. One of the German Shepherds walked around to the back of me.

Now they had me surrounded, like a deer that was going to be killed. Their growling was getting intense. They lowered their heads and put their front legs forward. They were about to charge. I had to act now, but what could I do?

I was drawing blanks. The only thing my body wanted to do was run, and that may be my only option, but I had to be smart about it. What dog was closer to me, and which way should I run? I slowly turned my head to the side to see which dog could potentially attack first, and then I saw it! I saw the shimmer of the shiny front gate.

My way to leave this compound. It was no more than 100 meters away from me. *Grr, ruff, grr, ruff* the dogs growled. They were getting ready to leap. Decision time! Without thinking twice I charged at the dog that was in front of me. It caught it off guard and it left running away.

My adrenaline was at full swing now, and I was up and sprinting to the fence. My mind was filled with so much adrenaline that I had forgotten about the second dog, until it bit the back of my winter jacket.

It was latched onto me, but I threw my leg up to the side and kicked the dog on the jaw. It let out a whimper and let go. I continued to run, I was only 50 meters away from the gate. I could practically taste freedom.

Thirty meters, twenty meters, I was only one jump away from climbing that fence, and then I stopped dead in my tracks. *Electrical fence, climb at your own risk.* Fuck! It would be impossible to climb without getting severely shocked; or maybe even killed.

Grr, ruff, ruff, grr, and I had no time to find another solution. The dogs were right behind me again, so I continued running, but I was getting tired. My initial burst of adrenaline was wearing off. What should I do? Think, Max, think! I panically searched the dark night for a solution, but I found none. This was it. My body was too tired to continue. I would be mauled to death.

My legs cramped up and I fell to the floor. The air was knocked out of my lungs. I tried to stand, but it was useless. My body had no energy left. It was over for me.

Tears rolled down my cheeks as I waited for the dogs to sink their teeth in my bruised skin. I prayed that they would not maul my face.

As gruesome as it sounds, I wanted my parents to at least be able to identify me.

Funny, they say your life flashes before your eyes when you are on the brink of death, but that was not happening to me. All I could think about was the pain that I was going to cause my parents and loved ones. I prayed that they would not suffer too much, and I closed my eyes and waited.

Phwwwwwft, phwwwwwft, phwwwwwft. Huh, what was that sound? *Phwwwwwft, phwwwwwwft, phwwwwwft.* Could that be a whistle? I dared not to lift my head, but after a few seconds the noise of dogs growling disappeared. The growling was replaced by the sounds of footsteps, human footsteps.

What was going on? I carefully picked up my head from the floor. "I do not wish to cause you harm." "I am here to help." It was the way that they spoke that made me trust them.

Something in me knew that this person was good. Plus, this man was not being attacked by the dogs. They must be someone that knows the dogs well.

I tried to stand to meet this stranger, but I fell back to the floor. He quickly kneeled down and put my arm around his shoulder, and he helped me up.

I carefully looked at him, but it was tough to really make out how he looked since it was dark. From what I could see, he was about six feet tall and weighed around 180 pounds. He looked to be around thirty years old give or take a year since he looked mature, yet with no visible wrinkles. His hair was blond, and surprisingly he had very tan skin.

"You need to come with me." "There is a warrant out for your arrest." I had to repeat the words that he said in my head. His thick French accent made it difficult to understand what he was saying.

I asked him to repeat himself in French, "Est-ce que vous pouvez répéter?" He nodded and spoke slower. "There is a warrant out for your arrest." I had definitely understood him now.

What do you mean by there is a warrant out for my arrest? I was genuinely confused. Why would I be arrested? Had the Daxes figured out that I left already and falsely accused me of stealing money from them?

No, they wouldn't do that because if they did they knew I would accuse them of kidnapping me, and that is not a fight that they would want to get into. It would ruin their "image" of being the perfect family.

I was about to ask the man why there was a warrant for my arrest, but then he yanked my hand and pulled me toward him. "Alexandre Dax called my boss, Paul." Wait, who is Paul? "Paul is the older man whose car you snuck into." Oh. "Alexandre Dax told Paul that you killed Kaoly." At that very moment I knew my life had forever changed.

Time stood still. I felt every hair on my body stand. I saw the individual blades of grass move in the cold night breeze. I saw the pores on this man's face. I felt my heart thumping. I could count the beats from the pulses in my head.

My fingers felt tingling. My vision started to get blurry, and then I fell. I simply fell. My legs became jelly. My arms felt like cement blocks, and I could not keep myself from falling.

I do not know what happened next, but instead of hitting a hard floor, I was now on a soft mattress. Where was I? My mind was a blur. Was I dreaming? I pinched my skin and it hurt. I was definitely awake, but I could not see anything.

I was in a dark room. That much I knew, but how I got here was a mystery to me. I couldn't remember anything before I fell. My mind was scattered. I felt scared, but I would not feed into the fear. Instead I lifted myself off the soft bed, and I took a deep breath. It was time to figure out where the heck I was.

I put my hands right out in front of myself and I carefully started walking. Within ten feet I reached a rugged wall. I quickly moved my hands around until I found a light switch. I switched it on, and a dark purple light filled the room.

It took my eyes a few seconds to adjust, but when they did I was not staring at much. I was in a tiny room. There was nothing in it, but a small bed. The only thing that stood out about the room was the white door. It was a big steel door. It looked like a door used to keep someone in, or to keep someone out of the room.

Oh no, I must be a prisoner here, but who had locked me up? I searched my mind for the answer, and then it all came back to me like a slap to the face. The blond guy! The dogs, the Daxes, poor Kaoly being dead, and worst of all being accused of murdering Kaoly!

All these things had been too much for my mind to handle, and I had fainted. The blond guy must be working for the Daxes, and that is why he had me locked in this room. However, that didn't make any sense as my memories rushed back to me.

This blond man had saved me from being mauled to death by the dogs. His voice had been kind and considerate, and to top things off I had awakened in a soft bed. I was also not gagged or tied like when the Daxes had me kidnapped.

I felt confused. I had to know if I was a prisoner or not. I ran for the door, and with sweaty hands I turned the knob. The door opened. I carefully peeked into a bright hallway. It looked bright as day out there.

"Well good morning, Max?" Huh? "Are you feeling better?" "You have been asleep for ten hours now." "Is it okay if I come into the room to talk to you?" I nodded yes, and the blonde man came into the purple lit room.

Who are you? I asked him. "My name is Mathieu, and do not worry, I am not here to hurt or harm you." He had a soft smile on his face as he spoke to me. It made him seem trustworthy, and it made me less tense to speak to him.

Mathieu, did I pass out? "Yes, I brought you here to get some rest." Thank you so much. I really appreciate it. He smiled at my gratitude. "Do you know why you fainted?" Yes, I fainted because of what you said to me. Please tell me that it is not true. He turned his gaze away from mine, and he spoke in almost a whisper.

"I am sorry, but it is true." "I cannot sugarcoat anything to you." "You are being accused of murdering Sophie Daxe's au pair, Kaoly." "The police are looking for you." I rubbed my temples as he spoke. His heavy French accent was not easy to understand, but there was no doubting what he had said.

Mathieu, are the police on their way to get me, now? I did not kill anyone! I yelled. Why are they doing this to me? My voice cracked with my frustration and fear. Please tell me you did not call the cops.

He looked at me with sympathy in his eyes. "Do not worry." "I haven't called anyone." "I believe that you did not kill Kaoly." I don't know what it was in the way he said Kaoly's name this time, but it hit me hard.

Yes, I was being accused of murdering someone, but at the end of the day Kaoly was dead. I may not have known her for long, but she was a good person. She had dreams to overcome the odds, and now she was gone. Tears rolled down my face, and I tasted my salty tears on my lips.

How did she die? "I am not sure, but she was murdered." Again I felt light headed, I stumbled back, but this time Mathieu ran to me and helped me stay afloat. "Let's take this one step at a time." "You have to put yourself first right now, or you will continue to faint and get sick."

Why are you helping me, Mathieu? You have never met me before. Why are you being so kind to me? I was in no position to be asking questions, but I was genuinely curious.

The past four months I had been ridiculed and treated like a slave. I was not used to being treated like a person, like an individual, especially by a stranger. My hope in humanity had drastically declined.

"The Daxes have visited this home many, many times." "I have seen how they treat their workers." "I have seen how they have harassed their past nannies and au pairs." "I have overheard incriminating conversations that they have had with Monsieur Paul."

I was trying to absorb everything that he was telling me, but when he said he had overheard "incriminating conversations" I had to interrupt him. If you have overheard the Daxes and Paul having these conversations why are you still working for him?

"I know this is not an excuse but I am a single dad." "I have a three and a half year old daughter." "She is my pride and joy." "I want her to have a better life than I did." "I grew up dirt poor, and it was tough."

"With Monsieur Paul I have a small house in the back of his garden." "He is paying for my daughter's day care." I nodded my head as he spoke. I knew it was not my place to judge him, but still I couldn't help but judge him. Working for people that you know are evil is not a good thing, but he was helping me now, so I guess he wasn't wicked. At least I hope he wasn't.

"I am helping you because I am not someone who stands by and watches while someone gets hurt." "I may know some of Monsieur Paul's and the Daxes' dirty secrets, but that doesn't mean that I agree with them, or would ever help them in causing harm." "In fact, if I ever saw them causing someone harm, I would help the person like I helped you." I guess that was a good enough answer.

"Max, I promise that I will do my best to help you get out of this mess, but right now you need to eat." "Your stomach is growling, and you cannot think properly on an empty stomach." I felt my cheeks get red as I heard my stomach rumble.

Mathieu smiled at me. "Shall we go have breakfast?" I nodded, yes to him, and he gave me a pat on the shoulder as he let me out of the purple lit room.

He closed the steel door behind us, and we entered his narrow hallway. "This house is tiny, but it is enough for me and my daughter." "All the rooms are at the beginning of the corridor."

"On the right is the kitchen, and on the left there are two rooms." "One of the room's is the main bedroom that I share with my daughter, and the other is the restroom." "I am sorry I only have one." That is fine with me, Mathieu.

May I go inside and wash my face off a little? "Yes, there is a fresh towel and some clothes that I have left for you on top of the sink." "In the meantime I will go ahead and make you some breakfast."

My eyes got teary again. "Are you okay, Max?" Yes, I am sorry. It is just that the last person to make me food was my mom, and that was months ago. I miss her, and I miss my family and friends.

"Oncle, but you are my family." I nearly jumped two feet in the air as a small ball of curly blond hair and chubby cheeks came over and hugged me.

It must be Mathieu's daughter. She was coming out of the kitchen, but why had she called me uncle? I gave Mathieu a confused look as the little ball of curly blond hair hugged me tight.

"Max, this is my Elodie." "She is so happy to finally meet her oncle." It took me a second, but I caught on. Mathieu must have told his daughter that I was her uncle. I played along.

Nice to finally meet you Elodie. "I am so happy to finally have an oncle!" "We are going to play so much together." Of course we are, Elodie. "Elodie, can you go wait for me in the kitchen, please." I need to speak to your oncle." The blond fuzz ball went running away.

"I have explained to Elodie that you are her uncle, and that you are visiting from another country." "She is so excited." "I have told her that you are here on a special mission to find the tooth fairy, but no one can know that you are here."

"She is so excited." Are you sure she won't tell anyone that I am here? "I promise you that she won't say a word." How are you so sure? "Well I told her once you find the tooth fairy that you will introduce both of them to each other." I couldn't help but smile.

Well, I guess that is a good reason to keep a secret. I mean who wouldn't want to meet the tooth fairy? She is rich! I said with a laugh. Mathieu's cheeks got bright red after my joke. "Yeah, well you should go ahead and freshen up so we can have breakfast." I grinned at Mathieu, and I walked over to the restroom.

As I entered the bathroom I immediately headed straight for the circular mirror that was hanging over the small gray sink. I took one long look at my face, and let out a sigh of relief. My bruises were clearing up.

My eyes were not swollen anymore, but I still had some redness to them. My lips were better too! Even my cheeks were back to their slender selves instead of looking like a chipmunk's cheeks.

Thank you, God. That ten hour sleep had definitely helped me recuperate. I just wish it had had the same effect on my skin color. I was still an unhealthy pale.

My natural skin tone was a light shade of brown, but right now I looked like I had not seen the sun in months, and sadly that was the case. Unfortunately, this also had a negative effect on my hair.

It had gotten much darker than its normal golden brown, and to make matters worse, I also needed a haircut. I looked like a pomeranian who hadn't been to the groomer in months. Oh well, at least my face had partially healed. My body on the other hand was a different story.

I gently took my clothes off and started to inspect it. I still had a huge purplish-blue bruise on the side of my rips. My back was still quite purple. My right thigh had a giant bruise the size of a baseball, and my biceps had scattered bruises.

All of my body hurt, but I did feel slightly better than when I arrived at the countryside house. I was slowly healing, but healing nonetheless. That made me feel better mentally, and with that positive attitude I headed for the shower.

I turned the valve to warm and I let the water hit my face. It felt magical. It felt like pure love. The warm water running down my body made me feel alive again, and then the guilt hit.

Kaoly was dead. Was her death partially my fault? Maybe if I had not left she would still be alive? Stop it Max! I told myself. It is not my fault. Somehow the Daxes, or Kaoly's rapist, Jacque had figured out about her pregnancy. It had to be one of them who murdered her, and blaming myself was not the key.

The key now was for me to get healthy, and the first step in doing so was getting some food in me. That way I could start to recover and not only clear my name, but also to get justice for the beautiful soul that was Kaoly and all of the other victims of the Daxes'.

Now was that time that I had to be strong, and confident. After all, I did have the evidence to use against the Daxes, and oh crap! Were the photos still in my coat? I had to check. I rapidly turned off the water and reached for the coat. I felt around, and they were still there. *Phew.*

Thank goodness, the pictures were still snuggled safely inside, and the letter that Kaoly had given me was still in my pants' pocket. Perfect, I had to protect this letter. This would serve as proof that Kaoly was fearing for her life. This card would help me bring down the Daxes.

Even with all the influence that they had, they could not shut down the evidence that I possessed. Their time was coming, and with that positive thought I reached for a towel and dried off. I then grabbed the white polo shirt, the blue sweater and the black jeans that Mathieu had left for me, and I changed.

Amazingly, everything fit perfectly; elevating my mood. It is crazy how a nice warm shower and a clean pair of clothes can elevate the mind. I was not feeling panicky anymore. In fact, I was feeling motivated.

My goal was clear. To go back home, and to report the Daxes for everything that they have done to not only me, but the countless victims like the ones in the photos; including Kaoly. Plus I now also had to report Kaoly's abuser, and Paul and his son.

They will all pay for what they have done. I just pray to God that Mathieu will be willing to help me. If he does it will make everything so much easier. In fact, I will ask him for help right after breakfast; which by the smell of it was done.

It was time to eat, but before leaving the restroom I quickly placed the pictures and cards in my newly borrowed jeans. I secured the cuffs, and then I walked out of the bathroom.

Chapter 9
THE PHONE CALL BACK HOME

To my surprise I was immediately blindsided by a jumping Elodie who had been waiting outside the bathroom for me. "Oncle, look you are on TV." "You are famous!" What do you mean Elodie? She grabbed my hand and took me into the living room.

"Look, oncle, look!" I stared at the TV, and I could not believe my eyes. My passport picture was plastered all over the screen. There was a headline over the top of my head that read, *Breaking News, American au pair is on the loose for murder.*

I fell to the couch in total shock. Mathieu came running over and grabbed Elodie. The news anchor came onto the screen, and began to speak, *Max is considered highly dangerous. He has killed a fellow au pair, Kaoly. He is on the run and is believed to be trying to flee the country.*

My hands were trembling. I could not believe what I was seeing and hearing. *We have first hand information that Kaoly was an au pair to Sophie Dax, who some of you might know is one of the owners of the Dax Wine and Champagne company. We have been granted an exclusive interview with the Daxes in their countryside home in Nantes. Take it away, Christille.*

Hello, everyone back at the studio, I am here with the Dax family in their beautiful countryside home. We wanted our public to know what exactly happened with this murder, and the Daxes have been gracious enough to grant us an interview. Let's speak to them now. Juliette, Alexandre and Sophie came into view.

Juliette looked like she was happy to be speaking to a camera, even though her beady eyes were "watery." Alexandre had a cold dark stare, and Sophie Dax looked mad. They were playing their part perfectly, to look like victims.

Firstly, thank you for granting us this interview. How do you feel, Madame Sophie with all that is going on? I know Kaoly was working for you. The camera zoomed to Sophie's face. "I feel like someone has cut my heart out." "Kaoly was more than an employee." "She was like the daughter I never had." "She lived with me for a year."

Fake all fake. Sophie was a total bitch to Kaoly. "Kaoly was about to start studying in France." "In fact, I had just finished paying for Kaoly's entire school year, but Max took that away. "He is vile and maybe he looks innocent on the outside, but remember to not trust a book by its cover."

"According to my sister in law, he even stole 5000 euros from them." It's incredible how easy they lied. My blood was boiling. The reporter handed the microphone to Juliette and Alexandre.

If I may ask, why wasn't Max reported to the authorities when he stole 5000 euros from you guys? Juliette spoke, "We had a serious conversation with him where he cried, apologized and begged us to not do it." "He explained to us the reason he stole the money was to buy medicine for his sick mother."

"This is really no one's business, but Max comes from a very impoverished family." "He showed us one of his mother's medical bills." "It was over 20 thousand dollars." "We felt awful."

"Regretfully we decided to forgive him, and we tried to move on like a family." "We saw him as one of us, as a Dax." "Unfortunately, he saw us as a bank." Juliette let out a fake sob while saying the word bank. Alexandre gave his wife a tight hug.

"We are sorry, Christelle." "This is very emotional for us, but in front of the entire nation I, Alexandre will take the blame for Kaoly's death." "If I had not been so trusting of Max, and fired him when he stole our money, maybe Kaoly would still be here." "Tears" were falling down Alexandre's pale face.

Christelle handed him a tissue. *Do not say that monsieur Alexandre, what Max did is vile and has nothing to do with you beautiful people. He will be brought to justice.* The segment cut back to the news anchor, but I could not watch anymore.

I felt like the room was spinning in circles. I stumbled forward on the couch. Mathieu ran over and pulled me towards him.

He turned the TV off and looked me straight in the eyes. "Max, you may have become public enemy number one, and your face may be plastered all around, but we will get through this." "You got that?" "You are innocent."

Something in Mathieu's voice made me feel better. He wanted me to believe him, and I did. There was no way that I would go down without a fight. The Daxes may have spilled lies about me on TV, but they did so with no evidence. I on the other hand had everything to take them down.

"We will prove your innocence, okay?" Yes we will, and thank you Mathieu for making me feel better. "You are welcome, Max." "Now let's finally have that breakfast!" He said with a laugh. Yes, please. I responded shyly, and I followed Mathieu to the dining area which in reality was part of his kitchen.

"Go ahead and take a seat." I pulled out one of the two chairs from the table. Umm, Mathieu there are only two chairs, but there are three of us. "Don't worry, Elodie has already eaten." "That little rascal is in the room watching TV."

Oh good, I am glad she did not hear any of the horrendous things the news had to say about me. "Let's not focus on that now, Max." "Let's enjoy this meal and we can figure out the rest later." I nodded in agreement.

"Here you go." He handed me a plate filled with heaven. Eggs with bacon, a buttery croissant and strawberries. I stared at the plate in disbelief. I could barely contain my saliva from dripping down from my mouth. Everything looks delicious! Mathieu smiled and handed me a cup of chocolate milk. "Well, bon appetit!"

I practically inhaled my food. It was gone in seconds. "You were very hungry, weren't you?" Yes, I was. I felt embarrassed. Mathieu was barely half way through his eggs, and I had finished all my food, including my cup of milk.

I am sorry for eating so fast. "Do not be." "You are going through a lot, and deserve this meal." "Besides, it feels good to have someone appreciate my food!" He tilted his head toward the hallway. Elodie was running toward the kitchen.

I started to laugh as Mathieu picked up Elodie. "Do you want some strawberries, Elodie?" "Non, merci papa." "You are such a picky eater, Elodie." "One day I will get you to eat something new." I smiled, and thought of an idea.

Elodie, if you eat an entire strawberry by yourself I will tell you the story of the beautiful princess named Elodie. Elodie's eyes widened. She grabbed the strawberry that her dad was holding and ate it in one gulp.

"When will you tell me the story, oncle?" She asked while yawning. Well how about you set up a space for me to tell you a story in your room and I will be there. She giggled and quietly walked off to the room.

"You are great with children." Do you really think so? "Of course, I wouldn't have said it if I did not believe it." Thank you, Mathieu. You do not understand how much that means to me. "Why is that?"

I worked with the Daxes for over four months. I babysat their children. I cleaned and cooked for them. I helped them with their homework, but not once did Juliette or Alexandre praise me. In fact I was reprimanded for not doing better.

"Well Max, my Elodie does not take easy to people, and she really likes you." Thank you, Mathieu. He smiled at me, but then in a serious voice he said, "Let's get to business." "I need to know all that I can about you." "Please tell me everything from when you first arrived with the Daxes to the day you came here."

Okay, but first let me tell Elodie her story. "Oh you won't have to worry about that right now." Why not? Mathieu pulled out his phone and showed me the live video camera of his room. Elodie was sound asleep.

Oh wow she fell asleep fast! I was surprised. "Yeah, this is her nap time, but don't worry she will remind you when she wakes up." "Shall, we start?" Yes.

I spent the next two hours telling him my entire story. I started by recounting the first day. The day they took my passport, and I shared everything in between like when Juliette threw bleach at my shirt for not drying the children's clothes well enough. I did not spare any details, including everything I knew about Kaoly.

"You have been through a lot, and I am sincerely sorry for everything that has happened to you." "I want you to know that you have an ally." "This injustice that has been done to you will not go unpunished, but we must be smart."

"You cannot just go to the police." "You must go to the *American Embassy* and report them there." I know. They are too influential in Paris, and after that news segment the whole country if not the world will be on their side. "Exactly."

"They were smart to have given that interview." "Luckily, you have one thing that they don't have." My evidence. "Precisely, and we have to protect that." How? "I will scan copies of all the pictures that you have and save them in a secure email."

Gosh Mathieu, I barely met you, but you are helping me as if I were a close friend or family. I know I said it before, but thank you from the bottom of my heart. Mathieu's cheeks go slightly red, but he looked content to be appreciated. I had a feeling that he did not get much praise either.

"Hey, I am sure you would do the same for me." Of course I would. "That makes me happy." He said with a smile, as he picked up the pictures and Kaoly's letter.

"I think I'll go and scan all these photos now while Elodie is still asleep." Okay, but while you are doing that, can I please use your phone to contact my family?

"Of course you can, but please call in private." I will. Mathieu handed me his phone, and I grabbed it nervously. My family would soon find out that I was not living a Paris dream, but a nightmare.

I felt ashamed, but I had to come clean now. I took a deep breath and started to dial my mom's phone number. The international dial tone came on, *bring, bring, bring.* "Hello?" "Max?" "Are you okay?" Mom, how did you know that it was me? "Who else would be calling at 1:00 a.m?

"Max, are you all right?" Yes, mom. "Are you sure?" "Why are you calling so late?" Mom, I just want to tell you that I am okay, healthy and safe. "But, but what?" "Tell me Max, please!" I hesitated for a second and then I blurted it all out. Mom, I am falsely being accused of murder.

"What?" "Are you joking?" "What happened?" My host family has falsely accused me of murdering someone. My mom let out a big gasp, and I heard her phone hit the floor. "This can't be happening, this can't be happening!" She yelled as she cried.

Mom, I don't have much time to tell you everything since I am using a friend's phone, but I want to tell you everything that I can. "This can't be happening to my baby." Mom! Please let me talk, I beg you. I yelled in frustration.

"I am sorry Max for losing my composure," she said through loud sobs. "Please tell me everything." I took another deep breath and told her all that I could. It was harsh hearing her cry and curse as I mentioned how I was treated by the Daxes over the past four months.

"My Maxi, I am so sad that you went through all of this." "It breaks my heart." "I want to kill those horrible monsters, but I know that would put all of us in danger." "I want you to know that we all love you, and we won't do anything stupid, so don't stress over us."

"I will speak with everyone tomorrow and we will keep our eyes open for any trouble." "I want you to know that I believe in you, and I know you will prove your innocence." "Remember, even though we are away, your entire family is here to support you."

Thank you mom. I'm sorry I ever came here. "Don't say that son, you had to do what you thought was right." "Sometimes in life things don't turn out how we want them to, but you will get through this, Maxi." "We are here for you."

Thanks mom. I gotta hang up now, but please remember to tell everyone to keep an eye out for any danger. "I will, and Maxi," yes? Please call me back as soon as you can." I will. Bye mom, "bye Maxi."

I put the phone down and stared at the white kitchen wall. I felt relieved and guilty at the same time. I felt relieved because my family knew the truth now, but I felt guilty because I had now placed my family in the ring of fire.

That said, my family was intelligent and strong. They would be okay. Besides, they were on a different continent far away from the Daxes. Yeah, very far away. I repeated only half believing myself, but that was enough to make me feel better, and with that I walked over to Mathieu.

Are you all finished? "Yes, I have scanned all the pictures, and I have uploaded them to a secure email." Yay, that is incredible Mathieu. When do you think we should go to the *American Embassy* in Paris? "Well, I have to go work now, but after work we can decide when and how we are going to get to Paris, okay?"

That sounds like a plan to me. "Wonderful." "Also, I see that Elodie is awake now, she'll eventually come out and want to play with you." "Don't worry I will come in at least once an hour to check up on her." "She knows the routine."

"All I ask from you is to stay away from any windows." "I do not want monsieur Paul or his son to see you, got it?" I got it, Mathieu. He came over and lightly rubbed my shoulder and left the house.

I went over and sat on the couch, and not even one minute passed when Elodie was right by my side. "Oncle!" "I am awake." "Can we play a game?" Of course we can Eloide. "Yay, let's play dress up." She grabbed my hand and took me to her room.

I think we played dress up for almost an hour. I was getting pretty tired when Mathieu came in to check up on Elodie. "Ma fille, tu es où?" "Je suis la papa!" Elodie went running out of the room. I followed her into the kitchen. She gave her dad a big hug as he was making her a sandwich.

"Go eat at the table, sweetie." "Max, when you get hungry you can help yourself to whatever you find in the kitchen." That is nice, thank you Mathieu. I will do that.

"Okay, I got to go now, see you in an hour or so." Hey, Mathieu, quick question before you go. "Yeah?" Does Paul ever get mad that you come into your house so often while you're supposed to be working? "Not at all." "Monsieur Paul knows that I look after Elodie by myself."

"He knows that I come check in on her at least once an hour just to make sure that she is safe." That blows my mind Mathieu. "Why, Max?" Well, you know the type of "business" he runs, yet he treats you like a human being. Unlike the Daxes do to their employees.

"You are right." "I sometimes forget what he does for work." "Well, I guess I try not to think about it." He slightly lowered his head in shame. I am sorry Mathieu. I didn't mean to make you feel guilty. In fact I want to do the opposite.

You are an amazingly good dad, and a good person. I hope to have your work ethic in the future. He flashed a shy smile at me as his face got red. "I am glad you think that way about me Max." "It gives me hope that I'm doing something right."

"And on that high note, I really need to be heading back out to work." "I'll be back in an hour or so." Sounds great, Mathieu. I'll be here waiting. "Perfect." He walked out the door with a smile.

I walked over to the kitchen to check up on Elodie. She was only half way through her sandwich. "Oncle, this sandwich is so good!" I am glad it's good, Elodie. "Do you want some?" No, it is okay.

You finish it all up, so you can grow up to be a big strong girl. I will be on the couch waiting for you so we can play when you are done, okay? "Yes, oncle!" She giggled and tossed her head in excitement causing her blond curls to jump up and down. She was so happy.

I, on the other hand, was a nervous wreck. I did my best to clear my mind, but it was hard. All I could think about was the shit hole that I was in. The longer I waited to report the Daxes and defend my name, the more people were going to hate me. The thought of that made my stomach start to turn.

I started to feel anxious. This is not good. "Here you go oncle." I jumped about a foot in the air, and stared down at a grinning Elodie. She handed me a Barbie like if she had not just scared the life out of me. It made me laugh.

What are we playing Elodie? "I am the princess and you are my best friend." "We have to rescue the queen from the evil monster who lives behind the refrigerator." I picked up the doll and followed Elodie all over the house.

Believe it or not, but I was actually enjoying playing "rescue mission" with Elodie. Mathieu came in a few times, and we both just ignored him and kept playing. It was so much fun that I forgot about my reality for almost two hours. Sadly, my truth came back to me all at once. It made me teary eyed.

"Oncle Max, why are you crying?" My cheeks were wet from tears. Desole, Elodie, I was just so happy that your queen Barbie was able to be rescued, that I cried tears of joy. I forced a smile for Elodie. She came over to hug me.

"Elodie don't you think you should let Oncle Max get some rest?" I turned around surprised to see Mathieu back in the house. I had not heard him come in. "Sorry for startling you." What gave it away? "Oh you know, your shoulders suddenly jumping to your head." Very funny. I laughed.

"Elodie go take your Barbie dolls into our room and remember to do your chores if you want us to go to the park this weekend" Elodie quickly ran back into the room.

"Max, I need you to take a seat." Oh no. My hands got ice cold. People only ask someone to take a seat when something bad has happened. What is it, Mathieu? "Please just remember that I am here for you, and we will get you out of this mess."

Mathieu, please just tell me. "There are strikes all over France going on right now." Wait, why are there strikes? "The French public wants you caught." "You are being called "The *Male Au Pair,*" *"Le Jeun Homme Au Pair."*

My stomach dropped to the floor. In the four months that I've lived in France I learned a lot of important things, and one of them was how the French love to strike. It's part of their culture, and it brings them together as a nation.

Unfortunately for me, that meant that I was a dead man walking.

Chapter 10

THE INFATUATION

If the whole country wasn't looking for me before, now there was no question about it. I was now the face of hate that united the population. That's the funny thing about us humans, we bond by having a common enemy. A.K.A me, and now there was no way that I would be able to get within fifty feet of the *American Embassy* without being hurt or arrested.

What do I do now? I yelled in frustration. "We will disguise you." "We will change your hair color." "We can add pillows in your shirt to make you appear heavier, and you can use my platform shoes to make you taller." "You will get into that embassy and you will present your evidence and clear your name!"

Thank you Mathieu, I said through shattering teeth. I had worked myself up so much that I did not notice my body shaking. Mathieu came over and hugged me. "I will protect you, Max." "Do not worry about anything."

He hugged me tighter into his chest. I could feel his pec muscles against my face. I felt awkward, and I pulled away cautiously. Did Mathieu like me more than a friend? I did not know what to make of it, but I could not focus on that now, so I decided to ignore it, and focus on what I have to do now.

Mathieu, do you have any hair dye that is not brown? "No, I have never used hair dye before." Okay I figured, but do you have bleach? "Bleach to clean?" Yes, do you have any? "I do, but wouldn't that damage your hair?" At this point I don't care. My hair needs to be changed.

"Okay, give me a second." I stared at Mathieu as he went to the kitchen sink and pulled out a small bottle of bleach. "Here you go, but be careful." "You can use the restroom to bleach your hair." Thanks Mathieu, give me twenty minutes please.

I headed to the restroom, but before I went in I stopped by Elodie's room. Hey, Elodie, I liked playing Barbies with you so much that I will dye my hair blond like yours and Barbie's. "Wow, oncle!" "Really?" Yes!

"Can I see you change your hair?" Hmm, I want it to be a surprise for you, so give me twenty minutes okay? "Okay, oncle." I'll be back. I left the room and entered the restroom. I closed the door behind me, and I took a deep breath and opened the bleach bottle.

I poured some liquid on my hands. And then I rubbed it onto my long golden hair. The smell of bleach was a bit overpowering, and almost immediately my head started to tickle. The changes were rapid.

Right before my eyes I saw how my golden brown hair changed color. Within five minutes I was a blond. I wonder if they really have more fun? I giggled to myself, but then my scalp started to burn a little. Quickly, I rushed to the shower, and I rinsed my hair clean of the bleach.

Carefully, I patted myself dry, and surprisingly when I ran my fingers through my hair it did not feel dead. That was a win in my book. The second win was that the color did not wash my face out like I thought it would.

In fact it made my dark eyes pop out even more. That stated, blond was not my color. I looked awful, but at least it made me look different. That was all that I needed. "Oncle, are you finished?"

Elodie knocked on the door. Yes I am Elodie. Close your eyes and stand away from the door. I waited to hear the tiny footsteps move away from the door and then I opened it. Elodie immediately started jumping up and down.

"Oncle, you look like Ken now!" Mathieu stared at me with wide eyes. Well what do you think, Mathieu? "Personally I prefer your dark hair, but you still look good, and different!" Well that was what I was going for, and hopefully soon enough I'll go back to my regular hair.

Mathieu gave me a wink and grabbed Elodie's hand. "Max, I am going to give Elodie her dinner, and when I am done we can talk about going to Paris." "Does that sound good?" Yes it does.

Also, take your time Mathieu. I'll go back to the guest room and try to get some rest. "Great, I'll come get you when I am finished."

Sounds fantastic, I said with a warm smile. Oh, and Elodie, please make sure you eat all your food okay?

"D'accord, oncle." "I want to be big and strong." I tussled Elodie's curly hair and I left the kitchen. I walked down the brightly illuminated hallway and headed into the purple lit room. Ironically enough, this time around the room felt peaceful and welcoming.

Maybe it was the purple light, or the fact that there were no windows, but it made me feel safe. Mathieu had definitely kept it that way to help someone relax because as soon as I laid on the bed my eyes closed. I was not planning to take a nap, but before I knew it, I felt a hand on my shoulder.

"Max, wake up." "You have to eat, and we need to talk about going to Paris." My eyes were heavy with sleep, but I opened them. Mathieu was smiling down at me. I am sorry Mathieu, I must have fallen asleep. "It's okay." "Let's go have dinner."

Where is Elodie? "It is 7:30 p.m, so she is asleep now." Wow, how long did I sleep for? Maybe forty-five minutes. Oh okay, that isn't too bad. "No it isn't." "A nap is always needed, but now, are you ready to go eat?"

Yes, please. "Well let's go." I followed Mathieu out the door, and straight into the kitchen. "Please have a seat." I took a seat at the table, and Mathieu brought out a pie looking thing that had a beautiful smell. It smelled like freshly cooked eggs and vegetables mixed with a hint of something sweet. Mathieu, this smells delicious, what is it?

"It is called a quiche." "Have you had one before?" No, I have never had one. "Then you are in luck." Did you make this, because it looks incredible. Mathieu grinned at me. "No, I did not make it." "There is a lady right down the road who cooks and sells them on order."

Wow, can I dig in? "Please go right ahead." I grabbed the fork that was on the plate and cut directly into the quiche. I took a small bite and I was in heaven. The taste was out of this world.

It was a mixture of sugar, salt and other spices. The bottom of my tongue started to water. The crunchiness of the crust was perfect too. It was not too hard or soft, and the taste of the egg was not overpowering.

Mathieu, this is wonderful! I yelled a little too excited. He started to laugh. "I am glad you liked it." "It is all for you." "The entire pie is yours." I did not know what to say, so I said the first thing that popped into my mind. Which was, Mathieu you are truly amazing, and I cannot thank the heavens enough for having sent you to me.

Instantly, Mathieu's face got bright red, and as he tried to say thank you his words came out in a stutter. Oh my gosh, I am so sorry, Mathieu. I didn't mean to make you feel uncomfortable with my flattery. "Oh, I, I am, not um, not uncomfortable."

"I, I liked, liked the compliment." He said with an even redder face. "It's just that it has been a while since a non-family member has shown true appreciation toward me." Well get used to it, Mathieu. I happily replied.

"Ha, I'll try to." "Is it okay, if I can give you a big hug?" Of course! He walked up to me and gave me a tight hug. "Thank you, Max." "You don't know how much I value your words." He stared down at me and blushed again.

I could feel his breath on my cheek, making me feel awkward. I think he really did have some sort of crush on me, or maybe I was just misconstruing a difference in affection between two distinct cultures.

For all I know he probably just liked giving tight hugs. Still, I moved my head to break the awkwardness, and thankfully he sensensed my weariness and he pulled away from the hug while changing the subject back to Paris.

"Well, Max, have you decided what you want to do?" The only thing I can think of right now is to go straight to the *American Embassy*. "I do not think that is a wise idea." Why is that, Mathieu? "For starters I can only take you to Paris at dawn."

"I start work at 7:00 a.m, so I would have to take you to Paris by 5:30 a.m, to be back here on time." "The other issue with that is the embassy won't open till 10:00 a.m, and I don't want to leave you out in the open like that." "The protests are all over Paris."

That isn't a problem, Mathieu. "What do you mean, Max?" I know someone that I can stay with until the embassy opens. "Who?" His voice got high and squeaky. His face trembled a bit. He was nervous for my safety. "Well, Max?"

My sweet old neighbor. She is eight-eight years old. "Oh." Mathieu said, and then flashed a big bright smile. "That is perfect." "She is the lady who you tutored, right?" Yeah that is her. I stared at Mathieu and his shoulders lowered as he let out a sigh of relief.

I got the feeling that he was excited that it was an older lady helping me, and not someone else. There was no denying it now. He definitely had an infatuation with me. It made me nervous, but when this was all over I would clear the air with him.

"Max." Yeah, Mathieu? "How can you be sure she will help?" It is not that I am one hundred percent sure that she will help, but she is the only one who was kind to me during my time with the Daxes.

Plus she is unaware of the outside world. She does not care to watch the news, only her soap operas. She never leaves her home but once a month when she goes to church. "How does she get her food?" She gets it delivered, so what I am trying to say is I do not think she knows of the commotion that is going on.

"I mean, everyone is talking about this, Max." "My parents even called me to gossip about it." "Don't you think her family would have called to talk about it?" No. She never got married and she only had one sister who died years ago. "I see."

"Okay then, it's settled." "We will head to Paris tomorrow." "Do you have a particular place in mind where you want me to drop you off?" Yes, there is a tiny park near *Notre Dame Cathedral* that is always empty in the mornings.

Beatrice lives near there, so I can easily walk to her apartment. "Wait, hold up a minute." "I just realized, Beatrice's apartment is in the Daxes' building, right?" "Are you seriously going to go back there?"

I have no other choice. "What if they see you?" The Daxes are so egocentric that they would never think twice about me returning back to the building. Plus, no one is awake at 6:00 a.m. in that building.

I can easily sneak into Beatrice's apartment without getting seen. Mathieu stared at me with worry in his ocean eyes. I felt bad, but he and I both knew that the risk of going to the embassy too early was higher than sneaking into Beatrice's apartment. At the end he understood.

"Okay, so tomorrow we leave at 5:30 a.m." Yes, that is perfect, and thank you again Mathieu for everything that you are doing to help me. I will pay you back one day. "No, I am not doing this so you can pay me back." "I am doing this because it is the right thing to do, and in a selfish kind of way because you remind me of a younger version of myself."

"I was a lot like you when I finished high school." "I had a travel bug." "I wanted to leave France for a year too, but I was pressured by my friends and family to stay." "I am from a small town in the South of France called *Saint Jean de Luz*, and everyone there is mainly a farmer." "I ended up not leaving, and this led to low points in my life."

"For almost ten years I was stuck in an awful abusive relationship with a woman I never liked." Why didn't you leave? "I didn't leave because everyone said I should be in a relationship, but guess what?" What? "When she gave birth to Elodie she left."

"Her exact words were, "You are lazy and I can do better." "I am taking the twenty thousand euros you saved up during these ten years." "Keep the baby." "She left me when Elodie was only two weeks old."

I am so sorry Mathieu! "Don't be Max." "When she left the veil that was over my eyes lifted." "I knew I had to get away from my small town, and I knew I had to get a better life for me, for Elodie, and for my parents."

"That's how I ended up here with Monsieur Paul." I now understood why he had turned a blind eye with all the wrongdoings of the Daxes and Paul. "My financial situation has gotten better, but you want to know something?" What?

"You have opened my eyes." How? "Life has thrown everything it has to stop you, but you still get up." "You have shown me that life isn't easy, but it is worth fighting for." "I have turned a blind eye to monsieur Paul for over three years because he had given me so much." "I can not keep doing that." "I will find a way out soon."

"I know that life will be harder for me and Elodie, but I am confident that I will succeed." "I want to start living my life unafraid, and in turn give Elodie the opportunity to live hers." I am so proud of you Mathieu. "Thanks Max, you really are special." "You have a light that shines over you."

"That is why the Daxes used you." "They saw that light and wanted it for themselves, but your light cannot be taken away." You're so sweet, Mathieu. I don't know where I would be if it wasn't for you.

"You'd be surviving because you are a survivor." I felt my cheeks get red. Mathieu smiled at me, and went to the living room.

I watched him as he pulled a gray zip folder from behind the TV. "These are the original pictures you gave me to scan." "I put them all in this folder, including the copies, my contact information, and the secure email login as well."

"I want you to call me as soon as you get to Beatrice's, okay?" I will, Mathieu. "Okay, perfect." "I'm going to bed now since we both have to get up early."

"Feel free to take a shower, or just go straight to bed, but please be at the kitchen by 5:25 a.m, okay?" You got it, Mathieu. I'll be there at 5:24. "Hahaha," he laughed at my stupid joke. "You really are something special, Max." "See you tomorrow, and have a goodnight." Goodnight Mathieu.

Chapter 11

THE RETURN TO PARIS

I waited for Mathieu to enter his room, and then I headed to the guest room. I felt tranquility entering the room, and for the first time in four months I felt like I belonged somewhere. It was bittersweet. I did not want to leave the comfort of this place, but if I cleared my name, maybe I could return and spend some extra days with Elodie and Mathieu.

I hung on to that lovely idea as I closed my eyes and slowly drifted to sleep. "Oncle, wake up." "We are going to Paris soon." I rubbed my eyes partially open, and a grinning Elodie was looking right at me. I couldn't help but smile. "Come on oncle, papa said you have to eat something before we go."

Okay, okay, okay. I am getting up now. Tell your papa to give me few minutes so I can freshen up in the restroom, okay? "D'accord, oncle." "I'll go tell papa that you are up now." Elodie ran out of the room giggling.

I reluctantly got up and made the bed. I put my shoes on and grabbed the gray folder, and I headed out the room. With my eyes half closed, I slowly walked to the restroom and closed the door behind me. The bright restroom lights stung my sleep filled eyes, so I turned on the sink to wash the sleep away from my face.

The second the lukewarm water touched my skin I was wide awake. Immediately I grabbed a towel and began to pat my face dry, while at the same time examining it. I no longer had any swelling or bruising of any sort. Thank goodness.

My body felt better too. Even though I still had a few bruises around my rib cage, but hey I was healing and that made me happy. "Max, we gotta get going in foure minutes, please hurry in there." Shit, I ran out of the restroom and made my way into the kitchen.

I'm sorry, Mathieu. I am here now. "It's cool." "I'm sorry for rushing you, but we gotta get moving now before Monsieur Paul wakes up." Oh you are right I said as we walked out the front door.

Is Elodie already in the car? "Yeah, she's comfortably sleeping in the backseat." He pointed down to his car. I could kind of make out her curls through the tinted car windows. "The second she steps foot in a car she falls asleep." "She reminds me of my father." He said with a laugh.

Or maybe like her father? I said as a joke. Mathieu couldn't help but grin, and he opened the car door for me. "Your chariot awaits." I felt a tad uncomfortable having Mathieu do that for me, but I thanked him and got in the car. He did a little bow and then got in himself. It made me laugh.

"Okay, Max I'm sorry to ask this, but can you please crouch your head until we get out of Monsieur Paul's property and into the highway?" "I don't want anyone spotting you." Oh of course, Mathieu. I tried crouching my head toward the floor but the glove compartment opened and blocked my path.

"Please don't take this the wrong way, but once that thing opens it won't close unless I remove the screws." "Unfortunately, we don't have time for that, so can you please just place your head on my thighs?"

I raised a concerned eyebrow at him and his face got bright red. "I know that sounded wrong, but it is the only way you can comfortably crouch down." I know Mathieu. I was just joking. I said with a laugh. Besides I am sure your thighs are cozier than having my head on my knees.

He let out a small laugh, and I felt a shiver go up his legs as I placed my head on his thighs. I wonder again what I had done to make him infatuated with me. Was it my sudden appearance, and shock value that I brought to his life, or even some sort of savior complex?

I don't know, but I will ask him once all of this is over. It was not something that I had to know now. "Max, did you hear me?" Huh? "I said, you can lift your head up now." Oh sorry, I was daydreaming. I felt like I was resting on a pillow.

"Well I guess my thighs aren't as muscular as I thought, but we are on the highway now." Mathieu smirkingly said. I lifted my head and stared out the window. We were definitely on the highway. The first part of the plan had gone accordingly.

Mathieu, how far are we from central Paris? "We are only about 25 minutes away because there are still not many cars out." Oh wow, we are almost there. I started to feel a little skittish.

"Max, I want to give you something." What is it, Mathieu? I stared at Mathieu as he reached into his pocket. He pulled out some bills. "It is not much, but this will keep you going for a few days."

He handed me five twenty euro bills. I looked at him with tear filled eyes. I cannot take this Mathieu. You have Elodie to look after. I am sure my sweet neighbor will have some food for me. "It is not for food, Max." "This is for any transportation that you may need to take, or anything you may need to buy."

Mathieu, I really do not know what to say, but just know that when all of this is over I will pay you back for everything that you did for me, okay? "You got it, Max." "I want you to know that you made a friend for life here." The same applies to you.

I undid my seatbelt and hugged him. I felt his body relax and his eyes brighten. "When you prove your innocence, would you like to come stay with me and Elodie for a few days before you go home?" I would love that, Mathieu.

He grinned, and we did not say anything after. He just continued driving and there was a weird moment of peace. A moment where I got to glare out the windows and enjoy the scenery. The views were amazing, especially throughout Paris.

The Louvre Museum was particularly pleasing during this time of day. It looked so large without all the people who are normally there taking pictures around the pyramid. The streets and bridges throughout Paris seemed to shine with beauty as the sun rose to the top of the sky.

It felt peaceful to look at. In a way it felt like I was seeing Paris through a movie, a zombie movie where there are no more people. Weirdly enough it soothed me, and it helped calm my nerves.

Which was welcomed because we soon arrived at *Notre Dame*. The huge cathedral was one of my favorite monuments of Paris. It has stood the test of time. Over one thousand years old, and not even the fire could burn it down. Truly a masterpiece of mankind.

"Well Max, we are here." "Where shall I park?" Do you see that little ally on the far right? "Yeah." You can get stationed there. The park is right next to that spot, and there aren't any homes near there. "Got it."

Mathieu pulled into the alley and quickly found a parking spot. "So this is goodbye for now, isn't it?" I don't know what to say other than, thank you. Thank you for everything you did, and are doing for me, Mathieu. I promise you I will call you once I get settled in. Please let Elodie know that I will see her soon.

Mathieu unbuckled his seatbelt and hugged me. He embraced me for almost a minute. I felt that he needed that hug as much as me. His life was changing too.

"Okay Max, it is 6:00 a.m." "The early birds will start going into work now." "You best be on your way." I nodded in agreement, and I gently pulled away from the hug. I grabbed my gray folder and got out of the car.

See you soon Mathieu. I closed the door behind me and waved goodbye. I watched as he drove off, and then I made my way over to the far edge of the park near the road. I took a deep breath and prayed that I wouldn't be noticed. I crossed the street and started walking to the Daxes' building.

A ten minute walk from here, but an exposed walk. I put my hoodie on and picked up my pace. A woman opening her convenience store smiled at me. I got shivers down my spine, but I kept my cool and smiled back. I continued walking and the more I walked, the more Paris came alive.

People were coming out of their buildings now, but no one was paying attention to me. I relaxed a little and I slowed my pace down. Soon enough I saw the Daxes' building. My stomach started to twist.

Something that I had not told Mathieu was that there was a code to enter the building. If they had changed the code then my chances of getting into the building unseen were slim to none.

Breathe in, breathe out, relax, Max, relax. I told myself. The code won't be changed. The Daxes fear nothing, so why would they even bother to change their code. I started to feel better, and I was only about two blocks away now.

"Monsieur, monsieur." My heart stopped. Was someone talking to me? I dared not to turn around and I picked up my pace. "Monsieur!" Yes, they were definitely talking to me. I continued to ignore them, but then I felt the hand on my shoulder.

My natural instinct kicked in and I turned my head. It was an older man. He had a smile on his face. "You dropped your twenty euro bill." "I have been trying to get your attention for the last minute." "Here you go, and oh get your ears checked out!" I smiled at him, but I dared not to speak. If I spoke he would know that I wasn't French. He smiled back and left.

I let out a sigh of relief, but shit I felt like I was a prey and everyone was the predator. It felt as if I had a giant red flag hanging over my head. What a horrible feeling. I would not wish that on anyone, well maybe on the Daxes.

Whose building was only across the street now. Here goes nothing, I clenched my fists together as I crossed the tiny cross walk. I was only twenty feet away, then ten feet away, and then I turned right. I could not enter yet. My nerves were through the roof!

I shakingly walked over to the local Asian store that was right next to the building. As I was about to enter the store, I saw a picture of me on the window. It was in black and white, but it was me. It was the picture that I used for my *Navigo card,* which is the card Parisians use for the public transport system, like the metro.

Underneath my face were the words, KILLER, followed by a small description. *Come join us at 11 a.m. for a mass protest near the Saint Michel Fountain. The government will catch this killer or we will not stop our protests.*

My heart started beating as fast as a humming bird moving its wings. My palms got all sweaty and I left the store. I was not safe out in the open. Nerves or no nerves I had to get to the Daxes building, so I forced myself over to the massive blue wooden door, and prayed that they had not changed the code.

I looked at the small silver keypad by the door panel and I entered the code, 24B65. *Bing, bing, bing* the door went. I pushed it and it opened. Thank goodness! I was one step closer, and with wobbly legs, I went over the doorstep and entered the building.

I was now in, and graciously the lobby space was empty. This was my chance. I walked over to the stairs. There was no way in hell that I would use the elevator, and end up getting stuck. Instead I quietly went up the seven flights of wooden stairs up to Beatrice's apartment and my old room.

Miraculously, no one noticed me, and with pens and needles throughout my body, I walked over to Beatrice's door and I knocked twice. I could hear her walking up to peek through the peephole. A few seconds later she was unlocking her door.

"Max!" "I almost didn't recognize you because of your hair." "What are you doing here?" "I thought you were going home?" "Isn't that what your letter said?" "I thought you had written that you were going home for Christmas and that you wouldn't be back until next year."

Beatrice, I need your help. She looked at me with confusion in her face. "Please come in." "Why are you crying?"

I stepped into Beatrice's home and stared into the giant mirror that was hung over one of the main walls of the apartment. I had not even felt the tears on my cheeks, but I was definitely crying. My eyes were puffy and so were my lips. My face was bright red. "Please, you are worrying me." "Are you okay?"

"Shall I call a doctor?" NO! Beatrice looked at me stunned. I had yelled at her without meaning to. I felt bad, but I was scared. Beatrice please can we take a seat so I can tell you what is happening to me? She nodded, and we sat down on her kitchen chairs. I then began to tell her everything that had happened to me since arriving in Paris.

Chapter 12

THE FLASH DRIVES

B eatrice listened intensely to me. Her frown lines hardened with anger when she heard how the Daxes treated me. Her mouth dropped down when she found out about Kaoly and the situation that I was now in. Her eyes were filled with tears when I told her about Paul, and she started to cry when I handed her the pictures of the Daxes' victims.

"Words cannot describe the sadness that I feel in my heart for what you have gone through." "I am not sure what this little old lady can do, but I am in your disposition for everything and anything."

"What do you need from me?" She said, as her hands trembled and her legs shook. She was visibly anxious. Was this too much for her? The last thing I wanted was for her to get ill over me.

Beatrice, I am sorry for involving you in all of this. I can see that it has affected you. Beatrice's laugh lines grew deeper as she smiled. "Don't worry about me Max." "I am stronger than I look." Are you sure? "Yes."

"Right now the important thing is to get you out of this mess, so let's take a look at the news to see if they are saying anything about you." I nodded okay, and I followed her with caution into her living room. Which was a challenge considering the state of her place.

Let's just say she prefers the "messy style." She had magazines all over the house. She had multiple small figurines that she collected scattered throughout her salon. Her couches were filled with folded clothes that she probably hasn't worn in years, and there were multiple colorful boxes throughout the living room.

Her home reminded me of an art exhibit, which makes sense since she used to be an artist when she was younger. I admired her for keeping her passion alive. It made me smile, and she must have caught me staring at her things because she said, "Some say my house is too messy, and I say it's my treasure box."

Beatrice, if your house wasn't like this it would not be your house. That said, I am not used to being in your living room, so where do you want me to sit? She looked at me and pointed at the sofa. "Sit there Max." She then moved some clothes off the couch and sat right next to me.

"Can you hand me the remote right behind your head?" I reached back and gave her the remote. She pushed the power button and immediately my face came on the screen. *He has not been seen for two days now. He is highly dangerous and persummed armed.*

Please we ask you all, if you see him report him to the authorities. My passport photo was switched to my Navigo picture, and then the news segment changed to a news reporter outside of the studio.

We are coming live from Paris near the American Embassy in Place de la Concorde. Even at this early hour people have begun protesting. They are demanding that the government catch this au pair killer.

The camera turned to show a crowd of hundreds if not thousands of people protesting right near the *American Embassy*. I couldn't believe it, and I simply fell to my knees. Beatrice came rushing to lift me up.

"Max, are you okay, dear?" No, I am not. I cannot go to the *American Embassy*. Look at all those people. What am I supposed to do now? My face started to feel hot. I was getting paranoid. My plan had fallen apart already.

"Let me turn the TV off." "This propaganda will destroy your mind if you do not stop watching it." Beatrice I am scared. My entire plan was to go to a neutral zone not infiltrated by the Daxes, and now that is down the drain.

"Don't worry, Max." How can I not worry, Beatrice? "The French always change where they protest." "Today they are protesting near the *American Embassy*, and maybe tomorrow they will too, but they will eventually change locations." "You will present your evidence there, don't you stress."

"You are strong and you are smart." "Justice will prevail." Beatrice looked so confident that not only did I believe what she was telling me, but I felt empowered. A profound sense of hope entered my body, and almost simultaneously a new perfect idea emerged in my mind.

Beatrice! "Yes, Max?" I know I cannot go to the embassy for now, but since I am in Paris, I might as well get more evidence against the Daxes. Not only to prove my innocence, but also to ensure that I take them down completely. "How do you plan on getting more evidence?"

I will go inside their home, and look for anything that I can use against them. "Max, that sounds dangerous." "You can get caught." Don't worry, Beatrice, I know the Daxes schedule down to the very last detail.

I know when the kids are at school, and when Juliette heads to yoga. I even know when Alexandre leaves and comes back from work.

Beatrice's shoulders relaxed. She knew that I had their schedules memorized to the last detail, but she still wanted to know my plan. "How will you break into their home?" Simple, through the front door.

I know when the cleaner comes, and I know his schedule. He always leaves the front door open the first hour while he is vacuuming the rooms. I could sneak in there while he cleans and try to find proof against them, then.

Beatrice looked at me with worry in her eyes, but then she stood up. She practically ran to her room and she came back with a small key. "I have a key to your room." Wait, you mean you have a key to my chambre de bonne? "Yes, the Daxes gave it to me just in case you ever got locked out."

"Do you want to see if you can find any evidence of wrongdoing in your room?" There is nothing in my room that I haven't already seen, but Beatrice! "What?" On the other side of my chambre de bonne is the Daxes' luggage room. Maybe something is hidden there.

"Unfortunately, I do not have a key for that room." We do not need a key. Beatrice looked at me with confusion. I mean, all we need is a hammer. Her gray eyes widened, but then she smiled.

"Here I was thinking I would have the most boring day, and then you show up." I hope that is a good thing, Beatrice. "Of course, Max." "Besides, aiding you helps me feel useful in my life."

"Now give me a second." She slowly walked into a closet that was by her kitchen. She opened the door and went inside. After a minute of rummaging around she came out with a metal hammer. "Here you go, Max."

Merci, Beatrice. When do you think I should break into their luggage room? "Now, since they are always gone on Sundays." You are right. By 7:00 a.m. on Sundays they are well on their way to their local fundraisers. "Exactly, so here is the key to your old room."

She handed me an older rustic metal key and I took it. "I will leave my door unlocked." "When you are finished just come back in." Thank you, Beatrice, but before I go, can I call Mathieu and let him know what is going on?

"Of course, here is the phone." Beatrice handed me an old gray house phone and I quickly called and explained everything to Mathieu. A few minutes later I was in front of my chambre de bonne.

With trembling hands I placed the key in the hole, and I prayed that it wouldn't get stuck. I turned the knob, and luckily the door opened with no issue. *Phew.* I swiftly went inside and turned on the light switch. The room looked exactly like how I had left it.

For some reason that made me feel good. This was my safe haven after all. That said, I was not here to reminisce. I was here to break into the luggage room to find evidence against the Daxes.

With my purpose clear in my mind I pulled out the small hammer from my pocket, and I walked over to the right corner of my room to assess how I would break into the other side. There was only one sure way, and that was to hammer a hole that had to be at least two feet tall and around three feet wide.

A tight fit, but the smaller the hole, the less visible it would be to prying eyes. With that assessment finished, I gently began to hammer away. Shockingly, it was easier than I expected, but annoying because of all the dust.

By the time I finished I had practically coughed my lungs out. The dust trapped in the walls was a tad too much. Hopefully I would not get any sort of lead poisoning from it since the dust and flakes in the walls had to be hundreds of years old.

Oh well, we would see. I shooed the rest of the debris out of the way and peeked into the luggage room. Amazingly, it was quite small. It was no more than ten feet across and no more than nine feet tall.

The size didn't matter though, it was time to get inside. I scraped the jagged edges from the hole and began to squeeze my way into the room. White crusted paint fell on my hair and face, which caused me to have a coughing spell. I waited for it to subside, and then I shoved my way into the luggage room.

Once in, I carefully stood up and cleaned myself off. I then immediately began to look around the room. Thankfully enough light was coming in from the large window on the ceiling that I did not have to worry about finding any light switch, which made my search easier.

Nevertheless, I did not have much to look through anyway. The entire room had nothing but bags. No frames, no cabinets, just bags. How plain and boring, I laughed to myself as I began to open all the luggage in the room.

Unfortunately, every single damn bag was empty. Shit! There was nothing else to search for in this tiny storage place. I gently rubbed my temples in frustration for coming out empty handed, but then an idea struck me. The pictures that I had found in the Daxes' countryside house were hidden under a tile, so maybe something was hidden here somewhere on the floor?

I glanced over to the ground, and woefully it was solid concrete. My luck, but wait! I looked up to the ceiling and the ceiling had removable tiles. Something in me told me that I would find my evidence there.

Immediately, I grabbed one of the large suitcase that was by the wall and carefully climbed on it. I reached for the tiles and touched the first four. They did not budge, but I would not let that stop me.

I continued feeling the entire ceiling, and finally near the window a tile moved. Bingo!

I cautiously pushed it out of the way, and very carefully I stuck my hand in the empty space. I began to move my hand to the left, to the right, and finally forward, and then I felt something! It was some sort of box. Eagerly, I grabbed it and I jumped off the luggage.

I stared in awe at the small box in my hand. It was no larger than seven inches, but it felt semi heavy. I wondered what it contained. My body was rushing with excitement. I had to get back to Beatrice's to inspect it, so I squeezed my way back into the hole, and made my way into the room.

Once inside, I gently put the box down and grabbed the medium size garbage can that was by my old desk. I placed the bin over the hole. It covered it perfectly. Good.

With my sweaty hands I grabbed the box again and walked out of the chambre de bonne.

I wobbly made my way to Beatrice's apartment, and swiftly I opened her door. "Max, is that you?"

Yes, Beatrice it is me, and I have found something. I waited for Beatrice to come to me. I could have easily gone and met her, but I did not want her to feel that I was wandering her home as if it were my own. "I am coming, Max." I heard her slippers swipe the floor as she walked.

"What is that box that you have there, Max?" That is what I found. Shall we open it? "I am nervous to see what is inside, but yes, let's open it." Where? "Here in the kitchen is fine, on the table." Perfect.

I placed the box on the table. Here goes nothing, Beatrice. She leaned in closer to the box. I pulled the lid back and opened it. We both stared at each other in confusion. I guess we expected to find pictures in it, but we didn't.

The box contained four different flash drives. I was stumped. I had not seen flash drives in over ten years. "What is that?" They are called flash drives, Beatrice. They were used to store videos and pictures before, but now all of that is stored online.

"Then why do they have these?" One reason, Beatrice. "What is that, Max?" Whatever is saved here is so sensitive that the Daxes don't want it online. Beatrice's mouth dropped open. Exactly.

Chapter 13
THE SURROGATE

Beatrice, may I use your computer? "Of course you can." "Follow me." I followed her to the corner of her living room where she had a small desktop. It was not much to look at, but it would do.

"Here you go, it is all yours." Thank you Beatrice. Now let's see if the flash drives work. I inserted the first drive into the usb port. I waited for the computer to read it.

Please work, please work. I silently prayed. *Ting*, the computer went. "What was that noise?" It means the computer just read the drive, Beatrice. "Is that a good thing?"

Yes, now let us hope that there is no password to get into the flash drive. I nervously moved the cursor to the flash drive folder. I double clicked the folder and it opened. There was no password. Thank goodness.

"Did it require a code?" No. "Okay, good." "What do you see, Max?" I did not know how to respond. I must have translated the title of the file to English incorrectly. It was too dark, but I had to make sure. Beatrice, can you read this please?

Beatrice leaned closer to the monitor and fixed her glasses. "Merde," she cussed in shock. "It says, *The Murder of Roman and Mylene's Surrogate Mother*." My body tensed in hearing the confirmation of the title. Beatrice, what do we do? Do we play the video?

"Yes, we must." I clicked play on the video and we started to watch it. A man with a mask over his face had a gun to the head of a woman. A pale woman who yelled in pure fear. "Please do not kill me!" "I will not tell anyone that I am the surrogate of the Daxes."

"I will not tell them that they forced me to carry their children because they could not conceive." "I will go back to my home in Lithuania, but please do not kill me!" "You stupid bitch." *Bam*, the man hit the woman with the side of his pistol on her forehead.

I immediately paused the video. That was Alexandre's voice. "There is no doubt about it." I took a deep breath and hit play again. "Look, bitch you are the one who made the mistake by telling your boyfriend everything."

"You broke our trust and now you will pay." "You could have lived such a fulfilling life as the Daxes' nanny, but you ruined it." *Bam, bam, bam* and there was blood everywhere. The pale thin woman fell backward. Her lifeless naked body recorded.

Gossebumps covered my body. What had I just seen? I turned to stare at Beatrice and she had tears falling from her eyes. "This makes sense now." "Juliette always spent her pregnancies out in their countryside home." "I guess it was because she never really was pregnant."

Beatrice, this is all too much, but I have to know more. "Me too." Can you hand me another flash drive? "Of course." Beatrice handed me the drive, and I placed it in the port. *Tring, tring*, ACCESS CODE. This usb was password protected. I removed it from the computer and tried another one.

Tring, tring, ACCESS CODE, same thing. I repeated that for the next two. They all required a code. "Something major must be hidden in them." I can't even imagine, but at least we have more evidence against them.

"That is what is important, Max." "Every substantial piece of proof that you get about their wickedness will help." "The Daxes are very wealthy and influential." "The only way they will be stopped is if the proof is just so in your face that people will start protesting to put them in jail." I nodded my head in agreement.

That is exactly why I need to get into their home because I feel like the nail on their coffin is hidden there. "You will find it, Max, but right now you need to rest your mind before trying to get into their home." "I don't want you getting caught because you want to rush things, okay?"

Beatrice had an empathic look on her face. She really did care about me. It made me feel happy, and emotional. I felt a lump form in my throat. Please, don't cry, I told myself. I did not want to lose it in front of Beatrice.

Thankfully she picked up on my cue and headed to the hallway. When she was there she said, "Tomorrow is a better day to sneak into their house." "Their kids will be at school and the cleaner will be there too."

Yes, you are right Beatrice. Plus Juliette will be at yoga and Alexandre at work. "Exactly, so how about we stop worrying about that now and have something to eat?"

My stomach growled at that very thought. Beatrice laughed. "It seems like your stomach agrees with me, and you are in luck!" "I made crepes and I have some nutella." "Oh, and I have some freshly squeezed orange juice as well." You do not need to tell me twice.

Beatrice served me three entire crepes, and I had two glasses of orange juice. My stomach was bloated by the time I finished. I felt bad, but so good at the same time. Thank you, Beatrice.

I feel so much better, and were those crepes homemade? "Yes, was there something wrong with them?" Oh no! It is just that they were the best crepes that I ever had in my life. Beatrice's smile filled her face. She loved to be complimented about her cooking.

"I am glad that you enjoyed them." "Now we have the entire afternoon to ourselves." "What would you like to do?" "Play a game?" "Call your family?" Can I really call my family? "Of course you can." I glanced at the clock. It was 10:00 a.m, which is 1:00 a.m. California time. It was late, but I needed to check up on my parents.

"I'll be on the couch reading a book if you need me." Beatrice handed me the phone and I dialed 0 and then 1, and then I entered my mom's phone number. The phone rang twice and, "Max?" Yes, mom it is me. Are you guys okay? "Yes, Maxi, we are okay." "I am glad you called me." "I wanted to tell you that the entire town is with you Maxi."

What do you mean mom? "Maxi, more than one hundred people showed up to the local news station to defend you." "They were trying to tarnish your reputation and say that you were a troubled youth, but they defended you." "The news anchor had to come out and apologize!"

"Maxi, I love you baby, but we can't talk too much right now." Why not mom? "There is an officer outside our house." "The French government aligned with the American authorities to try to get you." "They might be overhearing our conversation." "I love you, Maxi." "Please stay strong." "Your brother and sister are so proud of you."

The call ended. I put the phone down and sat at the kitchen table. I put my head in between my hands and just thought. I was happy that my family was safe, and I was prideful that my town supported me which was so unexpected.

I never felt that I fit in there, but when push came to shove they had my back. That meant that world to me. Unfortunately, things were worse than I thought. The American authorities were now working with French authorities to try to capture me.

Now more than ever I had to secure more evidence against the Daxes. This was no longer just a *France-Crime-Story*. I could tell by my mother's voice that it was now an international story for the capture of the killer au pair.

Panic started to loom over me. My leg started shaking, causing the table to move. "Max, come watch this movie with me." Huh? Beatrice looked at me with a bright face. She must have been observing me. She did not want me to panic.

I nodded and went to the living room with her. She put on an old French movie named *Cleo de 5 a 7*. The movie was better than expected. It was funny but dramatic and it was exactly what I needed to calm my nerves.

After that movie ended Beatrice wasted no time for us to do another activity together. She pulled out the card game called *French Tontine* and we started to play. She was ensuring that I stayed calm and relaxed. I appreciated her for it, and after the game I accompanied her while she had a late lunch.

When she finished eating, we watched the *Edith Piaf* movie. Beatrice almost killed me when I told her I did not know who Edith Piaf was. "This is a crime against humanity!" "Edith Piaf is an international superstar."

Her shock of me not knowing her made me laugh, but she was not lying. The movie was great, and I was filled with appreciation for French music. "Are you an Edith Piaf fan now, Max?" You can bet on it, Beatrice. "I am glad," she said with a laugh, but then her face turned stern.

"Now, how about you go and have something to eat since you skipped out on lunch." Hmm, I think that is a good idea, Beatrice." Do you happen to have any cereal? "Of course, it is in the first cabinet." Perfect, I will go have some.

"Good, in the meantime I will go shower and get your bed ready, okay?" Okay, Beatrice. I let her do her thing, and I went into the kitchen. I was pleased to see that Beatrice had the French version of *Chocolate Cocoa Pebbles*. I guess having a sweet tooth does not limit one to an age.

I poured myself some cereal and I ate it slowly. Once I finished I washed my dish and every single dish that was in the kitchen. "Wow, Max!" "Merci, for cleaning the kitchen." It is the least that I can do.

"You are too sweet," she said as she yawned. Are you tired, Beatrice? "Yes, I am." "I am going to call it in for the night." "I have made your bed on the sofa, and I left a clean towel in the restroom for you." "There are also some large pants and a sweater that you can wear folded on the sink in the restroom."

Thank you Beatrice. I am very grateful. "You are most welcome Max." "Have a good night." Good night, I whispered as Beatrice went into her room. I waited for her to close the door, and then I turned off the kitchen lights. I then headed to the couch bed that she had prepared for me.

I was also tired. In fact I was too tired to shower, so I dove into the newly made bed. I think I fell asleep before my head even hit the pillow. Who knows, but when I woke up I felt so well rested and motivated.

Feeling like I could take on the world, I got up and made the bed. I then took a nice warm shower where I inspected my body once more. I was happy to see that I no longer had any more bruises. I was healed and that made me content, so with a smile on my face I headed to the kitchen where shockingly Beatrice was already hard at work.

She was squeezing oranges and toasting bread. "Good morning Max," good morning Beatrice. "Did you sleep well?" I really did, and you? "Perfectly well." That makes me happy to hear Beatrice. It seems like you are an early bird. "Oh, I really am not, but I wanted to wake up early to make us a small breakfast before you go to the Daxes."

Aw, Beatrice you shouldn't have. "Oh, it is my pleasure Max." "It makes me happy to be able to help you, plus I was feeling hungry this morning." She said with a smirk on her face. "Now enough chit chat, go ahead and take a seat and help yourself."

I obliged and grabbed one toasted bread, and poured myself half a glass of orange juice. I reluctantly ate the toast. I wasn't a fan of it. Something in the texture made me dislike it, but the orange juice made me feel more energetic, which I welcomed.

"Do you feel ready to go?" Well, I would be lying if I said yes, but I have to. It is already 7:30 a.m. The kids should be on their way to school, and the cleaner should be arriving now. "What time will Juliette be back from yoga?" She comes back exactly at 9:00 a.m.

"Okay, so you need to get going now." I nodded my head in agreement and stood up. Beatrice came over and walked me to the door. "I will be here when you come back Max." Her lower lip was shaking. She was nervous. I felt awful for putting her in this position.

Beatrice I want you to know that if anything happens to me, I won't mention your name. I want you to be safe, and not involved in any of this mess. "Max, if you get caught I want you to mention me." "I could not give two shits about what happens to me." "What are they going to do?" "Throw a little old lady in jail for helping someone out?"

"I like to see them try." She said with a laugh as she walked me out of her apartment. "Please come back safely." She gave me a small hug. I will, and with that I made my way to the end of the hall right by the stairway of the building.

Chapter 14

THE FIGHT WITH GERALDINE

I took one small peek down the stairs to ensure that they were empty. They were. The people who live in this building are quite predictable with their schedules. Which was a good thing for me. However, my nerves were through the roof!

Every step that I took down on the rustic wooden stairs was like a slap to the face. I felt like someone would come out and see me. It made me sweat with fear, and by the time I reached the edge of the stairs on the fourth floor my shirt was moderately wet from all the perspiration.

Fortunately, no one saw me go down the stairway, and in even greater news the door to the Daxes' apartment was open like I had predicted! I could hear the cleaner vacuuming. This made me confident that the place was empty. This was my chance! I took a deep breath, and walked inside the home.

Immediately my stomach turned upside down by simply feeling the bad vibes of the place. The beige coloring of the walls was draining. The frames on the porcelain table from the 1800s made me feel like I was in a bad museum. I felt sick being in here again, but I had to shake it off.

The minutes were ticking away. The cleaner will soon come down to the first floor. I couldn't have that happen without checking the area out first. Afterall, the Daxes's master bedroom was on this level.

Without wasting any more time I took a right and entered their bedroom. *Creek, crack, creek crack* the floors went, as I passed the hall entrance to their room which led directly into the suite restroom.

A massive restroom that was split into three components. The tub, shower and toilet. Each contained in its own little room separated by a white wall. The sink and cabinets were on the opposite side of the toilet.

I decided to check the cabinets out first. I made my way to that side of the bathroom and opened each one. There was nothing but shampoos, deodorants and towels. My luck. Maybe there was something hidden behind the toilet.

I knew that people sometimes hid wads of money there. I dispensed no time and checked. I looked under the toilet and inside the water jug. Nothing. All empty. The restroom was a dud. It was now time to explore their bedroom.

The first thing that came into view as I walked into their room, was their king sized bed. It was carved out of wood. It smelled like winter oak. The bed was raised a couple of inches off the ground, which gave me a perfect view of what was under it.

There was nothing there. Shit. This was getting harder than I expected, I told myself as I opened the drawer next to their bed. I rummaged around inside of it. There were a few papers there. It looked to be nothing but bills so I put them back.

Stress and disappointment started looming over me. I still had not found anything. My heart started beating faster. I had maybe ten minutes left before the cleaner came down to the first floor, so out of desperation I began to feel around the walls.

Maybe there would be a loose piece in the marble of the walls, like in the floor and ceiling. My hands gingerly touched around, but there was absolutely nothing.

I only had one option left, the closet. The damned closet. The place where I had found my passport. I was dreading ever going back there. That is where Juliette had caught me right before this entire shit show started, but I had no other choice now.

I pulled back the two large doors of the closet and pushed them aside. The automatic lights turned on and I entered. I went straight for the drawer where I had found my passport and I opened it.

There were a lot of documents and I did not have time to read them all, so I pulled out the large folder that they were in and took it under my arms. I then commenced to feel the walls in the closet to see if any piece was loose, and there was a loose piece! The part on the far right corner felt hollow and shaky.

I gave it a knock and the piece of the wall bent inward exposing a hole. I was flabbergasted by what I saw. There were bags of money inside the hole! Neatly wrapped bags of euros in plastic sacks. There was at least over one hundred thousand euros there.

For the Daxes that is not much money, but the fact that there was liquid cash in the wall made me suspicious. I had to know if there was something else there. Thus, I stuck my hand inside and felt a soft bag. It almost felt like flour, so I pulled the bag out of the hole and my heart stopped.

Something in me knew that this sack contained drugs. It felt heavy. At least 3 kilos of what I assume to be cocaine. Shivers went down my spine, and I put the bag right back in the hole, while at the same time feeling around some more.

I moved my hands in all directions, and then I felt something that felt like another folder. I grabbed it and pulled it out. It was a small envelope no more than eight inches. It had to be important, but since I was low on time I shoved it into the larger folder that I had found just a minute earlier.

I would open it once I was back at Beatrice's, but now it was time to leave. I quickly stepped out of the closet, and I checked the time on the clock that was on the drawer by the Daxes' bed.

It was 8:28 a.m. I still had two minutes before the cleaner came down to this floor, and over thirty minutes before Juliette came back. Okay good, I thought to myself. Relax, Max, you still have time to get out, and with that I headed into the hallway that led out of the Daxes' bedroom.

Regrettably, right as I was about to leave I saw her. She stared at me with the evilest smile. The corner of her lip flared out. Her bucked teeth looked like they were ready to bite my neck off. She looked like a demon coming to get someone who sold their soul.

"Well, well, well." "Who do we have here?" "We have the convict." "We have the killer and the thief." I continued to walk toward the door. I was not going to sit around and wait for her to insult me. "Where do you think you are going?" Not one word, Max. Do not say one word to this waste of a person.

"Give me that folder NOW." I was face to face with her now. She had the exit blocked. How was I going to get her to move? I did not want to hurt her, but I had to get her out of the way.

"You aren't going anywhere." I had no choice. I would not get caught again. I grabbed her left hand and dragged her out of the way. "How dare a vermin like you touch me!" "You think you scare me?" *Bam, bam, bam.* I felt three slaps hit my face. She had hurt me.

That was the last straw. I would never let anyone hurt me again. I grabbed both of her arms and squeezed them tightly, and I dragged Geraldine, the host grandma to the bed.

You will never abuse me again you racist bitter hag of a person! She looked at me with fury in her eyes and I smiled back. All of you will end up in jail. You picked the wrong person to mess with, and if you think of hurting my family I will personally come back and hurt you! She looked at me with her mouth wide open as I flipped her off.

"You ignorant animal." "You will rot in jail." I ignored her comments and I quietly left the apartment. This time I did not slam the door behind me, instead I closed it gently and I walked back up to Beatrice's place as if nothing had happened.

"Max, are you okay?" I looked down at Beatrice as I straightened my body up. I must have looked like a mess. I felt my hair in my eyes. My body felt hot and my face felt flushed.

To top everything off I was out of breath. I put my finger up to let Beatrice know that I was okay, but that I needed a minute to catch my wind. She looked at me and waited.

After a few big breaths I sat on the kitchen chair. Beatrice, I had an encounter with Geraldine. She slapped me three times. "Are you okay?" "Did she follow you?" "How did you manage to escape?" I dragged her carefully to the Daxes' bed and left her to be, and no she didn't follow me.

Beatrice looked at me and started to giggle. "Well, I am glad she got what she deserves." "That bitter witch has been nothing but awful to me since we met." "She treats people like they are all beneath her."

"But I digress, I am happy that you made it safely out of there." "Did you find anything?" Yes, Beatrice, I found a large folder and an envelope. I pulled them out from beneath my arm and opened the folder. It contained several letters, but what caught my eye were the ultrasounds.

There were two ultrasounds. One of a boy, and one of a girl. They were three years apart. "They must be of Roman and Mylene." I nodded in agreement, and I flipped to the next page which contained a medical record. I began to read it. The record was of a 28 year old woman from Lithuania. "The surrogate mother."

"What does the envelope have?" I grabbed the small envelope and opened it. **RECORDS OF DRUG CLIENTS**. There it was in big bold letters. There was a list of over fifteen names. Each name had a small section and picture of the person.

It seems like they also sell drugs, Beatrice. She nodded her head and then gasped in shock. "This man!" Which one? "The first name on the list, look at his picture." "Do you know who this man is?" No, who is he? "He is the Chief of Police in the *Il de France* region." My fingers went cold.

Do you think he is working for the Daxes? "I am not sure if he is working for the Daxes, but he is on this list." "If this folder is true, he has bought drugs for them!" "It just shocks me because he does not look like a drug user?" I mean, he himself might not use them, but he could be disturbing them.

"You have a point Max." "You know, you certainly struck gold by finding this envelope." Why do you say that, Beatrice? "The one thing we French hate the most is when people in power over use their power." "The French people will rally with you Max, once this comes to light."

I hope what you are saying is true. "It is Max." "Once you present all of this to the embassy I am sure your name will be cleared right on the spot." I hope so, Beatrice. "Don't worry, Max." "I know what I am talking about."

Okay, I believe, *NEE, NUUH, NEE, NEE, NUH*. The noise erupted in my ears. It came out of nowhere, but it was clear that

it was the sound of sirens. THE POLICE BEATRICE! GERAL-
DINE MUST HAVE CALLED THE COPS!

Chapter 15
THE NEW AU PAIR STRIKES

"Go hide in my room!" I dashed to Beatrice's room as the sounds of the sirens grew closer. *NEE, NUUH, NEE, NEE, NUH.* My heart pounded in my chest. I don't know why I was so surprised. Of course Geraldine had called the cops, but for some reason it still astounded me.

However, I at least felt certain that she did not know where I had gone. She had not followed me when I left the apartment. Nevertheless, she probably suspected where I was. I couldn't be sure, but when the doorbell rang to Beatrice's house my body stopped moving, and my ears tuned in to the door as Beatrice opened it.

"Bonjour Madame Beatrice, I have your groceries for the next two weeks here." "Unfortunately, they did not have the blueberries in season yet, but the man at the store said next month." "Oh that is a shame, but do not worry." "You may come in and place the groceries in their spots."

I collapsed to the floor in relief from the realization that it was just the delivery man, but that was too close of a call. I had to prepare myself just in case I had to dash out of Beatrice's home, so I got back up and ready myself for anything. I then walked over to the bedroom door and pressed my ear on it. I needed to know what the delivery man knew.

"Madame, are you aware of what is happening?" "I have no clue, but I hope whatever it is, they stop." "The noise is hurting my ears." "Yeah, mine are hurting too." "Well I won't take any more of your time, see you on the next delivery." "Thank you sir, here is your tip." "You are kind, Madame." "Have a good day." "You too."

"Max, you can come out now." "He is gone." I heard Beatrice's voice but I was still too shaken to speak. "Max, did you hear me?" *DONG, DONG, DONG* the door went. Beatrice stopped talking, and slowly opened her front door.

"May we please speak to you Madame Beatrice?" "This is the police." Fuck. "The police?" Beatrice said with a hint of worriness to her voice. My body felt wobbly as the adrenaline rushed right through me.

I could not let them catch me. The chief of the police in this area was linked to the Daxes. There was no way I would survive. What should I do? Should I escape out the window? No, that would not work if there were police outside.

Damn, what do I do? I cried to myself, but I already knew the answer. There was nothing to do but wait. I kept my eyes closed and prayed. Please help me, God. I pleaded silently.

"We have reason to believe that Max is on the loose in this building, or was at one point here in this building." "Did you happen to hear any unusual activity at all? "Oh my goodness." "This sounds like it is getting out of control." "Is there reason that I need to fear for my life?" Beatrice was playing the perfect part. She was making the officers think she believed the Daxes and not me.

"No, Madame, we just wanted to update you because it is the right thing to do." "Well, thank you, but now I am scared!" "Will you leave an officer on guard in the building?" Beatrice was asking all the right questions." She wanted to know as much as she could.

"Yes Madame, he should be here this evening." "Also, the building is changing the entrance code, and here it is." "Thank you gentleman." "I need to sit down." "This is a lot to process." "Do you boys mind?" Beatrice played the part well.

"Not at all, Madame, but before we go, we also wanted to let you know that tomorrow there will be supporters of the Daxes in the boulevard." "The streets will be packed." "Oh no, that will cause a lot of disruption and noise!" "Don't worry, Madame it is only for one day, and by the night they will be gone."

"Oh okay, but does that mean they will quit protesting in the *American Embassy?*" "I think the protestors will change location in two days." "They can't keep the people in that neighborhood from working all this time." "You got that right."

"Okay, we are going to head out now." "Please, take it easy." "Go get some rest and if you see anything unusual call us." "You can count on me officers."

I waited patiently as the heavy booted footsteps left the apartment. Once I heard the door lock I walked over to the kitchen. Beatrice looked stressed. Her gray bob was frizzled out. "Max, sweetie, did you hear everything?"

Yes, I did. I said with a quivering lip. "Then you know we have to move now." "Here is the phone." "Call Mathieu to get you because you are no longer safe here."

I bobbed my head in agreement and grabbed the phone. I dialed Mathieu's number. The phone only rang once and he answered it. "Hello?" Mathieu, it is me Max, can you please pick me up at 5:00 p.m?

"Is everything okay Max?" As long as you come get me everything will be okay. "I will come." "Where do you want me to pick you up?" The same place you dropped me off. "Perfect, I will be there." Thank you, Mathieu, and see you soon.

"Well we have a couple of hours to spare." "I say we try to focus our minds on something else." How about we play some more card games?" I would love that Beatrice.

I followed her to the living room and this time it was me who taught her how to play a new card game. I taught her *Speed*, and I was glad she let me. The teaching helped me distract my mind from my reality. Beatrice, like Mathieu, were true angels.

By the time we finished playing cards it was a little over 3:00 p.m, and I volunteered to make us something to eat. I went straight to the kitchen and I pulled out all the ingredients that I needed for my plain vanilla cake.

I was excited to be making this cake not only to thank Beatrice, but to soothe my mental state. Baking always helped me to feel distressed and this time it was no different. As soon as I melted the butter my pulse got slower. By the time I had placed the cake in the oven my heart beat was normal.

"Max, do you want to play a few more rounds of *Speed* while your cake bakes?" Of course! I headed back to the living room and continued my game with Beatrice. It was a lot of fun, and when the oven timer went off I hurried back to the kitchen. I removed the cake from the oven, and I set up the table.

Beatrice the cake is ready, I called. Beatrice slowly walked over. "Wow, it looks delicious." "It is making my stomach rumble." "When will you cut it?" I want you to cut it, Beatrice.

"That is sweet Max." Well, this is only a small token of my appreciation, but just know once I get my name cleared I will give you what you deserve.

"Do not worry about it Max." "You were a gift sent to me." "My life was getting very lonely, and you brought a lot of excitement and happiness to it." "Now let's eat some cake shall we?" Yes, let's eat.

We slowly ate our slice of vanilla cake. It had a soft structure with a hint of butteriness to it. "This is such a good cake." "You have a talent for baking." I felt myself blush. I was not used to getting compliments, especially not during this point of my life.

Merci, Beatrice. I guess it is time that I should be getting ready to go. It's 4:30 p.m. "Are you ready?" I have to admit to you that I am scared. What if one of the Daxes sees me going down the stairs? "Wait a minute."

Beatrice stood up and walked over to the closet. She rummaged a bit and came back with a hat that had hair on it. "I had cancer a couple of years ago and I would use this wig-hat everywhere." She placed it on my head.

This will give you a better chance to not be recognized." Thank you, Beatrice. I"ll put it on once I start going down the stairs." It is a little itchy to have it on now. She smiled at me.

"How far do you have to walk? I need to walk ten minutes to get to the place where Mathieu will pick me up. "That is not too bad, plus it is almost dark out." "That way it will be harder for people to recognize you." That is what I am hoping for.

"Don't worry about it Max, and before I forget I need to tell you something." What is it, Beatrice? "I am here for you." "I do not care what time of day it is." "I will be here for you, okay?"

Beatrice, what did I do to deserve you? You are amazing, and I am forever grateful to you. I will do my best to call you once I get the chance to. Also, just know that you mean so much to me.

I grabbed one of her hands and squeezed it twice. Okay, I think it is time for me to get going. "Yes it is." "Did you grab your folders and box with the flash drives?" Yes, they are right here.

I picked up the folders and the box, and I walked to the front door. Beatrice opened it for me, and gave me a tight hug. "I will pray that the next time I see you, you are a free man." "See you soon, brave one." I wiped a tear from my eye and closed the door behind me.

I was now alone in the cold hallway. I felt exposed, so I grabbed the wig-hat and placed it over my head. The hair covered my eyes, but I parted it away. It was time. Well here goes nothing, I told myself.

I began to walk down the stairs. My body felt stiff. I was on edge. This was a busy time of day, and anyone could be walking down or up the steps. I felt scared that someone would see me.

The only thing that made me feel better was that the rustic wooden stairs made so much noise that I could hear anyone coming up or down them. Which would give me enough time to either hide or escape if need be.

I'll be okay. I reassured myself as I made it down to the fourth floor, the Daxes' floor. You got this, Max, I repeated again, and just as I was about to continue my steps down to the third floor I saw him.

My heart stopped beating. Sitting just a few inches from me on the stairs was a young man that I had never seen before. I was taken aback by his sudden appearance that I took one step back and slipped, causing my wig-hat to fall off.

I quickly tried to regain my composure, and just as I was putting the hat back on he saw me. Sadly, before I could react he was on me. He wrapped his arms around my stomach in a split second. He then yelled "I GOT HIM, I GOT HIM." In a clear English accent.

It was obvious who he was. He was the Daxes' new victim. Their new au pair. I felt pity for him, but as he tightened his grip around my waist I knew I had to take action.

Hey, listen! You do not understand, you are in danger with the Dax family! I yelled in frustration, as I pried his hands from my stomach. "It is you who does not understand." "I will hold you here till the police arrives, you dirty killer."

Shit, he was brainwashed. I could not reason with him like this. I had to set myself free, which meant that I would have to hurt him. Thus, I lowered myself to my knees causing the new au pair to get carried by me on my back. I was careful to not drop my folders or box.

I then rammed him to the wall with all my strength. He dropped like bricks to the floor. I looked at him, and said, "Just a word of advice, do not let them take your passport." "If they did go get it NOW." With those words said I dashed down the stairs, and to my luck the elevator was on the third floor, so I hopped right in.

I pressed 0, and down I went. As I reached the lobby I heard someone running down the steps, but it was too late. There was no stopping me because as soon as the elevator stopped I flew out of the building, and I ran.

I ran and I ran until I reached the street that led directly into the park where Mathieu would be picking me up. Once there I turned my head back and saw that no one was chasing me, so instead of running, I began to walk.

I calmly walked all the way to the meet up place, and just as I got there, Mathieu was pulling up to the parking space. I could see Elodie in the back. She was busy playing with her barbies that she did not even notice the car stopping.

I waited for Mathieu to park his car and then I headed towards him. He looked nervous. Hey, Mathieu, are you okay? "Merde, shit!" "You scared me, Max." "I did not recognize you with that wig."

Oh this little thing? I said with a laugh. It is just a disguise. "I see, but come in Max, hurry we got to go." "Monsieur Paul is hosting a dinner at 7 p.m and I think Alexandre Dax will be attending."

I practically dove into the car when I heard Mathieu say that. He then wasted no time and we were on the road again. Once we were safely out of the city and onto the highway he relaxed and apologized to me. "Sorry for the rude welcome." "I just wanted to make sure that we got out in time."

No need to say sorry, Mathieu. I understand, and I am grateful for you getting me with no notice. It is great to see you, and Elodie again. "I am also happy to see you Max, and I am sure Elodie is too." "Right Elodie?" "Yes, I am very excited papa!" "Oncle Max, can you play barbies with me?" Of course Elodie!

She handed me a doll and we started playing together. Mathieu occasionally looked at us with happiness in his eyes, and after about ten minutes of us playing, Elodie fell asleep. "Something about putting her in a car does the trick."

Yeah, the same would happen to me when I was a kid. "Max?" Yes, Mathieu? "Can you please take off that creepy wig?" "It is freaking me out." Oh, the brave and heroic Mathieu is scared of the little wig? I joked as I placed the wig on his head. We both laughed, but stopped suddenly as we felt the road become bumpier.

Which meant one thing, we were nearing Paul's place. Instinctively, I crouched down my body and sank to the floor of the passenger seat. "Please stay like that until I give you the okay, Max." "Got it?" I got it, Mathieu.

I waited to be given the okay as the pavement changed from extremely bumpy to pebbly. I knew we were entering Paul's place, but abruptly the car came to a complete stop. I smashed my head on the glove compartment.

"Max, I am so sorry but Alexandre Dax just got in front of the car, and is waving at me." "I had to stop." "I hope you are okay." "He is signaling me to get out of the car." "Do not move a muscle, please."

Chapter 16

THE SOLICITATION

How in the world am I supposed to stay still, Mathieu? If Alexandre is right outside! Do you think he saw me? What should I do? Do I go hide in the forest? I was panicking. "Max, I need you to trust me." "I am positive that he did not see you." "So I beg you, stay still, please."

Okay, I whispered as he looked at me with empathic eyes. "Max, you are safe with me." "I'll leave the door partially open so you can hear what we are talking about." "If it is something negatively concerning you, then you can let Elodie off and take the car." "Does that sound okay?

Yes, I said through sniffles. "Perfect, I'll be back." Good luck Mathieu. "I have all the luck I need with you and Elodie near me." He said as he winked, and then he stepped out into the dark evening. It was now a waiting game.

Sweat began to drip from my forehead and onto my lips as I waited for them to encounter each other, and after a few seconds the demon spoke. "Well hello Mathieu." "How are things?" Alexandre said with joy in his voice.

"Hello Monsieur Alexandre, I am well, and things are going good." "How about you? "Well, I am better now that I ran into you." "I have not seen you in almost a year!" "It has been far too long."

"Yes, Monsieur Alexandre, much too long." "What brings you to this neck of the woods?" "Paul is hosting a dinner party today, and I thought hey, you know who I haven't seen in a while?" "Mathieu!" "So I thought why not pay you a visit."

"I appreciate it, Monsieur Alexandre, and it makes me happy that you thought of me." "I am happy that you think so, Mathieu, because I have a proposal for you. "As you know, I have always been someone frank and to the point."

"With this entire Max situation my wife Juliette has not had much time to focus on certain parts of our marriage." "I mean the poor woman is so occupied trying to find that little bitch."

There was a long pause after Alexandre Dax called me a bitch, but then Mathieu spoke up. "Is there anything I can help you with Monsieur Dax?" "Yes, Mathieu, there is." "I noticed that you were on this certain app to meet people."

"I am not one to go on these apps, but like I told you, Juliette does not have the time for these types of things at the moment, and I am a man, right?" "Oui, monsieur, you are a man." "Good, well being a man I have needs."

Goosebumps went up my arms. Was he really trying to solicit Mathieu? Not only that, but in front of Elodie? Who luckily was still sleeping. I could not believe it, and it made my blood boil. That animal of a man had no self control. No respect. Plus he's married!

"What are you implying, monsieur Dax?" "I am going to stay the night at Paul's house." "After the dinner party I will come back here, and we will both have some fun." "I do not want to hear any complaining."

"I know you will love it." "I have caught you staring at me a few times before." "Monsieur Dax, I cannot accept that." "I am sorry." "Plus I have my daughter." "You do not have much of a choice, Mathieu."

"If you do not do what I ask, not only will I tell Paul to fire you, but to also put you and your daughter on the street." Mathieu must have been stunned because he started to stutter when he spoke.

"I, I, I, d, doo, do, do want, want, you, Monsieur Alexandre, but can we have fun in the forest?" "That way it is far from my daughter?" "Hmm, that sounds pretty erotic." "Okay we will take our fun there!" "I want you in front of your door right at 9:30 p.m, don't keep me waiting."

"Understood sir. "That is how I like them, obedient." Alexandre said with a sinister *Hahahaha.* Nothing more was said after that, and after a few minutes I heard the *thud, thud, thud* sound of footsteps approaching the car. I lowered my head in caution, but I knew it was Mathieu.

"Hey Max, I'm sorry to keep you waiting" "You can go ahead and pick yourself up." "No one will notice you now." I carefully lifted my head and looked into Mathieu's eyes. His ocean blue eyes were filled with tears.

Are you okay, Mathieu? "I just can't believe what Alexandre is proposing." "This will be a nightmare." "I am flabbergasted." I grabbed Mathieu by his shoulder and embraced him. Mathieu, everything will be okay. This may actually be a good thing.

Mathieu pulled away from the hug, and looked at me with surprised eyes. "What do you mean, Max?" Well, the Daxes, especially Alexandre, love their wine, and during their last party he was drunk beyond reason. I am sure he will be drunk tonight too, especially since he is staying at Paul's.

"Okay, but what is your point?" A drunk Alexandre is not as well aware as a sober one. If you can get him more drunk then maybe you can avoid what he has planned. Plus, you can possibly record a confession of him stating his crimes. Remember, they say the most honest people are drunk people.

Mathieu stared intensely at me. I could see the wheels in his head turning. "I think that may actually work!" "Let's go ahead and get to my house and plan this!" I'm right with you, Mathieu.

A few moments later we were outside his home. "Here are my keys, Max." "Can you open the door while I get Elodie out, and put her into bed?" Yes I can. I took the keys from his hands and got out of the car.

Shoosh, shoosh, shoosh. Immediately my face was greeted with cold arctic air. I shivered, and ran up the steps to the front door. I was not expecting it to be this cold, but wasting no time I unlocked the front door and entered Mathieu's home.

Shortly after that, Mathieu came in with a sleeping Elodie hanging around his neck. It was adorable. He really was a good dad. He gently walked over to his room to put her in bed. "She will be out all night." "At least that is one less issue to worry about."

I'm glad, I said with a smile. "Now how about we have some dinner before we sort out our plan?" That sounds good to me. "Perfect then." "Go ahead and take a seat, Max." I pulled a chair from the kitchen table and sat down. Matthew put two dishes in the microwave. "I hope you like what I made for dinner."

I am sure I will. You are a little chef after all. "*Haha*, oh it is nothing fancy, Max, just a Croque Madame." That is plenty fancy for me. *Bring, bring, bring* the microwave alarm went. Mathieu pulled the dishes out and handed me a tasty looking Croque Madame.

It had butter oozing from the sides of the bread. There was a fried egg on top. He had artistically placed a tomato around the sandwich. I was pleasantly surprised. See you are a chef!

"You are too kind to me." "I just hope you like how it tastes." I took a bite. The crunchy sound vibrated from the roof of my mouth down to my ear drums. This is delicious Mathieu, I told him with a stupid grin.

"I am glad you liked it, Max." "Shall we go over the plan?" Yes, I think you should get him more drunk than he will already be, and ask him questions that are direct and to the point. "Good idea." "Plus, if I get him drunk enough then nothing inappropriate has to happen between us." Exactly.

"Also, Max, you know that I don't like him like that, right?" He turned and looked at me with a smile. I turned away shyly, but then regained my composure. Mathieu, anything you do in your personal life is your choice. You don't have to explain it to me. "Oh I know, but I wanted to explain it to you."

I felt my cheeks get red. Thankfully Mathieu changed the subject." "I saw the news that the protestors will move from the American Embassy in a day or two, and once they move we will both go directly there." Merci beaucoup, Mathieu. I really do appreciate your help.

"No need to thank me." "This evil family needs to be taken down." "That said, I will go ahead and take a shower since it is 8:40 p.m. Which means Alexandre Dax will be on his way soon." What should I do, Mathieu? "I think it is best that you go to the room now." "Once I leave with Alexandre then you can shower." Okay, I will do that, and hey Mathieu, "yeah?" I just want to tell you, please take care of yourself. Please be careful. This man is dangerous. He is cold blooded. I don't want anything bad to happen to you.

Mathieu stood up from his chair and gave me a tight hug. I could feel his heart pounding. He was either nervous, or excited. I don't know which it was, but I let him hug his feelings out. Eventually his heart beat went back to normal and he let me go. "I will see you tomorrow Max, and thank you for letting me hug you."

No need to thank me, Mathieu. "I liked the hug. I felt safe. Mathieu blushed, and then he carefully walked into the restroom and shut the door. I, on the other hand, headed to my room. I wasn't tired, but I wanted to lie down.

I had an unsettling feeling. Alexandre had always been crude, but I did not know he was sexually promiscuous. The idea terrified me. Something horrible could happen to Mathieu, but then I remembered what Alexandre had told Mathieu.

He had said that Mathieu looked at him in a more than friendly way in the past. Did Mathieu actually want this, and now that he was in the situation he was regretting it? No, Max, don't think like that, I told myself. Regardless of the circumstances, victim blaming is the worst thing to do, and I will not do it.

Even if Mathieu was or is attracted to Alexandre, that does not give Alexandre the right to abuse his power over him. Alas, this is just all fucked up, and it feels like it is all my fault. If I never came to France maybe Alexandre would have never set his eyes on Mathieu.

No, no I have to stop thinking like that. It is not my, *creek, crack, creek, crack* my thoughts were interrupted by the opening and gently closing of the front door. It must be Mathieu leaving to meet up with Alexandre. I had to make sure.

I got off the bed and tiptoed all the way to the dark living room. I crouched down and put my ear next to the door. "Go ahead and take off your pants here." "I want to see and touch what you are working with." "Monsieur Alexandre, my baby is sleeping." "She may overhear something."

"Fine, let's go to the forest!" "Would you like some wine to drink?" "I brought some." "Uh, this isn't a date, Mathieu." "I am not gay!" "Let me get that straight." "My wife isn't putting out, and I am only doing this because I like dominating scums like you."

"Now come on, let's get moving on." The sound of leaves crunching and twigs breaking disappeared into the night as they headed to the forest. I was left dumbfounded.

Alexandre was truly gross. It took every ounce of my body and mental will to not go out the door and beat him silly, but I had to stick to the plan. Mathieu knew what he was doing. It will all work out, I reassured myself.

Unfortunately, I only half believed my own words. However, it was still enough to calm my nerves and keep my hope alive. Staying positive was the only thing that would keep me sane, and with that positivity in my mind I headed back to the room and got into bed. I closed my eyes and drifted to sleep.

Regrettably, I awoke numerous times throughout the night, and the last time I woke up, I could not stay in bed any longer. A feeling of dread loomed over me. It was like my sixth sense kicked in.

Something happened to Mathieu. I felt it. I rushed out of the room and headed to the kitchen. The clock read 4:00 a.m. Mathieu should be home by now.

I tiptoed to his room and gently opened the door. Elodie was sound asleep on his bed, but there was no sign of Mathieu. Fuck! He was not back yet. I had to look for him. I grabbed my shoes and a jacket, and I headed out the house.

Which way do I go now? Maybe they left footsteps? I looked down on the ground, and there were boot footsteps. Thank goodness. I followed the footsteps that lead to the forest by Paul's house.

I searched for over five minutes but then the footsteps disappeared. Where do I look now? "Help me, please someone help me."

Chapter 17
THE MURDER

Lying in a pool of his own blood was Mathieu. Mathieu! I yelled in fear. What happened to you? Even in the darkness I could see the blood all over his face and body. This could not be happening. Mathieu!

Don't die please. Elodie needs you. I fell to my knees and brushed his curly hair from his eyes. His breathing was rapid. His eyes were flickering. This was a nightmare. I had to save him, but I was no doctor.

I had no experience caring for others, but I had seen and read plenty of movies and books on how to treat wounds. One must put pressure on the wounds to prevent the blood from leaving the body. I immediately started to feel around his body.

The warm blood on my hands gave me chills, but I found two large wounds. One was on his stomach and the other on his chest. I took my jacket off and put it over the first wound on the chest. I then took off the sweater and put it over the wound on the stomach.

I turned to face Mathieu and his eyes were slowly closing. No! No! No! I will not let you die Mathieu, please fight for your life. The phone! Mathieu had a phone. I could call the police, and ambulance.

I frantically started to pat down Mathieu until I found his phone. It was snuggled inside his pocket. It was now or never. I did not care about what happened to me at that point. If the police came with the ambulance, oh well! I had to save him.

I dialed 112 which is the French equivalent of 911. The phone rang, *bring, bring*, "Hello, how may I help you?" Hello, madame, I have found a man lying in a pool of his own blood. Please, please, please send help to this address.

I gave her Paul's address and instructions on how to get to the forest. "Thank you, help is on the way." I hung up the call and put his phone back into his pocket.

Mathieu was shaking with violent shivers. He started to mumble something and then he spoke. "Please, hide." "Go to the house and hide." "I will fight for my life, and I will fight for Elodie, but for now, please go hide." I am sorry, Mathieu, but I am not leaving until I know that you are safe in an ambulance.

"You must go NOW!" Take my phone. I recorded everything that happened." "It is all in my gallery!" I reached for his phone again, and pulled it out of his jeans. "Now, go, allez!" I hesitated, but I knew he was right.

Mathieu, please, please don't die, and just as the words slipped my mouth I heard the sirens off in the distance. Mathieu, I hear the sirens! They will save you my friend.

I was surprised how fast they had responded, but then again this town was the size of no more than one thousand people. "Go, please, vite, Max!" "Look at my gallery." "Take care of my Elodie." "Tell her that I love her."

Quit talking like this Mathieu. You will be okay. He managed a small smile and then looked away. I ran from him as the lights of the sirens got closer. I hid behind a tree about one thousand feet away.

I wanted to make sure that the ambulance took him, and as awful as this sounds I wanted to make sure that they didn't cover his body. If they covered his body that meant he was dead. *Pin Pon, Pin Pon, Pin Pon* the ambulance noise filled the night.

Two people rushed out of it and brought over a carrier. I could not see very well but they were doing something to his injuries, and then they lifted him out of there with no cover! They were gone within three minutes, and I myself made my way over to the small pond that was in the middle of Paul's yard.

Once I reached the pond I placed Mathieu's phone down on the grass, and with all the strength that I could muster I hopped into the water. My body went into shock, but I frantically began to rub Mathieu's blood off of my body.

Sadly, I couldn't afford to let Elodie see me this way, so this was my only option. Thankfully, the blood washed out fast, and I hastily got back out. Wasting no time, I grabbed Mathieu's phone, and I ran back to his home.

By the time I reached his front door, my goosebumps were covered in goosebumps. Moreover, my hands were frozen, but still with numb hands I managed to not only open the door but also to lock it behind me. *Phew*, I was safely inside, and I took a second to bask in the warmth of the house.

Nonetheless, I had no time to waste, and I tiptoed straight into the restroom. Immediately, I grabbed a warm towel and I removed my wet clothes. Once I patted myself dry I folded my wet outfit and I set it aside. Now, I had to find something to change into.

Where, or where can I find clothes? I opened the drawer of the sink, and miraculously

my old dirty outfit from the other day was there. It was properly folded and washed. Yes! Thank you Mathieu, I whispered to myself while I put the warm attire on.

Feeling much better I walked over to the guest room. It felt nice and warm as I sat down on the bed. Regrettably sitting down was not such a good idea. I started to feel anxious. I pondered what could be going on with Mathieu.

My pulse started to rise and my breathing got heavier. I had to stop this feeling before I lost control, so I stood back up and walked around the house. I quietly paced around Mathieu's small house for almost ten minutes until I started to feel a tad tired and calmer.

I then made my way back to the room and got in bed. I clutched Mathieu's phone next to me and I closed my eyes. *Bring, bring, bring, bring.* Huh? What is that noise? *Bring, bring, bring.* The phone! It was ringing.

I opened my eyes and stood up. I reached for my shoes under the bed and grabbed the phone that had fallen in my sleep. The bright screen hurt my eyes, but it was a missed call. It was 6:30 a.m.

I dialed the number back. Hello, did you guys just call this number? "Bonjour, yes, can we please speak to Monsieur Christian?" "Monsieur Christian, I repeated?" "Yes, right before surgery Monsieur Mathieu asked us to call Monsieur Christian at this number." What? Who was Christian? I thought to myself, but then it clicked.

Mathieu had given them a fake name for me. Oh yes. I am sorry. I am still asleep. "No problem, it's still early in the morning." "We wanted to let you know that Mathieu had emergency surgery." My stomach fell to the floor.

Was this good or bad news? The person on the phone had such a neutral voice. "Monsieur Christian, are you there?" "I said we have managed to stabilize him." "He is currently in the ICU." Oh thank God, he is alive!

What happens next? "Well visiting hours are from 8 a.m. to 6 p.m." "You or any loved ones may come in during those times." Is there something I must fill out for him? "No, he gave us the consent for his surgery, and he has insurance."

Thank you God, I silently thought in my mind. Please if there is any emergency that comes up please do not hesitate to call me. "I will." I hung up the phone, and fell to my butt. He was okay. He was stabilized and in good care. That was a huge load off my mind.

It just sucks that there is no way that I could visit him. That said, I was sure he had his parents contacted. Mathieu was smart. He probably had the hospital call his parents and requested that they pick up Elodie. At least I prayed that that was what he did.

"Oncle, where is papa?" I jumped two feet in the air. Elodie was standing by the door rubbing the sleep away from her eyes. I nearly peed myself! I had not heard her come in. "Oncle, is papa working early today?" Good morning Elodie, no your papa had something important come up.

"What do you mean, oncle?" It is a surprise that he had hidden from everyone. "What surprise, oncle?" Your papa was selected for a gardening competition in Paris. He left last night and will be back later. "Papa left without telling me goodbye?" No, of course not.

He kissed you last night, but did not want to wake you up. "Oh good." Elodie gave me a big smile. "When will he be back?" Tomorrow, he will bring you a surprise. "Yay, a surprise!" "I can't wait." "Can I know what the surprise is?"

"Yes, your papa said if you behave well he will take you to Disneyland, but you have to be on your best behavior. I probably should not have said that because Elodie started to run around the entire room. She had the biggest smile on her face. If she only knew that her papa was almost murdered yesterday.

"Oncle can we go play Barbies right now?" Oh I almost forgot. Your daddy said you have to do your chores too. "Ah oui, I remember my chores, oncle Max." "I am going to clean my room now." "You will tell papa that I cleaned my room, okay?" I nodded my head and she ran out of the room.

It would take Elodie some time to clean her things, so now was the perfect time to look at the gallery in Mathieu's phone. With my heart thumping in my throat I opened the gallery up and saw that there was a fifteen minute video.

I hit play and began to watch. The video was black because the phone was in Mathieu's pocket, but the sound was crystal clear. The sound of footsteps walking and the wind howling made the video eerie. There was no talking until about thirty seconds in.

"It must be hard being such a busy and successful man, isn't it Monsieur Dax?" "You would have no idea even if I tried to explain it to you, Mathieu." "Your little brain cannot absorb all that information."

"Yeah, I guess you are right Monsieur Dax." "Take off your clothes please." "I want to get this over with now." The sound of a shirt and jeans being removed were heightened on the phone. It was like I was listening to an ASMR video.

"Yes, you have a good body Mathieu." "You know many of you lower class people have great bodies." "It is a shame that your mind isn't as strong." "Monsieur Dax, I am a bit nervous." "Do you mind if we have some wine before?"

"You think that I want to have a date before I dominate you?" "This is solely for fun and nothing more." "You should be lucky I am even here." "I am sorry." "I am just nervous, but I can't even imagine the stress that you are going through because of that stupid boy Max." "That's why I think a bottle of wine will calm us down."

"I already had plenty of wine, and yours is cheap wine from the looks of it." "Besides, you should not even talk about Max." "The only reason he is less of a human than you is because he is not French." "That said, that boy has heart and has the potential to change his life more than you do."

"It has been four days and they still haven't caught him." "He may be way below me, but he has surprised me with his will and drive, and that is something that you do not have Mathieu." "You are just a worker bee."

"You will always only be a gardener and nothing more." "Now get over here." I paused the audio. I was afraid to hear anything else. Plus I needed to absorb what I had heard. Alexandre Dax had given me a backhanded compliment, but he had spent forty seconds complimenting me nonetheless. That will look terrible for him in a trial. An accuser glorifying the accused.

That is not the norm. This video will serve as a contradiction to the interview he gave when I was first accused. People would see him as the liar that he truly was. Yes, thank you Lord. I couldn't help but smile from ear to ear, but then a wave of guilt engulfed me.

What was I doing? Here I was celebrating a small victory, while Mathieu was out there fighting for his life. That was not right, and I'm sorry Mathieu. I will find your evidence to send Alexandre behind bars.

I grabbed his phone again, and clicked play on the video. "You've wanted this since the day you set your eyes on me, didn't you?"

"Monsieur Alexandre, this is not right." "Shut up." "I do not want you to say another word." "Now get over here so I can feel you."

I paused the video again. I was fearful to hear what would happen next. I did not want to hear any sexual content, so I fast-forwarded the video to the last two minutes, and I braced myself as I hit play encore.

"Please, please don't kill me." "I will not tell anyone about this." "That is what they all say, now take this." **"AHHHH! IT HURTS."** "Lie here in the blood of your own filth." I heard footsteps leaving the area. The recording stopped.

There it was. We had Alexandre. He could not escape this. I felt emotional. My name would get cleared and Mathieu would get his justice. I just hope that I also had enough proof to send Juliette and Geraldine behind bars.

Which, I was *Knock, knock, knock.* I turned my head to the door. It was Elodie again. "Oncle Max, I am hungry." What would you like to eat? "Can I have Chocapic?" You want Chocapic for breakfast? Elodie gave me a mischievous smile. Chocapic was quite possibly the sweetest cereal ever, but you know what she deserved it.

Of course you can, Elodie. "Yay." She jumped up and down and ran to the kitchen. I followed her and grabbed two bowls of cereal. I was pretty hungry myself, and hey I also have a sweet tooth.

Here you go, Elodie. "Thank you oncle, and oncle can we also watch Bluey?" Of course! I rubbed her curly hair and turned the TV on for her. She looked so happy, but little did she know that her father was fighting for his life. Guilt loomed over me, but I forced a smile for her.

"Oncle, I am finished." "May I go to the living room and watch Bluey?" Yes, you may Elodie. She handed me her bowl, and I went over to wash it. As I reached to turn the faucet I saw a small blue Puegot pulling up to the driveway. There was an older couple in the car.

It had to be Mathieu's parents! Shit. They must be here to pick up Elodie, but they couldn't know that I was her. Elodie! I yelled. "Yes, oncle?" Do you want to play another game?

"Of course, what game oncle Max?" Well remember your daddy said if you do not mention me to anyone that you'd get a prize? "Yes, oncle I remember, and I will win that game." Okay this is the hard level of the game. Your grandparents are about to come in, and they cannot know that I am here, d'accord?

Elodie lifted one eyebrow in suspicion, but then said, "Oh you will surprise them at their home?" Exactly! You are such a smart girl. "Heheh, thank you oncle." "Will you go hide now?" Yes, I will. See you soon, Elodie. "Bye oncle, Max."

Bye, I whispered, and I dashed to the room right as the front door was being unlocked. "Elodie, tu es où?" "Mami, I am here." "Look at you sweet thing." "Come with me." "We are going on a surprise trip." "Wow, really?" "Will papi join us?" "Ye, yesss, yess." Elodie's grandma struggled to speak. She was hiding her pain.

"Do I need my suitcase?" "Yes, sweetie." "Let's go to your room." The sound of rapid paced footsteps vibrated through the entire house. She was definitely nervous. "Where are your sweaters?" "In this drawer, mami." The noise of drawers being pulled open shook the walls. I could feel the pain, anguish and overall distress coming from Mathieu's mom.

Something was not right. "Do, dddd, doo, you have everything, sweetie?" "Yes, mami." "Alright, let's go." "Your papi is waiting for us outside." "Can I say bye to the house, Mami?" "Yes, quickly, please." "Bye house," Elodie joyfully said as the door slammed shut, and not even a second later the sound of a car leaving filled the morning air.

They were gone as fast as they had come, yet I still cautiously walked out of the room. I made my way over to the kitchen window, and I caught the last glimpse of Elodie's curly blond hair on the passenger seat as they left the property.

Thank you Lord, Elodie was safely with loved ones. That was a load off my shoulders. She would be okay with her grandparents, unlike Mathieu. Something awful had to have happened to him since I last spoke to the hospital. His mother seemed too disturbed.

She had moved too fast. Was he still alive? *Bring, bring, bring*, the ringer of the phone brought me out of my haze. I walked back into the dark room and picked up the cell. Bonjour, "Oui, may I please speak to Monsieur Christian."

Yes, this is me. "Monsieur Christian we are sorry to inform you that Mathieu has passed away." The phone slipped from my hand and bounced twice on the floor. I collapsed on the bed in shock.

Time froze at that very second. It was as if the world stopped moving. I tried to process what I had just heard, but instead I stared blankly at the floor for what felt like a lifetime. I was a zombie, but soon I was brought back to life by the sound of heavy footsteps at the front door. Out of instinct I immediately grabbed my folders and box.

The front door opened. "Elodie, it is your uncle Paul, are you here sweetie?" My heart sank to the floor. Why out of all people was he here, and then a second voice. "Elodie, honey it is Monsieur Alexandre." "Can you please come here?" "We have a present here for you." What was going on?

"The little bitch isn't here." "She would have already come to greet us." "Are you sure, Paul?" "One hundred percent, the hospital did say Mathieu's parents were coming down." "Okay, well that is one less thing to worry about."

"Alexandre, are you sure that the nurse that you paid to suffocate Mathieu won't speak?" "Oh yes, he has murdered others for me in the past. "That said, I still want you to burn this hell hole up, just in case." "What about his parents, Alexandre?" "The hospital was only able to reach them after Mathieu died."

"There is nothing linking me to his death." "Don't worry Paul." "Anyway, burn this place up." "I'll buy you a new one." "Okay, Alexandre." The door slammed shut, and they loudly walked away from the house.

I was left dumbfounded. Mathieu was dead, and all thanks to Alexandre. Tears fell down my cheeks. I couldn't think or move anymore. I simply laid on the bed. The only thing that brought me comfort was the sound of wood burning!

Wait, the sound of wood burning? Fuck! The house was on fire! The realization brought me back to reality, and immediately I dashed to the front door. Thankfully, those bitches had left it open, and I could clearly see them heading to Paul's house.

What should I do? How do I get out of here? I frantically scanned the property and I spotted Alexandre's car right by the front gate. Immediately I ran to it, and to my luck not only was the driver's door open, but the car was on!

Bingo. Wasting no time, I dove inside the car and I set the clutch to first gear. *Boom, boom, boom* the roof of the house went into a small explosion. Flames were everywhere. The house was being burned to the ground. I moved to second gear and that is when Alexandre and Paul saw me.

Chapter 18

THE TRAIN RIDE BACK TO THE CITY OF LIGHTS

If I had a camera at that very moment to capture the look on Alexandre Dax's face I would have been the happiest man in the world. He had a look of fear on his arrogant mug. I enjoyed every second of his agony. It was blissful until he came running after the car.

With his bare fists he began punching the driver's door. "Come out this instant." "What do you think you are doing?" Don't respond to him, Max. Keep driving, I told myself. I continued forward and set the car into third gear.

Alexandre then jumped on top of the vehicle. "Stop right now, Max!" "If you stop I will call all the chargers off." "You'll be free to go back home." How stupid did he think I was? It made me laugh. I did not stop. I continued to pick up speed even as he punched the windows with his hands.

He could beat on the windows till his fists bled off, but I was not stopping the car. Especially after noticing that the front gate was closing. Paul must have hit the button to close the gate. No problem. I switched to fourth gear and sped toward the gate in hopes that Alexandre would let go, but he didn't.

With his body moving in all directions he continued to hold on to the hood of the car. He punched and punched the vehicle like if that was going to make it stop. I had to get him off, so I did something that in hindsight I maybe should not have done, but oh well.

I put my foot on the brake and pressed it all the way down. The car stopped instantly. I felt my body almost hit the steering wheel as the seat belt pulled me back. My head bobbled back and forth, and Alexandre Dax flew off the car.

He landed on the bushes right by the gate. I had no time to react, and I quickly restarted the car. I peeled rubber and I was out of the property. From the rearview mirror I saw Alexandre Dax standing back up. The look of hatred on his face was indescribable.

It made me smile as I drove on, but now it was time to refocus on the goal. Getting to Beatrice's was my only way of surviving, so that meant going back into Paris.

Unfortunately, the only way back to Paris at this time was by train. Which was a huge risk, but an even bigger risk was continuing driving this car. Which quite possibly was already being traced by satellite.

Okay, Max you gotta ditch the vehicle. I drove for three more miles, and parked the car a mile away from the train station in an area that was dense with shrubs. The place was ideal for ditching an auto, but not for walking because by the time I reached the station I had several cuts on my hands from all the thorns.

That didn't matter though, I was just happy to be here, and to see that the depot was jam packed. The more people the easier I could blend in.

Feeling more confident, I snuggled my folders and box tightly under my arm, and I walked over to the Kiosk machine. I bought a one way ticket to *Paris Gare de Lyon*. Thankfully, Mathieu's money had come in handy. *The next train would be approaching in five minutes.*

I took my ticket and went far behind the crowd of people that were lined up for the train. I wanted to make sure that no one saw me clearly, and I was happy to see that everyone was minding their own business. Good, I thought as I held in my tears.

I still couldn't fathom that Mathieu was dead, and poor little Elodie. She will grow up without the father who loved her more than he loved himself. I prayed that her happiness wouldn't be torn from her.

Also, I knew, *CHOO, CHOO, CHUGGA, CHUGGA,* the train cried as it slowly came to a halt, interrupting my thoughts. "Everyone in one line please." The conductor shouted as he opened the doors to the train.

People started to form one line, and then the conductor started to let everyone in. I followed them discreetly. My hoodie pressed to my face at all times. I tried to keep a nonchalant look on my face as I neared the conductor. "Billet, s'il te plait."

With a stiff hand and making no eye contact I showed my ticket to the conductor. Without looking at me he validated my ticket. *Phew*, that could have gone bad. Gratefully, it didn't, but now it was time to find a secluded area where I could sit.

I cautiously walked to the back of the train, and found an empty place where there were only a few people. I took a seat behind a man who was playing some sort of action game on his phone. Weirdly enough I felt pretty comfortable on the train because everyone had their faces tied to their phones.

That was a relief. At least they wouldn't notice me, and that's one less thing to worry about. "Doors, closing." The conductor blew his whistle and closed the doors. The train started moving. I pressed my head against the window to get a view of the town.

There was not much to look at when it came to views, but far off in the distance I saw three police cars heading this way. More than likely they were headed to the area where I had left the car.

They were too late to stop me here, but shit there was no denying it. The police would be waiting for me in Paris. It doesn't take a genius to look at the security cameras, and see that I bought a one way ticket to the city of lights. Fuck! I had not thought this through.

Nonetheless, I had a solution, and that was to get off this current ride and take another train back into the fashion capital of the world. That would throw anyone off my trail, but now the question is what stop do I get off at? One thing was certain, it could not be the first one.

They will easily guess that, and it cannot be the one before Paris because that would be too obvious. Hmm. I glanced at my ticket. There were a total of four stops before the city of love, and one of the stops was in a tiny village. Bingo, stop two it is.

Feeling a bit better that I had a plan again, I clutched my folders and waited for the minutes to pass until I reached my new station. *BOIS LE ROIS*, arrive dans une minute. This was my stop. I grabbed my things and I walked to one of the exits.

Surprisingly, no one even batted an eye in my direction as I passed by. Honestly, it shocked me how easily I was going unnoticed since everyone was a prisoner to their electronics. I could have worn a sign that said I was the killer au pair and no one would have seen. Well, whatever works for me. I laughed as the train came to a halt.

The big doors opened and I was the only one to get off. Not shockingly, the station itself was small and not much to look at. There was only a train platform, a vending machine, a monitor, and a ticket kiosk. In all honesty it didn't even look like a station, but at least it had a monitor showing the schedule for the rides today.

The next train going into Paris was in thirty minutes. Perfect! I had some time to spare, so I joyfully walked over to the kiosk and bought another ticket to the city of lights. Again, I felt ashamed for being happy, but the truth be told I really had enjoyed the short train ride.

Never in my wildest dreams would I have imagined this because the first and last time that I was on a train it had been pure hell. I recollect that it was a journey to Versailles, and I was with Roman, Mylene and Geraldine. I remember there were four open seats and they all sat down.

Innocently, I had tried sitting next to Geraldine, but she had pushed me to the floor. She then gave me a look of disgust and said, "Pigs do not sit next to queens." "Go find another seat, you vermin!"

I had never felt so humiliated. Countless people stared at me. No one defended me. I recall trying to keep my tears in my eyes, but it was in vain. I'll never forget the pitiful looks that I got.

The stares made me feel like I was less than everyone on the train that day. It was an awful experience, but this experience among several others have made me more motivated to bring down the Daxes. They will pay for, "Train to Paris arriving in five minutes." The automated speaker announced, interrupting my thoughts.

What the heck. Arriving in five minutes? I thought the monitor had shown half an hour? Did I really spend over twenty-five minutes reminiscing? I glared at the screen. Yes, yes I had. The train will be arriving in four minutes now. Okay, get it together Max.

I quickly rearranged my folders and made sure the box was safely inside my jeans. I then walked to the platform to wait for the train. There were now two other people waiting for it, but they were busy on their phones. Which was a good thing.

CHUGA, CHUGA, CHO, CHO, the train roared as it came to a stop in front of the platform. Before the doors even opened I could see through the windows how packed it was. It made sense. It was almost 9:00 a.m, peak work commute time.

The people looked annoyed to be in there. It was going to be a struggle to get in, oh well. The conductor stepped out and opened the doors. She signaled us to get in. Once again, I pressed my hoodie against my face as she validated my ticket, and I went inside.

Which was a mission in itself. A packed train is always a huge challenge in France because people will not move when someone comes in. You have to kindly "push them" out of the way, so that's exactly what I did until I reached the only available spot. Which was in the middle of the crowd.

It was a tight fit, and this wouldn't work because I could easily be identified. I had to move, but where? I quickly skimmed around the carriage, and when I turned my head to the left, a middle aged lady caught my eye.

She was sitting on a step as she intensely stared at her phone. I cranked my head to the side to get a view of what she was staring at so intensely. Oh shit. She was reading an article about me.

I held my breath. She was only about three feet to my left. If she saw me on the train my cover would be blown. That was a no no, so I hastily turned my head to the opposite direction and I kept it down. I then lifted up the collar of my sweater over my chin. I did not dare to look her way.

Instead I took Mathieu's phone out and acted like everyone else. Like a zombie who was glued to the screen. I started to feel more at ease, when out of the blue someone yelled.

"He struck again!" Everyone picked up their heads towards the screams of a guy who looked to be around my age. "The male au pair has killed and burned down the home of a gardener!" "A gardener who was tricked into thinking that he was a good person that should be helped!"

Unexpectedly, I did not feel anything from hearing the news that I was accused of murdering Mathieu. I expected to be charged with that crime, but at the end of the day I was the one who had video-audio of Mathieu stating in detail who killed him. I felt nothing but peace in hearing that accusation against me.

On the other hand, the people in the train began to go crazy talking to each other and viciously looking up the new information. It felt like I was in a circus watching the clowns run around in circles.

Little did all those people know that the "au pair killer" was on the train with them, and all they had to do was put their phones down. It's a shame, "Wait!"

The train got silent as the yell of a woman echoed throughout it. "This can't be right." I turned to face the lady. It was her, the one who was reading the article about me. "I do not think that he killed the gardener!" "This is too fishy."

"It seems like the male au pair is being blamed for everything!" "I believe the Daxes are pinning all this on him!" "He is their scapegoat." "Every time there is a disaster they are involved." "Things are not adding up." I was left in shock. She believed me, and ironically her outburst started a heated debate in the train.

It was chaotic, but it gave me the opportunity to sneak out from the middle of everyone, and amusingly hide behind that same woman. Her support made me, "Arriving in *Paris Gare de Lyon* in three minutes." "SPECIAL ANNOUNCEMENT," the conductor said through the intercom.

EVERY PERSON WHO DOES NOT HAVE THEIR LICENSE OR SOME SORT OF DOCUMENTATION SHOWING THAT THEY LIVE IN PARIS WILL BE HELD FOR FURTHER INSPECTION. WE APOLOGIZE FOR THIS INCONVENIENCE, BUT WE WANT TO MAKE SURE THAT THE MALE AU PAIR DOES NOT SNEAK IN TO, OR OUT OF PARIS.

Shit. The police were here in full force. What was I going to do? I had no false documentation to prove that I was living in Paris. I was screwed. My mind started spinning in circles.

I could not get caught. The police were not to be trusted in Paris. I had to make it to Beatrice, but how? Think, Max, think! The train slowly came to a stop, and then it hit me!

The middle aged woman who had defended me. She was my only chance. Maybe she could get me into Paris? Thus, I carefully followed her as she exited the train.

Thankfully, she was one of the first ones out. Which kept us from running into traffic. That said, she walked fast, so I had to exert myself as she headed to the barricade of police officers who were blocking the exit and entrance to *Gare de Lyon.*

I had to reach her before she got there, so I ran to her. It was now or never. She would determine my fate. I crossed my fingers and tapped her shoulder.

Please, I beg you to not scream. I am Max, the male au pair. I was on the train with you, and saw how you defended me. Her dark eyes widened. I want to let you know that I am innocent, and I am actually the victim in all of this.

Look, take a look at these folders if you do not believe me. I handed the folders to the lady. She took them with trembling hands, and began to examine them. She did not say anything for over a minute, but then she looked up at me.

She had tears in her eyes. She wrapped her arms around me. "I am so sorry that you have gone through all of this." "It brings me pain to see what they have done to you." "Look at you, you are just a child and they have traumatized your entire life."

Don't lose it Max, don't lose it in front of everyone. If I lose it now that will cause a commotion. I swallowed the lump that was in my throat and spoke. I need your help. I need to get into Paris to speak with someone who can aid me.

I finally have enough proof to take down the Daxes. She glared at me with her dark eyes and nodded as her eyebrows cringed up. "What can I do?" First, are you from Paris? "Yes." Okay, I need to pretend that you are my mother or something. That way they can let me into the city.

Is that okay? "Of course that is okay, and by the way my name is Paulette." I am glad to make your acquaintance Paulette, and I am sorry for meeting you during this awful time and under this situation.

"Do not apologize Max." "You have been through a lot, so I am glad that I can do what little I can to help you." Thank you, Paulette. Shall we cross the barricade now?

"Yes, but I want you to put on these sunglasses that I have." Why is that? "Your eyes are the most noticeable thing about you, Max." "Put the glasses on and no one will know it is you." I grabbed the glasses and put them on. We then slowly walked to the police barricade.

"Madame, may I see your documentation?" Paulette reached into her purse and gave her license to the policeman. While he inspected it, she grabbed my hand and brought me closer to her. "I am sorry officer, but can we hurry this along?" "I want to be home." "This au pair killer scares me!"

"Is this your son?" "Yes, and he is blind." "I need to go home." "Sorry about that madame." "Go on ahead." Paulette hugged me toward her as we walked out of *Gare de Lyon.* "We are out, Max."

Thank God, and thank you Paulette. She smiled at me and her laugh lines thickened. "My car is parked in the long-term parking lot." "We just have to take the elevator down to the 0 floor." "Don't you worry, I will also drop you off wherever you want in Paris."

That sounds perfect, Paulette, and thank you so much for everything. I will never forget this. She gave my shoulder a gentle rub after I said that. "The elevator is just over here." I followed behind her as she pressed the button to call for the lift.

Graciously it quickly came and we entered the hoistway. Paulette then pressed 0, and right as the doors were closing a man ran in. Shockingly, he pushed Paulette to the side of the frame as the hatch closed.

Chapter 19

THE SOUNDPROOF ROOM

"Hey, what is wrong with you?" "Shut up, bitch." Hey! Who do you think you are pushing, and talking to her like that? "Max, I'll get to you in a minute." My body froze. How did he know my name? Before I had a chance to react he pulled a taser out and struck Paulette. A bright light filled the elevator as her limb body fell to the floor.

Instinctively I ran to the button panel and pushed the emergency red button to open the doors, but it was to no avail. The elevator had started its descent, and it was almost at the parking-garage floor. "Seems like you're stuck with me." The man turned around to face me. It couldn't be. No, please, no God.

It was the same man from the airport! The one who had beat me mercilessly, not once but twice. He smiled a devious grin at me, and removed his frames. His beady eyes said it all. He saw me as his prey, but boy was he wrong. I was not going to go down without a real fight this time!

Before he had the chance to get close to me, I moved to the side so as to not injure Paulette's unconscious body, and then I jumped in the air. With all my force, I kicked him in his chin. His head thrusted back, and I was on him in a flash. I began to punch him in his face, and he fell to the floor.

Wasting no time, I jumped on him and swung away. He tried to get me off, but I was stuck on him like gum. I could see him losing consciousness with every blow that I gave him. It was enough. I stood up and picked up my folders that had fallen in my rumble with him.

I placed them back inside my jacket. Hopefully he had not seen them, but if he did, it did not matter. I would not be giving them up. "*Bing, Bing, Bing,*" the elevator doors opened.

"You'll pay for this." The airport assaulter said with a hoarse voice. I ignored him and dashed into the parking garage. "Come back here you little cunt!" I turned back to look at him. He was on the floor holding his face.

It brought me satisfaction, but now what do I do? I quickly scanned the parking garage and saw the emergency stairs! I sprinted toward them, but to my horror two large men got out of a car and ran toward me. One of them signaled the other to block the stairs.

Fuck! What now? Think Max, think. How can I escape? I rapidly looked around the garage again, and saw another elevator that was to my side. Without thinking twice I ran toward it.

Regrettably, the other man, not blocking the stairs, was on me before I even ran three steps. I had underestimated his speed. "You are not going anywhere." He said in a thick French accent as he yanked my arm toward him.

That truly pissed me off. I was done being the punching bag, so without hesitation I kicked him in the shin. He groaned in pain. I'm not going down that easy you bitch!

He gave me a smug look, and I swung my fist to his chest. Unfortunately, before I made contact with it, my body started shaking uncontrollably. It was as if I had been thrown into a washing machine. It took me a few seconds to realize what had happened, but then the pain kicked in.

The pain was electrifying. Electric shocks went up and down my body. I could smell sizzled hair and pee! I had soiled myself. Thanks to being tasered. "He pissed his pants." "*Hahahaha*, how funny, let's take a picture."

Tears rolled down my cheeks. Rage and hatred flowed through me. I tried to move my body again, but the electricity running through it made it impossible for me to move a single muscle on my own.

I was in misery and all I could hear were voices mocking me. I felt like a sideshow attraction. A sideshow attraction who could not stop bouncing up and down. With every shake my body took a toll, and finally I banged my head on the garage floor. Everything went black, and slowed down.

"Snap, snap, snap." My eyes fluttered open. My head was killing me. I had fainted, but I knew that I was no longer in the parking garage. I was lying on some type of wooden floor. Where was I? "Ah, I see you are awake now." "You have been quite the pain in the ass."

That cold shallow voice, it was her! There was no mistaking it. It was, Juliette. Her heels clicked and clacked on the floor as she walked her way to me. I tried to get up to face her, but my body was still wobbly from being tased.

"Oh, are you having a hard time seeing me?" "Not a problem my dear, Max." She pulled my hair down to my neck, which sent my head up toward her. The pain was immense. I felt myself get lightheaded.

My eyes fluttered as I fought to stay conscious, but it was hard because of the bright pink room that I was in. The color was intensifying my headache. Oh fuck. I knew where I was. There was only one place where I had seen such a bright pink before.

I was back in Paris in the Daxes' spare room. The spare room on their second floor that they made me clean once a week even though no one went in there. This room was soundproof. I could scream all day and no one would hear me.

"Well, I can tell that you know where you are at" I tried to look away from her but she held my head and made me face her. She stood over me with a bright smile on her face. Her hair was styled back in a high ponytail. Her makeup was light but visible.

"You have done well for a person of your status, but your time is up." "Did you really think you could outwit the Daxes?" "You may have fooled the police, but we planted spies to look for you on every train."

My heart stopped beating for a second. Juliette must have noticed a shift in my body. "Oh, and that sweet lady on the train, well she is dead." "Serves that dumb bitch right for trying to get in the way." My jaw dropped. "*Hahaha*, Max, you should have just let Alexandre catch you because now that I have you, you will suffer!"

Without reacting, without thinking and with all the hatred in my heart I spat. I spat on her face. Right between her two eyes. The look of horror on her face filled me with satisfaction.

She deserved it. After all, she would always let Mylene spit on me. This was just a taste of her own medicine. "You mother, *Tah, Tah, Tah*, she struck me with three slaps across the face. I wasn't shocked. She always slapped me, but at least this time I gave her a reason to do it. That said, it still hurt.

My face tingled and itched. I glared at her with hate. "You think you scare me?" "You are the one on the floor with pissed pants." "I can kill you with a snap of my fingers." Then do it! I yelled.

Enough was enough. I could no longer let her speak to me this way. You think I am afraid of you? If you kill me all the evidence that I have against your deranged and narcissistic family will come to light.

"*Hahaha!*" "You have nothing against us." "You are lying." I have no reason to lie. For example, I know what you did to your poor surrogate. Juliette's mouth dropped wide open. She took three steps backward and almost stumbled to the floor. She was in shock, and that made me happy.

So here is the deal, I told her. You Daxes will release me and I will be on my way. We can forget that this entire thing happened and just move on. Juliette looked at me with focus. I could see a crease forming in between her eyebrows; even with all her botox.

"You think I'm an idiot?" "As long as you have evidence against us then you will always be a problem." Slowly and intentionally she got face to face with me and smiled. "Burn in hell, bitch." "Enjoy the last hour of your life!" She screamed, and walked away. Slamming the door behind her.

The last hour of my life huh? For being from the "upper class" she sure was an idiot. She had just left me alone in a soundproof room. In a soundproof room! I couldn't help but laugh because escaping would be easy. All I had to do was make a small hole in the door, and then simply unlock it.

From there it was only a matter of dealing with her once I got out of the room. I was sure that her husband and gangsters were not in the house. If they were, I would have already been dead.

That said, I had to act now. I just need something hard to break the wooden door. I scanned the bright pink empty room, and saw the perfect thing to use. The heater! The old styled mounted wall heater had five polls. I could unscrew one and use it as a bat. Perfect!

I carefully stood up and walked over to the heater. I unscrewed the thickest side of the pole and yanked the piece off. It was a good three pounds and made of metal. This would do just fine, but before

I start hammering away I need to make sure that I had everything with me.

I opened my jacket and thankfully my folders were still there. I felt my pants and my box was there. Thank goodness. I guess pissing myself was a good thing. It prevented anyone from searching me.

All right, enough with the lollygagging it was time to get out of here. I headed toward the door and struck it. It only took three hits for me to make a hole big enough for my hand. I quickly removed the debris and I stuck my hand through the hole.

I felt the cold metal locks on the doorknob and I quietly unlocked the door. I had to be careful now. I was no longer protected by the sound proof walls. My heart was beating fast as I carefully turned the knob. Little by little the door opened.

The small squeaks that it made, made me sweat, but still I persisted. Finally after a few gentle pushes, I opened the door wide enough for me to fit through. I slowly squeezed myself through the porte, but before leaving the room, I looked in both directions to make sure no one was there. As I had predicted the coast was clear.

Perfect, and with no hesitation I ran out of the room, and I flew down the stairs. My body was full of adrenaline as I reached for the front door handle. "No, please don't go, Max." "I have missed you since you left." That soft voice. I turned around. It was Roman. The only Dax who was ever sweet to me.

His big eyes filled with tears. "I know my family treated you awfully, but you are the first person that I relate to in life." "You are the first person that showed me that there is more in life than money and prestige." "Please, come back and be our au pair again."

I should not have done it, but I spoke to him, and I spoke to him with the truth. Your family has done great harm to me. I cannot stay here. I am sorry Roman, but I want you to know that you are such a special kid. Don't lose your nice personality. He nodded in consolidation, and I opened the door.

Regrettably, standing in front of the door were Alexandre, Juliette, and two other men. The men rushed me, and grabbed me by the arms before I could react. They took me back inside. I screamed and yelled for help as Juliette closed the door behind us.

"Papa, let him go, let him go." "He did nothing wrong." "Let him go now!" "Juliette, please take Roman into his room." "He needs to calm down." From the corner of my eye I saw Juliette drag a crying Roman away.

"Here's how it's going to go." "We are going to have a little one on one conversation in the room you were just in." "If you don't agree I will blow your brains out right now." Alexandre pulled out a gun with a silencer on it. I stood frozen, and the men dragged me up the stairs. They threw me back into the soundproof room.

"Boys, go ahead and stand outside." The two large men left the room and closed the door behind them. "You are not leaving this room alive, but before I kill you I will give you a lesson in true dominance and humiliation." "Take off your clothes now, or I will slowly torture you to the point where you wish you were dead!"

I looked at Alexandre with pure hatred. He wanted to defile me to make a point. That was not going to happen. I'd rather die a million times before I let that occur! "Five seconds." He pointed at his watch and smiled.

I was not scared of him anymore. I straightened my body up and stared at him down. You won't do anything to me. I already told your wife of the evidence I have against your scum family. Your days of torture are over!

"Here is the thing, Max." "You have evidence against me, but you know what?" "That evidence will only get people talking about me." "It won't tarnish my name; let alone take me to jail." This man was full of himself. I had to laugh out loud.

He looked at me in surprise. "What is so funny?" You arrogant man. You kill like if it's nothing, but you murdered the wrong person this time. Mathieu recorded your entire interaction. I have video and audio evidence where we can hear you killing him, and incriminating yourself.

I glared directly into Alexandre's eyes to see his reaction to what I just had said. His lower lip quivered, but he quickly got that under control. He stared at me with pure fury. "There is no way you are getting out of here alive, Max."

Oh yes there is because if you kill me you are still going to jail. Do you think that I was stupid enough to not have saved all my evidence online somewhere? If I don't access my secure email weekly, then everything that I have against you Daxes will go out to every major police station worldwide. Not just to your corrupt police here.

Alexandre smirked. "Well I'll be damned." "It seems like you are smarter than we could have ever imagined." "I mean who would have thought someone like you would cause us this much headache."

"I guess we have some negotiating to do, don't we?" What do you have in mind? "Something simple and to the point." "We both come out together on the news tomorrow and say this entire thing was a misunderstanding."

"I will take the blame in falsely accusing you of everything" "You will go on TV and say that we are a model family, and that you understood why we did what we did." Okay, and you will pay for my flight back home. Also, you will donate money to Kaoly's and Mathieu's families.

Alexandre looked me up and down as I made my demands. I wonder if he knew that I was immediately going to accuse him once I got back to the USA, and once Kaoly's and Mathieu's families got their money. I could not tell, but I was sure that he was on to it. "I need to see you delete every piece of evidence that you have." Of course, I said.

Unbeknownst to him, I still have all my physical evidence. It didn't matter if I deleted everything online. Thank goodness. This was my secret weapon, and I would be using it as soon as I got what I demanded from him.

"Well, I guess we have ourselves a deal, don't we?" Yeah, we do. He came over to shake my hand, and the door busted open. "Who do you think you are?” “You are nothing, but shit.” “You think you can blackmail us?” “The great Daxes?”

“Well, you have something else coming. She came straight to my face. I saw how her left arm came up and formed a fist. She swung at my face, but she was not fast enough. I caught her blow with my arm and twisted her hand back.

I gently pushed her to the floor. I wanted to cause her some pain, but not hurt her. She was seventy after all, but she still had to be taught a lesson. “Ahh, she yelled as she hit the ground with a quiet thump.

Well it seems that someone was eavesdropping. Geraldine stared at me with fury in her eyes. “You will pay with your life for that.” Juliette ran into the room, and helped Geraldine up. “Maman, are you okay?” “Oh yes, better than okay.” “Especially after having killed that annoying old bitch who lived on the seventh floor.” What? “You heard me.” “I killed that bitch who helped you.”

Chapter 20

The Attempted Murder & The Murder

Geraldine smiled from ear to ear. Had she really killed Beatrice, or was it some sort of lie to piss me off? I eyeballed Alexandre Dax to see how he was reacting to what the vile woman was saying, but his face did not reveal much. He had a straight grin, dashed with a hint of cockiness.

He was proud of what Geraldine was saying, but I could tell that he did not know if she was lying or not. That said it was apparent that he was doing his best to not fully support his mother in law. The coward was sucking up his pride because of the "deal" that we had just struck together.

"Well are you going to just stare at Alexandre like an idiot, or are you going to say something?" I glared at Geraldine. She wanted a reaction from me, and she was close to getting one. "I made sure that the sale pute suffered." "Oh, and I let her know that she wasted her life trying to save a creature like you." "Hahaha, what a pathetic fool."

Her laugh sent me over the edge. Deal or no deal she had to get a taste of her own medicine, so I ran up to her and spit right in her face. Her eyes bulged out in surprise, and she began to scream as if someone was murdering her.

Her yells brought me delight, and before anyone in that room could react to what I did, I was out of there. I bolted out of the apartment, and I ran till I reached the seventh floor. Out of breath and with my thighs burning, I reached Beatrice's front door. Please don't be locked, I prayed. I turned the knob and the door opened.

Good, and without wasting any time I entered her home. Beatrice, are you here? It is me Max. Are you okay? I got no response. My stomach started to hurt. Something was off, but I had to keep my faith. She had to be alive.

Beatrice, I am looking for you. Did you fall down somewhere? Please answer me. I begged, and I began to search her entire living room and kitchen. She was nowhere to be found. That left me with one option, her bedroom.

I hurriedly walked toward her room and opened her door. My face went white. Lying on the floor with her hand twisted behind her back, and with her face filled with bruises was Beatrice. Her eyes were flickering. She was hurt, but alive!

Thank you Lord. "Mmmmaaaaxxx, is that you?" Yes, it is me Beatrice. What did they do to you? I whispered. She looked at me and managed to smile. "Geeettt the camera, Max." She grunted and stuttered with pain. Huh, what camera? With a shaking finger she pointed toward the camera that she had on her counter by her TV. I took the camera and Beatrice looked relieved.

"Thhhey hurrrrt me badly, but I'vvve beennn through worse." "I heaaard them commming up the stairs, and I hit recoorord on my cammmmera." "Geraldine's thugggs knocked mee out, and she musst thinknk that I am dead." "I want her to keeeep thinking that."

How did she know that you were helping me, Beatrice? We were so careful. "Theeree aree a loot off eyeess in this buiddling, Max." "Let'sss jusstt bee happy that we onlyyy gooott caught now." You are right, Beatrice but what should we do now then?

Weee will keeepp her tthhinnking that I am dead, butt youu muuustt geet goinnngg!" I can't! I have to call an ambulance for you. "NO!" "I will be fine." "Youuu on the other handdd areeenntt saffee here." "Iii donn't want youuu hurt." She said with a hoarse cough.

Okay, Beatrice, but before I go, can you help me decide on what I should do next. She slowly nodded her head. "What decision must you make, Max?" Well, before I found out that Geraldine had hurt you, I had struck a deal with Alexandre. "Whattt was tthhhe deal?"

In short, I must get rid of the online evidence that I have against them. Alexandre will then admit to falsely accusing me. All the charges against me will be dropped. Lastly, the Daxes will have to give money to Kaoly's and Mathieu's families.

"Matthieeu iss dead?" Beatrice said with a gasp. Yes, he was murdered by Alexandre. "Wow." Yeah, so that puts in me in a pickle.

Should I just go straight to the embassy and report them now, or do I stick the deal out for the future of Mathieu's daughter, Elodie?

"Onnly you caaan decide whattt is best, Max." "I trusttt you." "Also, youuu haveee my cameraaa as proof now too." "Sooo maaake your choice wisely, buttt mmaaake it fast." "Iii havvve faith in you." "Noww, go, beeffore they come here!" "I will beee fine."

Alright, Beatrice, I'll get going, but how can I be sure that you will be okay? What if they finish the job they started? "Theeey won't." "Geerraadline is cocky." "Sheee woonn't check on me." "I'mmm ceerttain, she will make my deattthh seemm like a breaakk in gone wrong."

I pray to God that it is true. "Trust me, Max." "I'll beee fine." "Nooww leave please." "I want you to be safe." D'accord, but promise me that you will be standing up tall the next time we see each other.

"I promise you." "Seee you soon, and donn't forget that I beelievee in you." Her voice choked as she smiled at me. I knelt down and stroked her tangled hair. She closed her eyes, and I left her bedroom. Quietly I walked over to the kitchen, and I carefully put her camera in my jacket.

I was feeling better. At least Beatrice would be okay for now. That said, it was time to make my decision! Think, Max, think. If I break my deal and go to the embassy my name would be vindicated with all my evidence, but that leaves Mathieu's and Kaoly's families with no money.

I know money shouldn't be the deciding factor in my decision, but I want Elodie to not have to worry about it. Ugh, what to do? *"Thud, thud, thud."* The sound of footsteps outside the door broke my concentration. I guess I couldn't make my decision just yet. *Slam!* Beatrice's front door shook open and Alexandre, Juliette, Geraldine and two of their guards rushed through the door.

"Oops I guess I don't know my own strength." "Now Max, I just want you to know what Geraldine did was on her own terms and not mine." Alexandre lowered his head and faked a sympathetic look. I did my best to not let it get to me as he continued to speak. "That said we struck a deal."

"I have contacted the news." "They will be here in an hour." "I need you to go get ready so we can say what we talked about." Hold up. I thought you said the interview was for tomorrow? "They want the news out today." "The government wants these protests to stop."

Alexandre gazed annoyingly at me. He was tired of me, but he couldn't do anything. I savored the moment. I would not let him off this easily. He would do everything on my terms now!

Ummm, you know what, Alexandre, sorry, but no. Our deal was for tomorrow, and do you not see what has happened? Geraldine just killed Madame Beatrice! This is no time for an interview!

"Now, now, there's no need to get into a pickle." Juliette interrupted our conversation, and came up to me. "Max, she was like 100, it was only a matter of time." "My wonderful husband did not break his deal with you." "He just amended it, and I have a few things that I want to amend to it too."

"This is what I want you to do," Juliette said. "You must confess that you did indeed steal money from us." "Also that you understand why the Daxes thought it was you who murdered all those people, and that you never experienced any negativity from us."

Fuck no. I already talked to Alexandre about what I was going to say. I will not say anything else. Juliette eyed me down. I could practically feel her stare burning holes through me, but she kept her mouth shut.

Geraldine on the other hand could not bite her tongue. "Enough!" She yelled. "Why are we taking demands from this vermin?" "Just kill him!"

"We can't maman." "Why not?" "You guys are murderers!" All our heads turned automatically to Beatrice's front door. The new au pair stood by the door. He was shaking from fear.

He was in shock. I was not sure how much he overheard, but he then yelled, "I am going to the police!" "Oh no you're not!" In the blink of an eye Geraldine reached for Alexandre's pocket and pulled out his gun.

She aimed at the au pair, and shot him point blank in the head. Blood squirted all over Beatrice's walls, and he fell like a brick to the floor. I couldn't believe it. It was the first time I had ever seen someone get murdered.

Time stood in suspense at that moment. I felt like I was *The Flash* seeing everything in slow motion, and that is when I made my decision. I would report the Daxes immediately to the *American Embassy*. This was too much, so with my decision made I ran out of Beatrice's apartment.

I heard Alexandre and Juliette call my name, but it was far in the distance. My mind was going a million miles an hour, and before I knew it I was out of the building. Cars beeped at me as I jay-ran across the road, but I didn't care.

I had one goal in mind now, and that was to take the metro to the consulate. Thankfully, the station was just across the street from the Daxes. Thus, I reached it in seconds, and wasting no time I flew down the steps into the building.

It felt cold in there, and it smelled like oil and gunk. It was over-stimulating, but at least it was not that packed. No one even noticed when I jumped the gate instead of scanning my nonexistent ticket to reach the train platform.

I started to feel hopeful that I would reach the American Consulate with no issues, but then trouble started. "Look at his shirt!" "It is filled with fresh blood." I felt several eyes look at me, and I looked down at my shirt. Shit. I had blood from the au pair all over me. I hadn't noticed.

"Hey, he looks like Max, the au pair." "Can it be him?" A woman loudly said. "Yes it is him!" Another person said. "Let's get him!" A man with a big belly came toward me and reached for my wet bloody shirt.

I was not having it. The days of people pushing me around were over, so using all my strength I jumped up and I slammed my two legs on this man's chest. He fell hard. This got everyone's attention.

Instantly three other people tried to grab me, but I was on high alert now. I moved to the edge of the platform. No one dared to come close to me, especially since the train was arriving in one minute. Instead all seven people there took their phones out, and they started to record me.

Perfect. I said out loud. Go on and give me a platform to speak, and I'll speak. "Then go ahead," a soft voice said, so I did. Hello to anyone watching this. I know that I have a bloody shirt, but this blood did not come from someone that I hurt.

This blood came from someone that the Daxes hurt. In this case, Geraldine. The Daxes are the true monsters. They killed Kaoly. They killed Mathieu, and countless others. I have been framed by them for far too long.

It is time that they be exposed for who they are. I have all the evidence I need to not only clear my name, but to send them and those working for them to jail.

In fact that is why I am going to the *American Embassy* now. I have proof that everything I am saying is true. *Chuga, chuga, chuga* the train was coming. I had to finish my speech.

Lastly, to my mom and family, if you are watching this, know that I love you. I am fighting for my life, but please stay hidden. The Daxes will try to hurt you guys! I love all of you.

With my speech finished, I turned to face all seven people that were there. They each stopped recording. Their phones were lowered. The soft spoken individual talked again. I turned my head to face her. "The media portrayed you like a monster, but you aren't one." "You are a victim."

Thank you from the bottom of my heart for saying that. I told her. She smiled at me, and then the man who I had hit in the chest came up to me. "I believe you too." He shook my hand, and then something miraculously happened. One by one all seven people in that metro came to me and shook my hand.

I was in disbelief. People believed me. People who had not even seen my evidence, but they believed me because they felt that I was telling the truth. I was overwhelmed with joy, but I managed to keep it at bay while the man who I had hit spoke.

"Please understand we always thought they were good people." "They donate to charities." "They have scholarship foundations, and help clean the environment, but all these murders involving them are too much."

"All the money they have and they can't keep their name out of trouble." "It makes no sense." Everyone shook their heads in agreement. The Daxes had murdered one too many people this time. This time I would truly be set free.

"Will you go to the *American Embassy* now?" Yes, and I want all of you to come with me if that is okay? "Oui, oui, yes, yes, of course, yes and when do we leave?" Now, but before we go I just want to thank you guys.

The past four months, and especially these last two weeks have been torture, but I finally see the light at the end of the tunnel. I promise you all that your support means the world to me, and it makes my heart happy.

They all began clapping for me as I finished my little appreciation speech. It was touching, and in perfect timing too because the screeching train came to a half before us right as the last person finished clapping. Ironically, it was the lady who had originally yelled at me.

This time though, she smiled and opened the train door for me. "I'm sorry." She shyly said. Oh, it's no problem Madame. Shall we go in? "Yes." I signaled for her to go in first, and right as she did the entire lights in the station went dark.

It was pitch black for about five seconds, but abruptly waves of light flashed all around me. Which were accompanied with rapid movement. The suddenness of it all left me bewildered, and then the cries started to happen. "Don't hurt me." "Please leave me alone." Men and women yelling in pain. It was utter confusion.

My instinct immediately told me to get away from the platform, so I kneeled to the floor and I crawled away from the platform until I reached a wall. I guess my intuition was correct because the clang of the moving train soon filled my ears, and then it was followed by a terrible sound.

A sound that couldn't be. A sound that I had only heard in scary movies. The crackling of bones being crushed. Oh, no, God, please.

Don't let that be. I prayed, but in my heart I knew that my ears did not deceive me.

Chapter 21
The Chaos at the Metro Station

People were being crushed alive by the train. They had been pushed to their deaths, and I was frozen in place from the fear and confusion that I felt. This was the end for me. My poor family would suffer so much from my passing.

"Don't give up, Max." Huh? Mathieu? Is that you? No, it's impossible. He's dead, but how had I heard his voice so clearly? "It hurts, help me!" Someone yelled. *"Stop them, Max." "Avenge us all."*

Maybe I was going crazy, but that was definitely Mathieu's voice that was speaking to me. For some strange reason "hearing" his voice helped calm me down. My fear disappeared, and I could now think clearly. It was the Daxes!

Somehow they had gotten control of this metro station and caused all this destruction. They had to be stopped. I owed it to each and every one of their victims to get justice for them, but in order to do that I had to get out of this hell hole. Luckily I knew how.

I had seen an emergency door before going to the train platform. It couldn't be more than a few feet away, so going against all my instincts I stood up and ran blindly in the opposite direction of the chaos.

Within a few steps of sprinting in complete blindness I spotted the red lights of the emergency door. "God, help me now," someone cried in pain. Their yells made me run faster, and just as I reached the door, the chaotic noise ceased.

Unfortunately this meant one thing, all seven people in this station had been murdered. Sadly, I had no time to stop and reflect. I had to get out, so with all my strength I pushed the rectangle panel in, and the door swung open.

Fortunately, no alarm went off like I had expected, but my luck did not last. Woefully, the door did not lead to the outside like I thought it would. Instead it led to a bright room. I rubbed my eyes to get used to the lightning, and before my eyes even got the chance to adjust, he spoke.

"Well nice to see you again, Max." My shoulders dropped. Standing right in front of me was Alexandre Dax and a man that I had never seen before. I turned to run back out, but the man shut the door behind me.

"I am sorry that my stupid mother in law acted like a fool, but do not worry she is not here." "Juliette and her are taking care of the poor au pair that they killed." I could feel my adrenaline pumping through my veins. Alexandre had a smirk on his face. He thought he was unstoppable.

"As you can see we are in a control room." I quickly did a scan of the room. There were nothing but buttons and panels all over the walls that showed live footage of the metro station, but wait! There was a door behind the computer desk.

It had a sign over it that said emergency exit only. If I could reach the door before they got me, maybe I could escape. "Don't even think about it Max, or I'll blow your brains out."

I guess Alexandre noticed that I was looking at the door. "Look, Max, you have really annoyed me." "I know you have evidence against me, but quite frankly I do not care anymore." "You want to know why?" Yes, I do. "Well, money speaks louder than morals."

"Look at this man here." "I had never met him before today." Alexandre tilted his head to the man in the room. "But you know what?" "I found out he was the director of the metro station, and all it took was forty thousand euros." "Forty thousand euros, and he did exactly what I told him to do."

Why are you telling me this? I asked him. "I am telling you this because people can be bought, and even with all your evidence against me, I can buy the jury." You can't buy everyone! I shouted at him. "True, but I can buy enough of them to set me free, and to have you convicted."

"Money can practically convince anyone to do anything." "Take a look at Mathieu." "On the outside he was your everyday sweet guy, but guess what?" "He knew of Paul's deals, and turned a blind eye." I did not know what to say, and as much as I hate to admit it, Alexandre was right.

Money had temporarily corrupted Mathieu, and if it can do that to him then it can do that to anyone. Fuck! The Daxes once again had leverage over me. I clenched my fists in frustration. "Clenching your fists are we?" "That means you understand that you are back to being ours."

"Hahaha, the Daxes always come out on top." Alexandre laughed maliciously. "Now come back with me, before I personally drop you off at the police station where you can get arrested." Wow. You are so arrogant to think you have all that power.

"I do have all that power, and just for calling me arrogant I am calling the police now to inform them that I have you in my custody." I don't care! Call whoever you want. I am not scared of you. I already told you that I have my evidence. "That evidence won't mean shit in the long run!"

Alexandre, I will admit that your money will influence a lot, but that doesn't mean you will win this war. "I have already won!" No, you haven't. All you did was re-level the playing field. "What do you mean?" He asked annoyingly, but in a concerned tone.

Simple, I go to jail, but the mighty Daxes will also suffer. Your family's reputation will take a huge blow when I accuse you all, and when I release my photographic and audio evidence that I have. People will stop doing business with the great Daxes.

No one will want to align themselves with a family of criminals being accused of murder, drug sales and who knows what else!

Don't believe me? For crying out loud people get canceled for the smallest things, and you think the Daxes won't? Especially when there is actual proof?

Alexandre's face grew red from frustration as he began to realize that I was correct. I guess he had not thought about the long term repercussions to his empire. "MERDE!" He screamed.

"You conveying little bitch." "You may be right, but do you really think that I care if I lose money, or friends?" I gave him a sarcastic stare. Of course you do, and so does Juliette! You two are the most self-centered people that I have ever met in my life.

Plus seeing your bank account dwindle will eat you and Juliette alive. You guys cannot afford to change your lifestyle. Living high and mighty is what the Daxes do. There is no way you will jeopardize that.

"*Clap, clap, clap.*" "I applaud you, Max." "I see that you will not fall for any of my little tricks." "Once again you have proven your cunningness." "I respect that, and I am willing to give you one more chance to make a deal with me."

"What do you say?" I wanted to flat out say no, but maybe striking a deal with this psycho would give me enough time to turn the tide in my favor again. I know I shouldn't be playing with fire, but I had to take the chance. I asked him to go over the deal again. "The deal has three mandatory components, but before I go into them, Monsieur the director, may you step out of the room?"

The director nodded and stepped out of the room. "Okay, the first part of the new deal is for you to say how lovely we are." "I want you to tell the public that we never treated you badly." "Oh, and do not worry, Juliette and I will come out and state that our accusation against you was false."

"Of course we will put all the blame on Kaoly." "I hope that isn't an issue?" Alexandre asked condescendingly. He wanted a reaction out of me, but all I said was "that's fine." "Okay, then, I'll continue."

"The second part of the deal is that you must finish your contracted year with us as an au pair." "You will return and work for us under the normal conditions that we already had." I cringed at that thought. Those conditions were awful, but all I said to Alexandre was fine.

"Lastly," he said as he lowered his face to mine. "This one is my personal favorite." He quietly whispered. "The last part of the deal is about you and me." My body shivered. "Oh don't get scared." "All I ask is to have fun with you whenever I please."

Once again the world stopped moving. All I could see were his dark gray eyes gazing at me like I was prey. My body trembled and I was speechless. "There's no need to worry, Max." "I won't hurt you like I did with Mathieu." "He was stupid, unlike you."

"You are not easy to get rid of, and I want to rule that mentality." Instantaneously I felt tears hit my cheeks. Why was I crying? No! I wouldn't be scared anymore!

The wet tears on my face mixed with my anger inside me brought me back to life. I looked at him straight in the face and yelled, THERE IS NO WAY IN HELL THAT I WILL EVER DO THAT! DEAL'S OFF!

"Don't be silly, Max." "If you do not agree to our deal I will go ahead and kill your family because if my life is going to change because of you, then I might as well make you suffer!" "So either you accept our deal or suffer the consequences."

You will never find my family! You psycho! "You think I can't find out where they are?" "I can pay whoever I want to find them!" "Someone will eventually accept my bounty offer for their heads, maybe even their friends, hahahaha!"

My head was spinning. He was right. My family couldn't hide forever. Someone would see them, and they would rat them out for the money. Fuck! There was no way around it. He had me cornered again!

I would have to play his sick little game; at least until I could get my evidence to someone with the proper authority that had not or could not be bribed. Sadly, that was easier said than done.

Especially since the *American Embassy* was out of the question due to the fact that Alexandre and the metro director had obviously overhead my plans. "You have one minute to accept my deal or it is off the table."

Alexandre interrupted my thoughts briefly, but I ignored him as I quickly thought of an option to save myself down the road. Hmmm, if I can't go to the *American Embassy* then where can I find someone with the correct credentials to help me?

Think, Max, think! "Thirty seconds." AH! I felt the pressure as Alexandre's eyes glued onto me. He knew I was thinking of a way out. "Twenty seconds." "Bon voyage to your family."

Bon voyage! That's it! The airport! The airport has government authorities from all over the world. I could look for help there when the time was right! That said, my help would have to come from someone that wasn't an American. That way Alexandre wouldn't suspect and bribe them!

Eureka! I had some sort of plan now, and feeling better I extended my hand out to Alexandre. Deal accepted. He shook my hand and smiled. "You see, no one messes with the Daxes and gets away with it."

"Now that we have our deal." "I want you to remove your shirt." "I am going to take pictures of you." I was stunned. I was not expecting him to demand that part of the deal so quickly, but I had no choice. I removed my jacket and I took my shirt off. I felt cold and sick to my stomach. Alexandre smiled as he began to take pictures.

"With these photos I can see the progress of how you fall from a confident young man to a lousy soulless guy." I felt tears wanting to escape my eyes, but I would not let them fall. There was no way in hell that I would give him that satisfaction.

"Turn your head that way, yeah like that." "Okay now face this way." "Can you lower your pants a little?" "Bend this way, and try to smile!" "Stand on your knees and look up at me."

I felt a pit in my stomach. He wanted to see the literal downfall of who I was as a person. He was slowly torturing me. What did I ever do to deserve this? All I wanted was a new cultural experience. I felt like a failure.

I hated Alexandre, and I hated the Daxes, and most of all I hated myself at that moment. I could have been back home enjoying my freshman year of university, but instead I was getting inappropriate pictures taken. I felt like a fool, but as the camera flashed in my eyes it brought me back into my senses. I was no fool, but an innocent victim.

A victim that would get his revenge on this piece of, "Put your shirt back on." Alexandre said as I tried to regain my dignity. "My chauffeur is waiting for us outside." "Also, Max, before we leave I want you to know that this is strictly a power thing, and nothing more."

"You are nothing, but a worthless sack of," the door shot open. "Monsieur Dax we must leave now!" "Word has gotten out that Max was seen fleeing to this metro station." "A mob is on its way." "We have maybe ten minutes tops before it gets here."

"Okay, let's go then." Alexandre shoved me out the door, and we quickly walked over to the car. The chauffeur opened our doors, and just as we were getting in I saw the silhouette of the mob coming in our direction.

It was not ten minutes away, but at most two minutes if that since I could clearly see it now. Thankfully the mob did not have a view of us fleeing the area. We were leaving from the back. They were loudly coming in from the front.

"Catch him now, catch him now, catch him now," the crowd roared. "Let's take a left up here in the light." Alexandre told the chauffeur. "We have to get away from the crowd." "Sir, wouldn't it be easier if I quickly drop you guys off at your building? The mob is still a good minute away.

"Don't be an idiot." "People can see long distances, and someone might be recording, so how about you shut the fuck up and keep driving until I tell you to stop." The chauffeur fell silent. There was an awkwardness in the air until Alexandre spoke up again.

"I have texted the director of the station to let the crowd know that Max was never in there." "Continue driving until I get an update." "I will, sir." We drove for a good fifteen minutes in silence, until Alexandre got the call.

"Are you sure everything is good?" "Uh, huh, uh, huh, got it, thanks." "The mob is dispersing now." "We can head back home." He told the chauffeur. "Okay, monsieur Dax." "The GPS says we should be home in twenty minutes because of traffic."

"Fine, I'm going to read, so don't disturb me." Alexandre put his head down and started reading on his phone. I, on the other hand, looked out the window.

I was momentarily happy. I was seeing the beautiful scenery of Paris once again, and I was ecstatic when we drove over *Pont d'Alexandre*. It is absolutely stunning. It is painted in gold, and it has many angel statues overlooking the city. It is a piece of art, and my personal favorite.

Which is ironic considering the shame that I suffered here. The first time that I visited *Pont d'Alexandre* Mylene had thrown a pile of leaves at my face, and of course it was right in front of her friends and teachers. She wanted to show her classmates that she "owned" me.

It was petrifying, but somehow this pont had made me feel calm in that chaos. I guess art does that, and that is one of the reasons I wanted to come to Paris. It is art at its finest. For example we were now driving through the seventh district. A district that looked like someone had hand painted it to perfection.

In another life I would get to enjoy this city at peace, but for now, "Yeah, Juliette, we are about seven minutes away." Alexandre broke my concentration. He was talking to Juliette.

"Is the new au pair taken care of?" "Okay, good." "That way Max can go to bed." "He has a big day tomorrow." "He will admit to everyone how sweet we really are." "Hahaha!"

The laughter that erupted from Alexandre was infuriating. I could even hear Juliette laughing. She probably thought I was the stupidest thing alive, but whatever. I didn't care, and I continued to soak up the last few minutes of Paris until Alexandre handed me the keys to my old room. We had arrived.

"Monsieur, Dax should I leave you in front of your building or descend with you into the parking lot?" "Leave us here, no one is in the street." The chauffeur parked the car right near the entrance of the building. Alexandre got out of the car, and I followed him over to the front entry.

By the time I reached him he had entered the last digit on the control panel and was pushing the door open. "Welcome back home."

He said sarcastically as we entered the lobby. Thanks, I quietly whispered.

"Oh cheer up, Max." "You'll have a great time with us." He maliciously winked at me, and it made my body automatically tense up. "Oh relax Max, and just to show you how nice I am, you can go ahead and go up to your room, but make sure you are at our place by 7:30 a.m. tomorrow."

"Oh and before I forget, Juliette has left clothes on your bed." "Wear those clothes." "I want you to look presentable for the interview." Okay, I will. See you tomorrow, I tirelessly said, and I headed up the rustic wooden stairs.

By the time I reached the seventh floor I was completely exhausted and ready to crash, but I immediately regained my energy when I saw Beatrice's front door wide open. Yes! That meant Beatrice had been right when she said Geraldine's plan was to make it seem like her "murder" was a break in gone "wrong."

The opened door proved it. I was giddy with glee, and I dashed into her apartment. Beatrice, Beatrice, are you there? There was no answer, but I knew she was in her room.

I carefully stepped around the broken plates, cups and TV and made my way into Beatrice's closed door. I knocked three times, and she responded. "Come in Max." I opened the door, and I was so happy to see her that I instantly started balling.

Chapter 22

THE DEMISE OF THE SWEET NEIGHBOR

"Oh, don't cry, Max." "I'm alive, bruised from head to toe, but alive." She tried joking, but I could tell she was in pain. Beatrice, is there something that I can do to help you? She looked at me and smiled. "You are sweet, Max, always thinking about others, but honestly I am okay."

Are you sure? "Well, I will feel one hundred percent better when we get you your justice." Oh. Sadly, that won't be for a while Beatrice. "Why not?" I had to strike a deal with Alexandre so he wouldn't kill my parents.

Beatrice looked at me with empathetic eyes, but soon those eyes turned cold. "Max, forget your deal with him." "We have to go to the *American Embassy* at this very moment and report the Daxes." "I can order a taxi, and we can now."

Unfortunately, that's not possible. "Why not?" Alexandre overheard me talking to some people in the metro. These people believed in my innocence, and I told them my plans. They are all dead now. Killed by the order of the Daxes. "Those sick inhumane things!" Beatrice's wrinkles deepened as her face filled with anger.

"Max, the Daxes will never stop." "They are too powerful, and full of hatred." "They will never honor their part of the deal." I know Beatrice, but as long as I cooperate for now I have time to plot out my plan. "Max, you may have the best plan in the world, but they will abolish it."

"They must be taken care of pronto!" "There is no other way." What do you mean? "They have to be killed, Max." "That is the only solution to free yourself, your family and everyone you care about."

"The Daxes must die." Beatrice was trembling as she was speaking. She was dead serious, but as much as I hate the Daxes, I was no murderer. Beatrice, I cannot kill someone. "I know you can't Max, but I will."

"You are too sweet to ever do something like that to someone, but I have had enough." "I don't care if I am thrown in jail." No! I cannot let you do that Beatrice! "Do not worry about me, Max."

"I have lived a long and happy life." "I have done everything that I wanted to do in my time." "As a matter of fact, I was ready to go before you came." "My life had become dull." "You were the first person in at least six years to take a genuine interest in me, and I want to pay back that happiness you have given me."

I do not need to be paid back. I did it because you are a great human. "Max, you are a great human, and that is why I want to save you!" No, Beatrice just no. We will figure out another way. She gently smiled at me. "I do not want your life to be hell." "I want you to have the best life possible."

"My decision is made." "I will be the one to exterminate the Daxes from this world." "Enough is enough." I bit my lip. I did not know what to say, or even to do. "Please, just know that this won't be your fault." "It will be mine and the Daxes' only."

Beatrice I really can't have you becoming a murderer please! *Aaahhn, hooah*, I yawned without meaning to. "I see you are tired." "How about we finish discussing this tomorrow before your inter-view?" Only if you are open to changing your mind! "If it means you can go rest then I guess I'll be open for another solution."

Thank you Beatrice. I gave her a small hug and wished her a good night. I then headed back to my room, and just like Alexandre had said, the light gray suit lay folded on the bed. The outfit looked elegant and expensive.

Figures, the Daxes probably wanted to trick the world into think-ing that they gave me nice stuff. Well, just to give them a huge FU I jumped on top of the outfit and went to bed. Comically, I awoke to one of the most restful nights that I had had since being in France.

Hmm, must have been the silk in the suit, I laughed as I tried to figure out what time it was. I couldn't check Mathieu's phone since it was dead, but based on how much light was coming in through the blinds I could guess-estimate. It had to be around 6:00 a.m. to 6:30 a.m.

Which was perfect! That meant that I had a good thirty minutes to speak to Beatrice before my interview. So without delay I got out of bed, and I marched my way over to her home.

I quietly squeezed my way through her open door and went inside. Beatrice, it's me, Max. I am here to finish our conversation from last night. I waited a couple of seconds for her response, but there was nothing.

Was she still asleep? I glanced over at the clock on the stove. It was 6:10 a.m. There was no way she was still asleep. Maybe she was changing? Only one way to find out. I walked over to her room, and I quietly knocked on her door. Beatrice, are you here?

Zero response. Okay, I am coming in. I opened the door, and her room was empty. Where was she? Had she gone out to kill the Daxes, or had she gone to the hospital? I had no clue, but what I did know was that I had to get out of this apartment.

I felt uncomfortable being here alone. *"Bam, bam, bam,"* the sudden sound of something being bashed against the wall made me dive under Beatrice's bed. "You conniving sack of old bones, you crazy bitter old witch." It was Juliette!

I could hear her screams coming from the living room. She sounded tired and like she had just gotten out of a fight. "I killed your mom because she TRIED to kill me!" "I should add that she failed, and as did you." That was Beatrice's voice!

I carefully peeked from underneath her bed. What I saw terrified me. Beatrice had blood all over her face. I could barely recognize her. Her clothes were torn, and Juliette had her by her hair. It was obvious that she had dragged Beatrice up here.

Slap, slap, slap. Juliette began smacking Beatrice, viciously. All Beatrice could do was take her blows. Her head was bobbing back and forth. I could not just sit around and watch this. I began to drag myself out of the bed, but Beatrice saw me. She nodded no.

She was sacrificing herself for me. Tears ran down my cheeks. "Your end is here, you old bitch." "You think you are so smart, poisoning my mom?" "I am going to blast your head open."

Juliette pulled Beatrice's head to the ground, and placed her foot heavily over it. One of Beatrice's teeth fell out from the pressure. "I hope you get tortured in hell." She then reached down into jacket and pulled out a handgun.

"Say your last," my instincts took over. I rose up from underneath the bed and tackled Juliette with fury. She gazed at me with confused eyes as the gun slipped from her hands, and onto the floor. I pushed her aside and went to grab the gun, but right as I was about to grab it someone snatched from my reach.

It was snatched up by Beatrice's bloody hand. "You're one step closer to freedom." Beatrice told me, and then she pressed her hand on the trigger and shot Juliette point blank on the forehead. It was as if time itself froze again.

Blood splattered all over the room, and even on me. Part of Juliette's skull flew to the other side of the room, and she fell backward.

Her left leg lay twisted, and her right arm stood as stiff as a board in the air.

I stared in horror, but Beatrice did not. She looked at me with sorrowful eyes and then said, "I had to do it." "I am sorry." "It is not your fault, and you were not involved." "Do not worry, okay?"

I started to feel dizzy. I was slipping out of consciousness, but the sudden feel of Beatrice's cold wet hand on my arm brought me back to reality. "You have to get out of here." No, I have to take you to the hospital! "No, I am done for."

Quit saying that, Beatrice! You are not going to die. Beatrice slowly lifted her shirt and showed me the stab wounds that she had in her stomach. She was going to bleed out. "Don't worry about me." "I just pressed my emergency necklace, and the police are on their way." "I will tell them everything."

I stared at Beatrice as she talked, but I was not really paying attention to what she was saying. All I could feel and hear was the pain that she was going through. Her whimpers of hurt reminded me of an injured child. An innocent child that was doing its best to be brave.

"Max!" I jumped two feet into the air. "Are you hearing me?" Yes, but there's no way in hell that I can leave you here on your own. I have to wait for the police and ambulance to come.

"NO, please go away!" "My time has come, and there is nothing you or anyone else can do, but please do not let my death go in vain." "I need you to succeed in your life, please do that for me, okay?"

I will Beatrice, but I beg you, fight for your life. I kneeled down and held her hand. She squeezed it and smiled, "I will do my best." "Now go, but before you leave make sure you wash all that blood on your hands and face off."

"I don't want anyone blaming you for this." I will, Beatrice. She smiled, and pushed me toward the kitchen. I quickly went over and washed my face and hands. I then headed back toward her, but she was not having it.

"Leave, Max!" I reluctantly walked out of her house and into my room. With a lump in my throat and a pain in my stomach I sat on my bed. I sat and I let the rays of the sun hit my skin. It was cathartic, and it made me feel comfortable in all this hell.

Maybe Beatrice will survive, "*boom, boom, boom.*" The sound of heavy footsteps running up the stairs penetrated my ears. "*Bash, bash, bash*" the sound of Beatrice's door being kicked open startled me. "Madame, are you okay?" "Look at that pool of blood, of course she is not okay."

"Madame, can you hear my voice?" "Grab the stretcher." "There is someone else here!" My heart stopped. The stretcher? Was Beatrice dead? "It was the Da da da." "Who, madame?" "They stabbed me." "They hurt me." "Madame, what are you saying?" "She's going into shock!"

"Grab the oxygen mask!" "It is too late Thomas." "She is dead." I fell to my knees and onto my side. My head hit the floor, and everything went black.

Chapter 23

THE TRUE AU PAIR KILLER

"Wake up, Max, wake up." My eyes flickered open. I carefully picked myself up off the moving cushioned floor. Wait, the moving cushioned floor? That makes no sense. I had fainted on a hardwood floor. Where was I, and who had called me? I rubbed my eyes to clear my vision.

I saw two big seats, and a mirror in front of me. I was in a car! "Well look who finally decided to wake up." That voice! It was Alexandre. He must have found me on the floor when I lost consciousness. My body tensed up. Where were we going?

I tilted my head to the left to see out the window. I wanted to get a sense of my location, but all I saw were trees. Trees in all directions. Oh no, was he planning to kill me, and bury my body in the forest? Did he think that I had harmed Juliette?

"Max, you seem worried." "Don't be, the kids are here with me." "I was just telling them that you decided to come back as our au pair." Roman popped his head from the back seat, and stared at me happily.

"I am so happy that you are coming back to be our au pair." He smiled from ear to ear, and in turn my body relaxed slightly because I knew Alexandre would not harm me while the kids were around. At least for now I was safe, but I wondered, what excuse had Alexandre told the kids about Juliette? Surely, they did not know of her death since Roman was too excited.

"Max, did you hear me?" Oh no, sorry Roman. I still feel a little dizzy from my nap, can you repeat yourself? "Of course." "I said, even Mylene is happy that you are coming back, and she promised to be nicer." "Isn't that right, Mylene? I turned my head back to look at her, she was rapidly nodding yes.

"Dad, told us that you are staying until June!" Roman was giggling with joy. If he only knew how sick I was feeling inside. "Max, you are like a big brother to me, and even to Mylene." "She may be arrogant at times, but she will learn."

"I promise you that I will do my best to help educate her." "Especially since mom won't be out of the rehab center until next June." There it was. Alexandre had lied to his kids about Juliette.

He must have told them that she was addicted to drugs. This was smart. It gave him plenty of wiggle room to move the date of her return. For all the kids know she could die of an overdose, or need more months in rehab. He is skillfully coneyving.

"Kids, Max is still a tad dizzy." "Let him rest for now." "Okay, daddy," they both responded. I looked at the rearview mirror and

Alexandre maliciously smiled at me. It made my skin crawl. He seemed too excited. Had he done something to me while I was asleep? Shit, had he taken my evidence? There was only one way to find out.

Cautiously I put my hands inside the side of my pants, and felt around. Oh thank you God. My folders were still tucked in my pants. Mathieu's phone and the usbs were still safely secure. Even Beatrice's SD card from her camera was still safely in my pocket.

Thank goodness. I let out a huge sigh of relief. "Everything okay back there, Max?" Yes, everything is fantastic Alexandre. "Swell." "Oh Max, before I forget, can you stay back a minute when we arrive, so I can have a word with you?"

Uh, a word about what, Alexandre? I asked him nervously. "Oh, just about the meeting that we were supposed to have, remember?" I felt a pit in my stomach. I had forgotten about the interview.

There had been a lot at stake there. From my name being cleared to the Daxes reputation being saved. "Well, Max, is that a yes or a no?" Don't worry Alexandre, I will stay back so we can talk about it. "Perfect!"

About twenty minutes after that conversation we reached the driveway of the house. *Creech, crack, creech, crack* the sound of the tires breaking branches in the dirt road filled my ears as the car came to a stop. We arrived in the countryside.

Alexandre put the vehicle in park, and unlocked the doors for the kids. "Roman and Mylene, make sure you unpack." "I better not see a mess when I go up and check on you guys." "Okay, papa" they both said as they walked out of the car.

Alexandre stared at the kids until they were safely inside the house. Once they were in, he immediately turned around to face me. "Here is the NEW deal." What do you mean "the new deal?" "Well, since that old bitch killed Juliette I had to change our terms and conditions.

How? "I am not dropping the charges against you until the end of the academic school year for the kids." My entire world shattered once more. Again he had changed the rules. I could not keep my cool, and yelled at him. THAT WASN'T THE DEAL! YOU CANNOT DO THIS!

"Hahahaha!" "You killed my wife, so now we have a new deal based on that situation!" I did not kill Juliette! "You may not have killed her with your own hands, but because of you she is dead, so be happy that I am still nice enough to make an agreement with you."

No, it's not that you're nice enough! You just know that I have proof against you that will also come to light! "You know, Max, I'm getting really tired of you raising your voice at me, and disrespecting me." "From now on, you will talk to me in a normal tone, and you will have to start using monsieur before my name!"

I will never call you monsieur again! "Oh no?" He quickly reached for his phone and shoved it to my face. I could not believe my eyes. Right on the screen was my family. They were all tied with black ropes and duct tape on their mouths.

I could see the tears falling from my sister's eyes. Her daughter was tied to a small chair. That was it. My family was under the Daxes' mercy.

"Go ahead and tell them something." "They can see and hear you." I did not know what to say. I was stunned. "Cat got your tongue?" "How about you tell them that you will start listening to me, to keep them safe.

I slowly nodded yes, and I began to speak to my family. I'm so sorry that you guys are there. I promise I will do everything Monsieur Alexandre asks of me. You guys will be set free. "Now that is more like it!"

Alexandre laughed and put his phone away. He then grabbed my chin forcefully. "If you play nicely you will be rewarded." "If you do not play nicely then well, just maybe one of your family members will have to suffer." Then I'll just expose you! "No you won't because I will kill them if you do that."

My hands were trembling. I wanted to rip his throat out, but instead I looked him straight in the eyes and said, *I will make sure that Roman and Mylene have a great Christmas vacation.* "That's more like it, and before I forget, here you go."

He handed me a phone. It was a black *Samsung Galaxy Ultra 24.* Why are you giving me this? "This is my present to you." "It will keep me in constant communication with you, which is crucial for your new role." What do you mean by "my new role?"

"You are now the new Juliette." "You will no longer be the kids' au pair, but their new mom!" "Hahahahahahaha." His awful laughter penetrated my ears. "Now, what do you say when someone gives you something?" Thank you Monsieur Alexandre for the phone. "You are welcome, Max."

"Now get going, and help the kids unpack." He rudely shoved me out of the car and laughed at me. "Oh, we will have a lot of fun!" "Your emasculation starts now." I did not bother to react to his comments.

Instead I hurriedly walked over to the house. I was beyond scared, but I still had faith. My family may be tied, but they wouldn't be killed. Even Alexandre wasn't that stupid. He wouldn't risk that, but I wouldn't poke the bear either. I will do what he asks until I can set them free and get away to the airport.

Alexandre may have the upper hand right now, but I was nowhere near out of the game. That thought made me relax, and without further ado, I climbed up the rugged steps to the third floor where the kids' rooms were located. I then knocked on one of the doors. A raggedy hair, Mylene came out. She tirelessly looked at me and said, "When are you picking up my trash in my room?"

I looked at her intensely, and responded, "I cannot do it for you, but we can work together and help clean up your room." The reaction on Mylene's face said it all. She scrunched her eyebrows together and put her hands on her hips. She had not appreciated my answer.

She immediately started crying. "I want my maman back." "I want her back." "Where is she? "Let me talk to her on the phone please." Her body was shaking, and her tears were rolling down her cheeks.

Her face was getting bright red. She was having a panic attack. I tried to hug her but she pulled away, and that is when Roman came running over. He hugged her and held her close to him. Within two minutes she was calm again.

"Are you ready to let Max help you clean your room?" Mylene nodded yes. I smiled and followed her and Roman into her room. We quickly worked together and put her clothes in her drawers. I made her bed and I picked up the trash on the floor. Within ten minutes everything was clean.

Well we did it guys, and all it took was a few minutes. "Can we play a game now?" Mylene asked. Hmm, how about we clean Roman's room first and then play the game. "I already cleaned it, Max, but instead of playing a game can you help us make a Christmas cake?" "Our mom always made a cake with us when our winter vacation started."

"Please, Max, please, I would love that." Mylene's enthusiasm caught me by surprise. She was jumping up and down. She wanted this cake too. It made me happy. Of course I will help you guys. Shall we go now? "Yes, yes!" I followed the kids down the stairs, and as we neared the kitchen we all stopped dead in our tracks.

Cooking something that smelled delicious was a woman that we had never seen before. "Who are you?" Mylene asked. The woman turned her head to face us. She looked young, and a bit timid.

"Oh, hello, Monsieur Max, hello Monsieur Roman and Madame Mylene." "I am Madame's Sophie's new au pair." My heart stopped, this au pair looked so much like Kaoly. She had long black hair and a thick accent. She sounded like she was also from Vietnam too.

"It is a pleasure to meet you all." "Monsieur Dax has informed me to tell you guys to go sit at the guest dining table" "Sorry, but we are here to make a cake." Mylene rudely answered. "Don't worry, My-lene, let's let her do her work." "We can make our cake tomorrow."

Roman affectionately took his sister's arm and walked her to the guest dining room. "Ugh, I hate her! "She is not letting us make our cake!" She is so ugly!" "Mylene please don't say that." "She is just doing her job, that dad ordered her to do, okay? "D'accord." Roman rubbed his sister's head and pulled her seat out for her. He then pulled a seat out for me.

You are too kind, Roman! I'll be right back to join you guys, but first I will help the new au pair finish cooking, okay? Roman nodded in agreement, and I went back into the kitchen to help the new au pair.

So what is your name? "My name is Blessie." Nice to meet you Blessie. She smiled as she grabbed plates out of the vanity. I counted seven. That meant we would be having two additional guests. "It is overwhelming to meet you in person, Max." She quietly whispered as she sat the plates down.

Don't be overwhelmed by me. I am just a regular guy. Not the monster that I have been painted out to be. *Ding, dong, ding dong,* the doorbell rang. "Excuse me, I have to get that." Do you need me to do something while you go greet the guests?

"No, I am okay." "Don't worry about me." "Go sit with the kids." I did not argue with her. I knew how she felt. She was feeling the pressure, so I let her be, and I walked back to the dining area.

The kids were joyfully playing a game of rock paper scissors. I played two rounds with them by the time Blessie came back in with the guests. "Please take a seat there." "I will be back with the food."

"Oh you are just the sweetest thing." My blood stopped flowing. That voice. I looked up, and standing not even three feet from me was the disgusting, perverted creep who harassed, and more than likely with the help of Alexandre of course killed Kaoly.

That murderous scum of a human. The bald man, Jacque! I could not contain my rage, and I gave him a dark glare, but he did not notice. He was too busy undressing Blessie with his eyes to pay me no mind. All while his poor wife was standing right next to him!

My eyes were twitching with anger. My heart was beating faster and faster. I wanted to yell to the seven winds that I knew that he was a disgusting killer, and I would have if Alexandre had not walked into the room at that very moment.

Chapter 24
THE HUGOS COME TO DINNER

"Welcome, my beloved, Jacque and Anne." "I am glad to have the mighty Hugos here with us, to help kick off our Christmas vacation." "The pleasure is all ours." Jacque, aka, Kaoly's perpetrator said with a huge smile.

"No, the pleasure is truly mine," Alexandre said in a loving tone. "Oh, and before I forget Juliette sends her love to you guys." "She is truly happy to be getting the help she needs, and she is especially thankful to you for helping her into rehab Jacque."

"I'm so glad." "Please let her know that she does not need to thank me." "I am happy that she is getting control of her life." "It was heartbreaking for me to see her misusing pain medication with Kaoly."

"Kaoly was truly a bad influence." There it was! This was their plan. They would kill two birds with one stone. They would make out Kaoly to be a bad influencer who got Juliette addicted to painkillers. It was the perfect scheme, and they had just laid the first seed of doubt in the kids' mind regarding Juliette's "addiction."

This was beyond evil, and I couldn't help but give Jacque a hateful look. He noticed, and looked directly into my eyes. He was trying to read me, so I quickly looked away, but he began to speak to me.

"I am pleased that your name will eventually be cleared, Max." He looked at Alexandre and they both laughed. I felt sick to my stomach, until Anne spoke up. "I knew you were a good kid." "I'm glad you are back with the Daxes, and I am sure the kids are happy you are here." I stared at the kids and they both smiled.

"See, their smiles say it all." Anne said, while looking down the hall, and at her watch. "Sophie seems to be late." "Oh, Anne, you know Sophie, work comes first." "She may not even make it to dinner." "Oh that is too bad." "Yeah, well at least she asked Blessie to cook us an amazing meal!"

"Speaking of an amazing meal, when do we eat?" Jacque asked, cheerfully. "Let me call out to Blessie." Alexandre responded. "Blessie we are ready to eat!" He yelled across the room. Blessie immediately came with a tray that had six plates filled with Cordon Bleu and some sort of tomato sauce.

She handed each of us a plate, and the awkward dinner got started. A dinner where Jacque kept undressing Blessie with his eyes every time she passed by him. His glares at her became so uncomfortable that eventually Alexandre had to start redirecting Jacque when it became obvious that the kids were noticing.

"So, Jacque, are you getting Anne anything special this Christmas?" "My baby will get whatever she wants." "Right, babe?" Anne blushed. "The only gift I want is to be a mom." *Cough, cough, cough,* Jacque nearly spit his food out.

"Are you okay sweetie?" "Yes, I am sorry." "My food must have gone down the wrong pipe." Yeah, right. He had choked because he knew he had killed his unborn child. A child that his wife wanted, and maybe couldn't have.

"Who knows, Papa Noel may make that dream come true this Christmas?" Alexandre chimed in. Anne looked at Jacque, and in turn Jacque hugged his wife. "We will never stop trying, baby." Anne's bright green eyes filled with hope, and my mind filled with clarity.

It was obvious why Jacque had killed Kaoly now. He must have found out that she was carrying his child. A child that his wife so desperately wanted. It would have killed her if she knew that he had impregnated another woman.

Which makes this entire situation so fucked up. Like why cheat when you care about your wife? Let alone kill! It really makes no sense, but what does make sense is why he and Alexandre are friends. They are two peas in a pod. A pod that had to, "Max?" "Did you hear my question?"

Huh? I shook my head in puzzlement. Once again I had been so caught in my own thoughts that I had not heard someone speaking to me. It was Anne. She was staring at me with her face filled with curiosity. Her crows feet deepened as she waited for me to respond.

I felt myself get red. Sorry, Anne. I did not hear what you asked. All this talk about Christmas has me daydreaming about my family. May you repeat your question? She smiled at me, causing her laugh lines to crease. "Of course, I can."

"I asked, what do you want for Christmas?" The question took me aback. I felt everyone's eyes staring at me, causing my instincts to take over. Thus, I said the first thought that popped into my head.

The only gift I want is to speak to my family. "Why can't you speak with them?" "Don't you have a phone?" "Oh he does now." "I just got him a phone," Alexandre said. "Oh that is great then." "Do you want to call your parents after dinner?" "Maybe we can say hi to them?"

Before I even got the chance to respond to Anne, Alexandre butted in. "Um, unfortunately he can't call his family now." "His phone has no service, and won't have any service until we get back to Paris."

"Oh, that is no issue, Alexandre!" "I have my old phone with me." "I can let him borrow it until you are able to get his set up." "I mean, as long as that is okay with you?" Anne suspiciously asked Alexandre.

I almost laughed out loud at that very moment. Alexandre had made a stupid mistake. He should have told her that my family was busy. It would have solved everything, but he gave her a stupid fixable excuse. He was stuck in a corner now, and had no choice, but to cave in.

"That would be a good idea, Anne." He forcefully smiled. "Perfect." She dug into her purse and pulled out an *Iphone 14*. "Here you go Max." I did not take it until I looked at Alexandre to see what to do.

He gave me a nod of approval, and I took the phone. I was giddy with joy. Merci, thank you so much, Anne. I really appreciate this. "You are most welcome." "When do you want to call your family, Max?"

"How about he calls them when we finish dinner?" "Oh, and speaking of dinner, Blessie, please bring the dessert out!" Alexandre nervously called out. He was in a panic. "Excuse me everyone, I have to accept this call." "I will be right back." "Don't start dessert without me!"

He practically ran out of the room. I knew where he was going. He was going to get my family un-tied and ready for the call. That made my heart happy. Speaking to them would be the perfect Christmas present, and I owed it all to Anne.

Anne, who strangely enough had a look of fury in her eyes. That took me by surprise. She has been cheerful all night, but then I noticed the reason why. Jacque had gotten up and walked over to Blessie. He was helping her place the flakey buttery croissants on the table.

"Jacque, why don't you come back and sit here." "You are bothering the young lady." Anne said in a stern but gentle voice. "Oh, dear but I like to help." Jacque responded. Anne stood up and gently got in between Blessie and Jacque. The tension in the air was razor sharp.

It then hit me that Anne knew of her husband's way, at least to an extent, so was she also his accomplice? Or was she an innocent bystander like Mathieu? I was not sure yet, but one thing was certain at that very moment Anne hated Jacque.

Jacque kept putting his hands on Blessie's shoulders, even when she shrugged him off, and as Jacque set the last buttery croissant on the table he asked a gut punching question. "May you please show me where the guest restroom is, Blessie?"

"Of course I will Monsieur Jacque." Blessie naively responded. There it was. This was going to be the downfall of Blessie. "I will be back, my beautiful Anne." "I need to wash my hands." "Some of the croissant flakes got on them."

I could not believe what was happening. I could not just stand around and do nothing. I guess Anne must have noticed my worry because as I glanced at her, she gave me a look that said, "please follow him."

Not that I needed that look. I was already halfway out of my seat. Blessie was not going to suffer the same fate as Kaoly. Her life would not be ruined as long as I was there. Jacque, I called out. Wait for me. I need to wash my hands too.

The look on Jacque's face changed from complete happiness to annoyance in a split second. His laugh lines harden. His crow's feet thicken, and he simply nodded. There was nothing that he could do, so we both followed Blessie to the guest restroom.

"Here you are guys." "I'll be right outside waiting for you two to finish." "Thanks, Blessie," Jacque grunted annoyingly as I followed him inside the massive restroom. It reminded me of one of those bathrooms you see at malls.

It had two sinks with a big mirror wedged right in the center. The floor was covered in white marble, and the walls were hand painted with designs of forest creatures. It is a beautiful place isn't it? I asked Jacque.

He looked at me and with a neutral face said, "Yes, and next time please do not offer to go to the place that I am going to." "I like to do things alone." Got it, I said slightly sarcastically.

Thankfully he didn't catch my sarcasm because he was too busy rushing out of the restroom. By the time I dried my hands and got out of the bathroom, he was already "accidentally" stumbling into Blessie.

He gently fell to the floor with her. His hands around her waist, and his head was in between Blessie's breasts. "Oh, I am so sorry, Blessie." "I must have slipped right out the door." "It is okay, Monsieur Jacque." Blessie said as she tried to stand up, but Jacque was not having it.

He scooted his body on her, and pressed himself in between every one of her crevices. I could and would not let this happen again. I ran to Blessie, and extended my hand to her. Blessie took my hand and Jacque was forced to get off of her.

I could practically see the fumes coming out from the top of his head, and I savored that moment. This clown was not going to hurt someone else on my watch. "Are you two ready to head back?" Jacque did not even answer. He was already on his way back.

Which was perfect. This gave me some private time with Blessie. I had to give her some sort of warning of what she was up against. Hey Blessie, "yes, Max?"

If something ever makes you feel strange, please let me know as soon as possible okay? Blessie looked at me and smiled. "Of course," but that was not enough for me. I stopped walking and grabbed her wrist as Jacque near the entrance of the guest dining area.

"Blessie, if you ever feel uncomfortable with anyone let me know, okay?" Blessie stared at me with confusion, but quickly nodded okay. I let go of her wrist. I felt bad for scaring her, but now at least she had a fighting chance, and that was enough for me.

So with that, I headed back into the guest dining room. "Are you ready for us to talk to your family, Max? I was caught by surprise, as a chirpy Alexandre greeted me with a question. "Well?"

You mean right now? "Of course. Before I could even answer, Alexandre hit "call" on the phone that Anne had given me. Everyone at the table had their eyes glued on me. *Bring, bring, bring.* Alexandre handed me the phone as the video call connected. My mom came on the screen.

She was in her bed. Her hair was tied in a ponytail. Her cheeks were red and I could see hints of smeared makeup in her eyes with a dash of sweat on her forehead. I felt awful. She must have been the only one forced out for the call.

"Maxi!" "I am so happy to see you, my handsome boy, but is something the matter?" "You usually do not call this early." It was 1:00 p.m. back at home, and I normally did call my family at that time. My mom was just playing her part. She had to end the call as soon as possible.

Oh mom, I just wanted to introduce you to some of my host family and their friends. They are eager to meet you. Is dad at home? "He is at work, Max." My mom slightly lifted her left eyebrow.

A look she usually gave when she was getting annoyed at us, but I knew that this time it meant that I had to end the call now, so I wrapped things up. Before I say good night mom, this is Alexandre.

He has been nothing but kind to me. I pointed the camera to Alexandre. He waved at my mom, and said, "Nice to meet you Madame." "The pleasure is all mine," my mom responded.

Mom, these are the host kids I work with. Roman waved hi to her, and Mylene completely ignored her. "Oh Max, you guys are having dinner?" "You should have told me." "You all need to eat before the food gets cold."

Yes mom, you are right. I miss you all. Please tell everyone that I said hi, and let them know that I will call back in two days for Christmas Eve. I felt Alexandre's eyes prying at me. I was not supposed to do that, but whatever, I had just secured a call with my family for Christmas Eve. I would deal with the consequences later.

"That sounds perfect sweetie." "I love you Max, and I will tell everyone." "See you then." "Goodnight." Bye, mom. I hung up the call and stared at Alexandre. He gave me a nod. He had approved of the way that I handled the call.

Good, at least for now I could worry less about my family, and thankfully, Alexandre did not seem to mind me scheduling a call. Hopefully that meant that my family would be released soon because at the end of the day, I was under the Daxes mercy anyway.

Aaahhnn, hookah, Mylene yawned, followed by Roman. "Kids, you two should go to bed." Roman and Mylene nodded and got up. "Max, can you come read me a story before bed?" Of course I will, Roman. I will be there soon, so go get dressed for bed.

He and Mylene dashed out of the kitchen and up the stairs. I will excuse myself too, I told Alexandre, and the Hugos. "See you tomorrow," Alexandre said. "Have a goodnight, Jacque responded.

"Max," yes Anne? "Before you go, I want to reset the password on the phone that I gave you." I walked toward her. "Oh, don't worry, I will walk with you while I reset it." She quickly got up and followed me out of the dining room.

As soon as we were out of view from Alexandre and Jacque she grabbed my arm. I was caught by surprise. "Here you go," she whispered. She handed me a small flip phone. "This is a trackless phone."

"No one will know when you use it." "I want you to call me after Christmas and I want you to tell me everything you know about my husband, okay?" I was speechless. I had no clue what to say or what to think, so I nodded my head in confirmation, and she left back into the dining room.

She left me with a sense of renewed hope. Now more than ever I was convinced that Anne was another Mathieu. Two people caught with the wrong crowd, but trying to make things right. I smiled at that thought and I headed up stairs to the kids room.

"Wait, Max, before you go up stairs." I turned around and saw Alexandre running up to catch me. "Before you go read to my kids, please hand me the Iphone Anne gave you." Without hesitation I handed him the phone.

"Well, there's a good boy." "Nice and fast." "Just how I like it." "I will see you tomorrow at eight a.m." "Make sure the kids are down and ready for breakfast by then," and with that he left.

Chapter 25

THE FLIP PHONE

Well, Alexandre, you may have taken the first phone Anne gave me, but you sure as hell did not take the second. I silently giggled, as I made my way up the stairs to the kids' floor. Hopefully they would be tired by the time I got up there.

Today had been a long day, and I could barely pick up my legs at this point. Thankfully, as I reached their rooms I was pleased to see that Mylene was fast asleep in her room. Thank goodness.

One down and another one to go, and with that I quietly tipped-toed over to Roman's room. I gingerly opened his door, and he was eagerly waiting on his bed for me. He was smiling from ear to ear.

Well thank you Roman for being so responsible and getting into bed yourself. I told him. "You are welcome, Max." "I also got Mylene to bed." Yes, I figured you did. Thank you for that.

"De rien, now it's time to read my book!" "It is one hundred and ninety-two pages, do you see?" He opened the book and showed me page one hundred and ninety-two. Wow, yes I see. You are getting to be such a great book lover. He smiled and handed me the book.

I could not believe my eyes. It was, Old Yeller. Roman! "Yes, Max?" This book was probably the one of the first chapter books that I ever finished myself. "Really?" Yes! "Okay, let's read it now please!" I opened the book and started to read it.

Charmingly enough, I didn't even get the chance to start the third page by the time Roman was sound asleep. He must have been tired too, so I quietly stood up and turned his light off. I left his room, and checked the time on the flip phone. It was 11:30 p.m. Now it was my turn to go to bed.

I cautiously headed down the stairs to "my room." In other words, the au pair room that Kaoly and I had to share. I hated that room, and I hated the fact that I would have to pass all those Daxes' portraits again.

It was no coincidence why the Daxes' put their portraits near the room of their "servants." It was to belittle them, and to show them who the true bosses were. Well, fuck them. This "no name, no one" will become their downfall.

I will show them what a motivated and kind individual, "Hey, Max." AHH! I screamed and jumped in the air as I reached the last step of the stairs. "Oh, did I scare you?" I had my hand over my heart. It was Alexandre.

He was at the base of the stairs in his pajamas. "I didn't mean to scare you." He sarcastically said. "Are you off to bed?" Yes. "Oh, but it's not even 12:00 a.m. yet." "It is much too early."

Yeah, well, my head really hurts, and I feel tired. "Oh I know what will help with that headache." "Come I have some medicine in my room." My body went cold. He was up to something terrible. I had to be careful on how I responded to him.

Thank you so much for the offer Monsieur Alexandre, but really it is okay. I think I can sleep off the headache. "Nonsense." He grabbed my hand and pulled me out of the hallway. I felt my fight or flight instinct kicked in. I was scared.

I did not want to go with him because I knew what would happen. I knew that I would be scarred for life, but sadly I had no choice. "You'll see once you get to my room you will feel more comfortable."

I forcefully followed him, but then my curiosity got the best of me. I had no clue where the Daxes' master bedroom was. Where was it? I had to ask. Where is your master suite? Alexandre stopped and smiled at me.

"Juliette and I remodeled this house in a way to make finding our room hard." "You know, just for security reasons." "Ironically our bedroom is hidden right in the center of the main living room."

He tugged me along to the main living room. I had only been here a couple of times since most of my time was spent in the guest area of the house. I was starstruck at the beauty of this space.

The room contained a beautiful golden colored piano. It had leather sofas, and expensive looking hand paintings. "Here we are." Alexandre said. I turned my head in confusion because he was pointing at the wall behind the piano. I do not see the room, Monsieur Alexandre. "Wait and see."

Alexandre pressed one of the tiles on the wall, and the entire wall opened. It completely pulled apart right in the middle. Bright lights went on and there was the room. It was a massive chambre.

Quite breathtaking, but even more mesmerizing was the fact that the room was underground. To get to it you had to go down a stairway. A marble stairway, and down at the bottom was the place itself.

Wow. "Yeah, a place fit for a king and his queen." I heard Alexandre speaking, but I was still starstruck. The room had four doors that I could count. It was like a maze. The doors probably led out to a tunnel or something.

Strangely enough, what made this place even more overwhelming was the fact that it also felt cozy. The room was carpeted and not floored. There was even a giant bean bag chair in the corner by a bookshelf. I was taken aback by the immensity of it all.

Sadly, I was brought back to reality when I felt a hand touch my thigh. I jumped in surprise. It was, of course, Alexandre. He was rubbing my thigh! I clenched my fists together in anger.

This was not the first time he had touched me inappropriately, but this was the first time that he did it as if it was nothing but normal. I wanted to knock his head in, but I couldn't. I had to be calm. I had to do it for my family.

He began to rub my shoulders. "You should take your shirt off to get more comfortable." "It will help your headache." I felt a lump in my throat. Till this very moment I had avoided anything going further than groping, but now I was doomed.

No one was here to save me, and I had no choice. I began to remove my shirt. The look on Alexandre's eyes was terrifying. He looked mad with power. He was not attracted to men. He just wanted the power of controlling someone. That is what turned him on, the control of it all.

My shirt was off. I clutched it in my hand. I felt like a dog. I felt like a dog that had just been yelled at by its owners. "Come inside, I will give you something for your headache." He had the grin of a devil on his face. I hated him.

I wanted him dead, but I began to go down the stairs. I felt guilty even though I was the victim. "Papa I had a nightmare, papa where are you?" In an instant Alexandre pulled me by the arm and dragged me behind one of the sofas in the living room. "Stay here and do not move a muscle!"

"Mylene, I am in my room." "Come here dear." I heard small footsteps running to the living room. "I could make out Myelen's figure as she neared Alexandre Dax's room. "Papa I had a horrible nightmare that mom was dead." "That she had been killed."

"Oh, sweetie do not worry about that." "Your mom is alright." "We can call her on the phone tomorrow if that is what you want." Of course that was a lie. Juliette was dead, but Alexandre would obviously get someone to fake her voice for a call. Or maybe even use AI.

"Papa, can I sleep here with you tonight?" "I think it is best that you go to your room sweetie." "Papa, please I want to sleep with you." Mylene was sobbing. This time she was not faking it. There was a long pause on Alexandre's end, and then he spoke.

"Okay, Mylene, but just for tonight." "We cannot have this become a bad habit." "You have to be a brave girl." "You are a Dax after all, and mommy would not like for you to be scared." "Okay papa, I promise you that tomorrow I will start being a brave girl."

I watched them go into the room. It took a minute for the walls to completely close, but when they did there was no evidence that the wall had ever opened. *Phew,* I let out a sigh of relief, and I carefully got up from behind the couch.

Thank you God, I prayed quietly. I had been saved again, but I was not sure how lucky I would get from this point on. My body shivered at that realization. The realization that I did not even control my own physique, but I forcefully shook off that truth for now.

I could not afford being depressed because if I fell into that rabbit hole I would never get out. So without further ado, I quietly walked over to the au pair room, and ever so tactically I went inside.

I mutely passed a snoring Blessie as I made my way to my bed, and before I knew it I was out cold. I don't even remember how I fell asleep, but I am pretty sure I was dead gone before my body ever touched the rough mattress. *Bring, bring, bring.* Huh?

Ugh, the loud sound of Blessie's alarm woke me up. I still felt tired. I opened my eyes half way and checked the time. It was 5:00 a.m. Gosh why was she getting up so early I wondered.

Ugh, who cares. I did not have to get the kids downstairs till 8:00 a.m. I still had time to sleep, so I set my alarm to 7:30 a.m. and closed my eyes. *Bring, bring, bring* my alarm went. I grabbed Anne's phone and turned it off.

I rubbed my eyes, and removed my blankets. Still with my eyes half closed I made it to the restroom, and I washed the sleep from my face. I then brushed my teeth, and slowly but surely I fully awoke.

Now fully awake I took a good look at my face, and to my happiness it was healed. My cheeks even had some of their plumpness back. Regrettably, the color to my face was still gone, but that was normal. It was winter.

At the minimum, I looked "normal" again. Well, that is if you call someone with a bird nest for hair normal. I desperately needed a haircut. My bangs were starting to cover my eyes. Which in reality wasn't such a bad thing.

At least the sorrow that my eyes showed would be hidden. Sadly, I still could not see the spark that was normally in my big dark eyes. All I could see were shallow pools staring back at me. It made me sad, but I was determined to get the shine back, and step one was playing the role of the perfect au pair.

With that said, I left the restroom and headed up the stairs to the door. As I reached for the metal handle, the door slammed open. Barely missing my face by an inch. "Where have you been?" "You should have been outside helping Blessie right at 5:00 a.m.

A yelling Sophie Dax got right up to my face. It pissed me off. I did not have to listen to her. I didn't even have to be polite to her. She was not Alexandre, and the relationship she had with Alexandre was on eggshells.

Excuse me Sophie, but firstly I do not work for you. Secondly, please knock on the door before you barge into someone's room. I could have been changing. The look of rage on her face was almost terrifying.

"You think you can talk back to me you little bitch?" I decided to ignore and moved past her, but she blocked my exit. "I want you to know that you are nothing but a piece of shit." I ignored her statement, and she spit on my face. It took all my strength to not spit back at her, but after a few seconds she started to walk back out of the hallway.

I immediately wiped the spit off my face, and I watched as she left the corridor. *Boom, boom.* Blessie accidentally hit Sophie on the shoulder with her arm. *Slap, slap, slap.* "You dumb bitch!" "Watch where you are walking." "Next time I will kill you if you ever dare to touch me again."

"I am so sorry, Madame Sophie." "I did not hear you coming down the hall." "Whatever!" Sophie cried and left the hallway. A tearful Blessie held her face. Her cheeks were bright red from Sophie's slaps.

Why do you stay with her, Blessie? Why not leave? "My family is dirt poor." "Beyond dirt poor, and I must stay here in order to one day get a better job." Blessie, are you even enrolled in a language course here? "No, I am not." Then how will you ever get a better job in a country that is not yours, without some sort of education?

"I have a plan to seek asylum this coming New Years when Sophie goes on holiday for two weeks." "Of course I will not tell her anything, but I will seek asylum and wait for the process." "In the meantime I will do what I am told."

I felt bad for her. She reminded me so much of Kaoly, but there was nothing that I could do, but warn her. Blessie, please be safe and watch your surroundings. "I will, Max." "I have to go freshen up if you excuse me." I nodded and she went inside the au pair room.

I on the other hand left the room, and headed to wake the kids up. By the time I reached the second floor I could hear that they were up. A screaming Mylene was arguing with Alexandre. "I want a tree now, papa!" "Sweetie, our tree won't come until Christmas day."

"Don't worry, Mylene, that is only two days away." Roman chimed in. "No, I want it this minute!" "We always had the tree before Christmas when maman was here!" "Well, sweetie this time maman did not have time to buy it in advance, so it won't arrive until the day of Christmas."

Uh huh, Uh huh, I silently grunted as I cautiously entered the room. "Oh good, you are here." "Please deal with this because I have work to do!" Alexandre said as he walked out of the room. Leaving me with a crying Mylene, and an annoyed Roman.

Chapter 26

THE DEPARTURE OF BLESSIE

Hey, Roman, can I speak to you real quick outside? "Yeah, what's up Max?" What do you say we make a compromise with Mylene? "What do you mean?" What if we decorate one of the pine trees outside? That way she gets to decorate a Christmas tree, and also learns how to wait for the real one.

"Wow, that is a great idea Max." "Can I tell Mylene?" Of course you can. "Great, let me go tell her." He ran back inside the room, and a minute later he brought Mylene out. She glared at me with her beady mischievous eyes, but then a hint of a smile appeared on her face. "Max, is it true that we can decorate a tree outside?" Yes, how does that sound? Before I could react she hugged me.

I was caught off guard, "Christmas, Christmas, Christmas!" It was the first time in my life that I saw her truly happy, and acting like a kid. That was a good step in the right direction. "When can we decorate the tree?" She asked me.

How about both of you clean your rooms, and after breakfast we can decorate the tree. How does that sound? They both nodded their heads and ran into their chambres. I could not help but smile.

It was nice to see them being responsible, and amazingly not only did they clean their rooms, they also cleaned the restroom. Needless to say, I felt like a proud au pair.

"Max, we are done!" "Can we go have breakfast now?" Mylene eagerly asked. Of course! Let's go. We hurriedly went down the stairs, and we dashed into the dining room. Alexandre was there to greet us.

"Kids, please take a seat, so I can tell you guys something." Roman and Mylene grabbed a chair, and looked at Alexandre with impatience. "Well, dad?" Mylene asked. Alexandre cleared his throat, and said, "I will be gone the entire day today, and I will be back tomorrow in the afternoon."

"Where are you going papa?" "I need to head to the south of France for a meeting that must be held in person." "I want you kids to behave, and to listen to what Max says." "Especially you, Mylene."

"Remember, Santa will take away your toys if you do not listen." "No, please don't say that!" "I will listen papa." "Okay, perfect." "That is what I like to hear sweetie." *Clap, clap, clap.* "Oh what a sweet family moment." Sophie laughed, "But don't tell me you are leaving my beautiful niece and nephew alone for Christmas, Alexandre?"

"Papa, you will be home for Christmas, right?" A nervous Roman asked. "Of course I will be." "Don't listen to your aunt, Sophie." "She is just mad that I have to attend all the important meetings for the company."

"I am not mad, Alexandre." "I just find it hard to understand." "Dad left you with 70% of the company because you are a man, but you do not deserve it!" "It is me who has kept our great Dax Winery thriving." "All you ever do is throw parties, and meet with the people after the deal is made."

"Oh sister, I see you are feeling quite catty this morning, so let me bring you down a level." "Don't forget you have the easy work." "You take care of our winery, but I take care of the social aspect of the Dax Empire." "You would absolutely crumble from that pressure." Sophie dogged Alexandre with pure hate.

It gave me satisfaction. "Anyway, sister, it is the holidays, so I will be nicer, and give you a compliment." "Which is?" "You chose a great au pair." "Look at the food she has prepared us." A shy Blessie came with a tray of crepes, accompanied with eggs on the side, and freshly squeezed orange juice.

"You are right, Alexandre." "I know how to choose au pairs unlike you." Sophie mockingly glanced at me. "You can make fun of Max all that you want Sophie, but he is special." "He is very intelligent, and most importantly the kids love him." "Right kids?" Roman rapidly nodded yes, and after a few seconds of staring at me, Mylene agreed.

Damn, Alexandre must truly hate his sister if he is out there complimenting me, I thought. "Well it was nice chatting with you Sophie, but I have to go meet with the Rives, in Bordeaux." "Uh huh, you just don't want to talk with me, but whatever!" "I'm used to it."

Alexandre rolled his eyes at her comment. "Yeah, that's what I thought." "Anyway, what time will you be back tomorrow?" "I will be back no later than three in the afternoon." "Okay, just don't forget to bring back some wine for Christmas dinner." "You got it Sophie."

"Alright kids, I am leaving." "Come here so I can give you two a hug goodbye." Mylene and Roman stood up and gave Alexandre a tight hug. He then playfully whispered, "I am counting on seeing Max alive by the time I come back."

The kids laughed, but I did not find it amusing. "Oh don't be scared, Max." "You will be fine." "Now, help me with my luggage." I grabbed his small bag, and I followed him to the front door of the house.

"Thank you." "Now, just a friendly reminder, I do not want you to do anything stupid while I am gone." "Your family is still under my control." Yes, I know. "Good, and if you manage to have everything in place by the time I come back tomorrow I will release your family for Christmas." Really? "Yes!" That would be amazing! I answered in a high pitched, overly excited voice.

"Hahaha, Yeah, I thought you would like that." "Now before I go, is there anything you need?" Yes, where are the Christmas decorations? "They are in the basement right next to the bar." "Thank you Monsieur, Alexandre.

"Oh, I love it when you call me Monsieur Alexandre." "It makes me want to dominate you even more." "Oh, and when I come back we can finish where we left off last night." Shivers went down my spine, but I forced a smile for him.

The last thing I wanted to do was jeopardize the release of my family. "Well, see you later." Bye, I said and I walked back to the dining area; desperately trying to shake his comments off.

Thankfully seeing the kids peacefully enjoying their breakfast helped ease my mind. "Max, now that papa left can we decorate the tree?" Mylene asked while a piece of egg hung from her mouth.

Yes, but first you two need to take your time and eat your food. I am going to search for the decorations now. "Okay," Mylene said grumpily. Roman gave me a wink, and I smiled at him as I headed to the bar area.

Luckily, I did not have to walk much to get there. The bar was just across the hall from the guest kitchen, and mysteriously built right underneath the bar was the basement. The entrance of course was hidden from plain view, but I knew where it was.

The basement door was underneath the welcome mat of the bar, so I carefully kicked the mat out of the way exposing the metal bottled doorway. With a bit of a struggle I pushed the three large bolts out unlocking the door of the basement.

It opened with a squealing sound. The noise hurt my ears, and my eyes got irritated as the automatic lights of the dungeon came on. I waited a few seconds for my eyes to adjust to the light change.

Once they were adjusted I made my way down the fifteen flights of stairs until I was in the basement. *Barf.* It smelled awful down here. The stench of rancid milk hit my nostrils like a bullet.

Why did it smell so bad? I began to look around for the source of the smell, but all I could see were boxes scattered all around the large gray room. Ugh, I gagged as I began to look for the decorations.

Gratefully, I spotted them almost immediately in the darkest corner of the basement. They were in a shiny box that said Christmas Decorations. I rapidly walked over there, and as soon as I reached the box the overly powerful smell started to make my head hurt.

It was definitely coming from this side! I had to see what this smell was. I moved the Christmas box out of the way, and right behind it were three large white bags. *AH, AH, AH, AH!* I yelled instinctively.

Sealed in a tight see-through bag was Juliette and Geraldine. They looked like they were sleeping! They did not look dead at all. They were so well preserved, but right next to them in a partially opened bag was the au pair.

His face was unrecognizable, and the only reason that I knew it was him was because of the clothes that he was wearing. His skin was green and was starting to come off. I was throwing up before I knew what I was doing.

Never in my life had I seen such horror. Why, why, please God tell me why someone so sinister as Alexandre would do this? Why would he do this to his dead wife? Why would he do this to his children? Why?

Oh, then it clicked. He wanted Juliette's body persevered for when he faked her death as an overdose. It was the perfect scheme. That said, why did he want Geraldine preserved? I had no clue, and quite frankly I was too in shock to care.

All that I could see and think about at that moment was the poor au pair. His body more than likely would be dumped somewhere outside of Paris. Alexandre probably just didn't have enough time to do it yet, or maybe he purposely brought his body here.

Wow, how awful and despicable, and simply plain evil. He probably wanted me to find his body down here to teach me some sort of lesson. He was a mind playing buffoon. If he wanted to make me sick and scared for my life he surely achieved his goal.

I was so stricken with fear at that moment, that my mind went blank. I completely forgot where and who I was. I only came out of my haze when I heard Roman and Mylene shouting for my name. Crap. I couldn't have them come down here. I am coming, I yelled.

I wiped my tears away. I did not want the kids to see me like this. "Do you need help Max?" Roman shouted from a distance. "Ew, what is that smell?" Mylene asked. Her voice echoed inside the basement.

There is a dead skunk down here, so stay up there! I yelled at them. "Eww, should we bury it?" No, I will ask the cleaner to take care of it Roman. "Are you sure, Max?" Yes, but I do need help from you guys. "With what?" When I reach the top of the stairs I need both of you to grab the Christmas decoration box from my hands.

"We are on it," Romain said. Okay, perfect. I am coming up now. I quickly grabbed the Christmas decoration box, and headed up the stairs. The box itself wasn't too heavy, so the kids had no problem taking it from my hands. Once they grabbed it I carefully got out of the basement, and I bolted the door shut.

I breathed a huge sigh of relief as fresh air hit my nose. "Are you okay, Max?" Yes, Roman. It was just too smelly and gloomy down there. "Can we decorate the tree now?" An anxious Mylene paced back and forth. Of course we can, and guess what? I said, trying to shake off what I had just seen.

"What?" We are going to decorate this tree into three sections. One section is for you, and the other is for Roman, and the top part will be a mixture of both your tastes. How does that sound? "That sounds awesome, Max." Roman giggly said.

Great, so now comes the fun part. Let us choose which tree will be the lucky Christmas tree. "I have an idea." Roman and I turned our heads in surprise to see Mylene making a recommendation. Usually she is no help. It felt good to see her start to grow.

Roman gave her a pat on the shoulder and then asked her, "What do you recommend, Mylene?" Mylene broke off on a run and yelled, "Follow me!" We ran right behind her, following her to the back yard. She stopped right in front of a large beautiful tree that faced the back of the house.

It was an Evergreen Tree. "This is the one." Wow, Mylene, this tree will be perfect. "Hehe, I know." She happily jumped up and down. "Can we start now?" Yes, I will leave both of you to decorate the tree, and I will be back in thirty minutes to see how you two are doing.

Does that sound fair? The kids were opening the box before I even finished my sentence. They didn't even notice as I made my way back into the guest kitchen. Good, this would give me some alone time which was much needed. Plus, the kitchen window would give me a direct view of the kids.

Perfect I thought as I entered the kitchen. Woefully as I stepped in the cuisine my hopes of having thirty minutes to myself faded because right in front of the refrigerator was a chaotic Sophie throwing blow after blow to an unprotected Blessie.

In the blink of an eye Sophie grabbed Blessie by the hair and dragged her to the floor. I watched in horror. She pulled Blessie by the hair to the front of the house. I ran to catch them. She was going to pull all of Blessie's hair off. STOP! I yelled at Sophie, STOP!

You are going to pull her entire scalp off! "I do not care!" She yelled out of breath. "This little bitch was using me!" "I overheard her on the phone with her mom!" "She was planning to leave after Christmas in order to seek asylum!"

"She was planning to leave me!" I looked down at a crying Blessie. Her face was red, and her eyes were swollen from the blows that Sophie had given her. That wretched Dax. She swung her fist once more and nailed Blessie in the stomach.

Arrete! I screamed. If you do not leave her alone, I will call the police! "Oh you will call the police on me?" "You are no better than this piece of shit!" "You were doing the same thing as her!" "You filths only use us Daxes for our influence and money."

"As a matter of fact I think I will call the police myself!" Okay, go right ahead and we can have a conversation about the Daxes' business practices. Which I may add, I have evidence of. Sophie stared at me with intense hatred, but she let go of Blessie's hair.

"Blessie you have three hours to get ready." "I am dropping you off at the airport." "You are going straight home, and I will tell immigration that you were using me, so they can revoke your visa forever!"

Blessie was sobbing uncontrollably now, but there was nothing I could do. I was sure her "student-au pair visa" would be revoked. A host family could ask for visa termination if they broke their contract early with the au pair. Sadly, Blessie was screwed. She had sacrificed so much just to be sent right back home.

"You know you have been nothing but an omen to our family." "But I am glad that you are making my brother's life a living hell." "I appreciate that, but I will tell you one thing, Max." "Get in my way again and I will kill you!"

I do not want any trouble Sophie. She eyed me down and threw one last kick at Blessie. She then walked away. A humiliated Blessie stood up and ran out of the kitchen. I felt awful for her, but I had to go back and check on the kids.

I peeked through the kitchen window and they were well in their way decorating the tree. They did however look to be struggling with adding the lights, so I decided to go out and help them. "No the lights don't go this way," Roman told Mylene. "Yes," that is how maman does it." Mylene responded. Wow, you guys are doing such a fantastic job!

They both jumped about two feet in the air, dropping the lights. They had not heard me come in. It made me smile. For the first time since I had been here they were actually acting like normal kids. Kids who got scared. Kids got excited, and kids who were finally allowed to be imaginative and creative.

"You scared us, Max!" Roman came over and handed me an ornament. "What do you think?" I think it looks amazing, but maybe we should add the lights together, once the entire tree is decorated.

What do you guys think? Mylene smiled and nodded. "Max, we asked the gardener to bring a small ladder so we can climb the tree and decorate the top together." You will need my help for that part. "No, the gardener will hold the latter for us." "We want you to be surprised once the tree is finished." "So go back inside," Mylene yelled.

Before I could answer they both began to push me out of the way and back into the house. Okay, okay, I am going! I said while laughing my way back inside the home. Well, as long as they are busy decorating the tree, I might as well go check up on Blessie.

I walked toward the au pair room, and as I neared the hallway of the Daxes' portraits I began to hear Blessie cry. I felt bad for her, but honestly the best thing for her was to be back home. At least that way she would survive, and on second thought I would just let her be.

This was something that she had to figure out herself, so I reversed my way out of the hallway, and I walked back to the guest kitchen instead. It was almost lunch time, so I might as well make the kids their meal.

Hmm, but what to make them? They were picky as hell. Eh, I would find something in the cupboards. I began to open the wooden cupboards, and luckily the first thing that caught my eye was a box of ramen noodles.

Perfect! They definitely liked this, and even though it wasn't the healthiest choice, it was the easiest. Moreover, Alexandre wasn't here to tell me otherwise, so I quickly grabbed five bags of ramen and placed them in a pot. I filled the pot with water and I left it on the stove. I would heat it up once the kids were hungry.

Cool, now that lunch is settled, and the kids are busy I can finally relax a bit. Maybe I could even watch a tv show? I pulled out Alexandre's phone. Please, don't have Youtube blocked, I prayed. I opened the app and it worked! Yes!

Almost instinctively I typed *Sabrina the Animated Series*, and clicked on the first episode. It started to play. Gosh I felt so happy. At least for this short moment I would have peace. Something that was a rare commodity for me these past months.

"We are leaving in five minutes Blessie!" Sophie's yells interrupted the ending of my episode. So much for having alone time. "I am coming Madame." I heard Blessie pulling her luggage as she opened the front door.

I cautiously stood up and peeked through the hallway. Sophie was walking into her car, and a sad and tired Blessie was dragging her two luggages down the pebble walkway. "Well, put your luggage in," Sophie said.

Blessie lifted the luggage into the trunk and closed it slowly. She then stepped into the car, and Sophie wasted no time. She drove off. The only thing that remained was the dust that her tires left behind.

Poor Blessie. Her future was uncertain, but at least she was in a better situation than I was. She was getting out before anything serious happened to her, and that made me feel good. Besides, she was better off with her family. At least there she would not be scarred.

Chapter 27

THE MOST HEINOUS DEFILEMENT

Well now that they are gone, I might as well go heat up the ramen. *Grumble, grumble, grumble,* my stomach growled at the thought of eating. Hmm, I guess even my tummy knows that it is lunch time. I laughed at my own joke, and I made my way over to the cuisine.

Once there, I set the pot of ramen to a medium simmer. It would take no more than five minutes to cook. That was the perfect amount of time to go and get the kids. They were probably hungry too considering that they were out in the cold decorating a tree.

Kids, I yelled, through the kitchen window. It is time to have lunch. "No!" "Not yet!" They cried. "We are not done!" If you guys don't come and eat, then I may go and take a sneak peek at the tree before it is done." "No, please!" Roman shouted. "Okay we are coming."

That is what I thought, I said to myself while smirking. It felt nice that the kids wanted to impress me. They had never done so while Juliette was around. As bad as this sounds, her death was probably the best thing that could have happened to them.

"Max, we are here." Roman said. "Where is the food?" I'll bring it right out. Please go take a seat with Mylene at the guest dining room. They bolted toward the dining room, and I grabbed three bowels and served the ramen. Surprisingly enough, before I even had the chance to sit down myself they were done eating.

Wow you two ate fast! "Yes, we want to finish the tree," Roman chimed in. "Also, you can't see it until we are done." Mylene said with a stern voice. Um, okay, so shall I stay here until both of you are finished? "Yes, Max." "We will come and get you." Well, okay Roman. Both of you be careful on the ladder.

"We will," they both said, and after that they were out the door. Yes, peace and quiet, I silently laughed as I sat down and ate my ramen. All while watching another episode of *Sabrina*. I wouldn't have asked for a more perfect lunch if I could.

Unsurprisingly, for that brief moment my heart was happy, but before I knew it the kids were running right back inside the house. "Max!" "We are finished!" "Come see," Mylene cried.

She grabbed my hand and walked me to the tree. Again, I was taken aback by her sudden kindness to me, but I didn't question it. I happily followed her to the backyard where I was blown away by the sight of the tree.

There were golden and silver balls all around it. There were lights wrapped around the entire tree. There were even blue and red ribbons around it, and even though the sun was barely visible, the colorful lights on the tree shone like little stars. It looked amazing, and it felt like Christmas.

You guys did an excellent job. I am proud, but there is one thing missing. "What is that?" Roman asked. A star! "What is a star?" Mylene looked at me confused. I was about to answer her, but Roman did. "C'est une étoile, Mylene."

"Max, I want a star!" "I want one too, Max, but the problem is we don't have any in our decoration box." That isn't an issue, Roman. You and Mylene can build one together. "Yes, that is a perfect idea." Roman was smiling from ear to ear, and Mylene was jumping up and down.

"We have a lot of crafts in our art room Max." Great, shall we go and make one? "No." Why don't you want me to go help you, Roman? "It will be a surprise again." He smiled at me. Well in that case make the biggest and brightest start that you guys can make. I will be waiting right here for you two.

They both nodded their heads and dashed away to the third floor. Once again I was by myself, so I went back inside the home, and without hesitation I turned on my cartoon again. What a way to forget my troubles, I thought, when suddenly I was taken back to reality.

"Where are my enfants?" I jumped up, startled by Alexandre. "Surprise to see me?" Yes, I thought you were coming home tomorrow? "I was able to get everything sorted out with the Rives just as I arrived at the airport, so I came back." "Now where are my kids?"

"Roman, Mylène vous êtes ou?" They are making a star for the tree. "Okay." "Roman, Mylene come down here." He shouted up the stairway. The kids came running down. "Papa, you are here!" "Yes, my baby girl." "My meeting got canceled." "Yay." Mylene shouted.

"That is great," Roman added." "Look dad, we are making a Christmas star." Mylene said while hugging her dad tight. "Oh la la, what an idea." "Can I see?" "No!" Roman quickly said. Mylene and I will put it on the tree we decorated, tomorrow morning for all of you to see."

"D'accord, parfait, but now I need you two to go get dressed." "We are going to see a play, and after that we are eating at a fancy restaurant." "The play is in an hour, so hurry up and go change." The kids walked back up the stairs, and Alexandre came back toward me.

"Max, I am sorry, but you cannot come with us to the play, let alone the restaurant." "It is too fancy for you, hahah." He scornfully laughed. Whatever, I thought in my mind. I couldn't care less, in fact I was happy to not be going.

"Oh, but don't worry you can go out and eat dinner at one of the Ma & Pa restaurants near the house here, hahaha." "In fact, just to show you how much of a nice guy I am, here are twenty euros." He placed the twenty euros in my pocket and continued to laugh at me.

He was maliciously trying to belittle me. I bit my tongue. I wasn't going to give him any sort of reaction, and he was about to antagonize me more, but the kids walked down the stairs. "We are ready, papa." "Okay, perfect, go wait for me in the car." The kids left the house, and Alexandre came closer to me.

He licked his crusty lips at me. It made my skin crawl. "Oh, don't be scared, Max, hahaha." "I just wanted to remind you to clean the kids' rooms." Is that all, Monsieur Alexandre? "Well, if you see anything out of place go ahead and tidy it up, other than that I'll see you later." He winked at me and left the house.

I was relieved to be alone, but this time I had work to do. I headed up the stairs and started cleaning Mylene's disastrous room. It had clothes all over the floor, and her dolls were thrown all around, but it wasn't anything that I couldn't handle. Within half an hour her room was spotless.

Now it was Roman's turn. I opened the door of his bedroom and even though it wasn't as dirty as Mylene's room, it was still filthy. There were dirty socks and sheets in every corner. Plus it smelled, oh well. I got straight to cleaning and twenty minutes later I was finished.

Well, that wasn't too bad, but what do I do now? I pondered. Hmm, maybe I should start on breakfast, for tomorrow? Yeah, that would be a good idea. It would free up my morning too, so without further ado I went to the kitchen and I got straight to work.

I pulled a bag of flour out of the lower cupboards. I then got two eggs out, some milk and butter. I mixed all my ingredients in a large bowel and then I sealed it up. The batter was ready, and they would be having crepes for tomorrow!

"Max, come here!" Ah! I nearly dropped the batter. I turned around startled. A screaming Sophie was walking my way. I went over to meet her. "Here is the bag of clothes that my brother asked me to get you." "Make sure you wear it for tomorrow by 1:00 p.m."

"Oh, and try not to ruin our Christmas tomorrow with your presence." Does he want me to wear this for Christmas? I asked, confused. "No shit, that is what I just said." I took the bag, and ignored her rudeness.

Thanks for the clothes Sophie. Oh, and Sophie, can I ask, did Blessie make it on the plane? "That bitch is on a flight straight home." Okay, thank you.

Sophie left the living room, and disappeared to who knows where. I myself also left and went to a little pizza place that was about twenty minutes away by foot from the Daxes' house. It was as Alexandre had said, a Ma & Pa place, but unbeknownst to him, this little place probably served better food than wherever the hell he was going.

To be honest this Ma & Pa restaurant had made the best pizza that I had ever had in my life. The pepperoni was crispy and the crust was crunchy. The cheese was perfect, and it wasn't overly greasy. I was left very satisfied, and with a bittersweet feeling.

The last time I had eaten a pizza was right before coming to France. My parents had thrown me a going away party and that is what they had served. Oh, if I could only turn back time. I would have never come to France, but no. Thinking negatively was not going to get me anywhere.

I had to be smart and have faith. I would get out of this hell, but now it was time to go back to the prison. It was almost 8:00 p.m. Alexandre and the kids would probably be arriving soon, and I wanted to get back to the countryside house before they got there, so I left the restaurant in a hurry.

I actually ran all the way back to the countryside house, and it felt amazing moving my body. It helped relax my mind, and it gave me a sense of control. I welcomed that peaceful feeling, but what I did not welcome was the sweat that was all over my body.

The twenty minute run had drenched me. It was time for a quick shower, so I made my way over to the au pair restroom and I hopped into the shower. I turned the handle to medium, and I let the water flow over me.

The lukewarm water felt amazing on my tired body. It felt like weight was being lifted from my physique. I closed my eyes and let the stream hit my face. My mind drifted into nothingness as the steam of the shower made everything foggy inside the restroom. It felt therapeutic, and after a few minutes of that I began to wash my body with soap.

The soap smelled like fresh maple leaves. It was all too perfect, until I heard footsteps. My body tensed up. Was that someone? Who is there? I shouted. "It is me, Max." "Do not worry, I locked the door behind me."

I repeated the words that he said. "It is me," my entire life stopped at that point. I felt like I could see in five dimensions. I felt like I could see through my own skin. The footsteps drew closer.

There was nothing that I could do at this point. It was either this or get my family killed. My tears began to fall, but they were consumed by the water of the shower pouring over my face. I tried to cover my naked body, but it was useless. The shower door opened. It was Alexandre Dax.

"Max, that shower is much too big for only one person." "Plus it is better to shower with two people that way we save water." "We are in a climate crisis, didn't you know?" He glared at me with his predatory eyes.

He was savoring this moment of power. He was enjoying this moment. I had caused him so much stress, and now I would pay for it all. He wanted to humiliate me, to de-masculate me. He wanted me to lose hope and become a mindless robot. A robot who did not know that it had no free will.

He started to remove his shirt and then his pants. His underwear were last to go. He was smiling. I couldn't handle it. I turned the water off, and tried to leave the shower. He put his hand out to block my escape.

"Where do you think you're going?" I am finished with my shower Monsieur Alexandre. There is no need for me to stay here anymore. I tried to go around his arm, but he moved with me. "No, you are staying here, Max." "We have a lot to talk about."

He stepped into the shower, and turned the water back on as he brushed his body right next to me. I felt disgusted and violated just by the touch of his naked body on mine. He turned around to face me. "You will always be a nobody to me."

"You killed my wife." "You tarnished our family name." "You have caused incredible damage to the Dax legacy, and now you will have your punishment."

He grabbed my arm and twisted it to the back of my head. It hurt. I wanted to punch him right in the face, but I could not defend myself. If I did, my family would suffer the consequences.

"Here we go." He whispered in my ear. I didn't respond. I was nothing but a dummy, a robot, a mindless drone to him. I closed my eyes, and left my body. I left my entire being at that moment. It was like I was an observer seeing through someone else's eyes.

I saw the tears rolling down my cheeks, but the pain. The pain was too intense to not live through. It felt like I was being ripped open. I remember screaming and being told, "Scream louder." It was disgusting.

I felt anger and guilt flowing through my body. My used body. I don't know how long it lasted, but I was in that shower long enough for the lukewarm water to turn ice cold. In fact, it was that ice cold water that brought me back to awareness.

Alexandre was gone, but the torture he had done to me was visibly present. There was blood all over my legs. I had bruises on my thighs. Instantly I began to cry. I grabbed the soap, and I cleaned myself until my skin started to fall off.

Yet, I still felt dirty. My body was shaking. Shaking so bad that I could not breathe. I felt like I would have a heart attack. *You will get through this.* Mathieu? Is that you? Had I heard his voice again, or was I hallucinating?

I don't know, but the thought of his presence being there with me helped me calm down a bit. I was able to catch my breath again, and my pulse went down. Feeling a little more composed, I got out of the shower and put my clothes on.

I then made my way over to my bed and I was out cold. I don't know how long I was out for, but I woke up sweating and confused. Had I dreamed it all? Had it all been a horrible nightmare? I got my answer within a second. I felt terrible pain in my downstairs area.

Cautiously, I touched myself and I felt something wet. I ran to the restroom, and I stared at my hand. There was fresh blood on it, and to my horror there was blood all over my pj bottoms. What had this monster done to me?

I immediately took my pants off to see, but there was too much blood to get a clear view. I guess I could shower again, but truthfully speaking I was scared to see what I had gone through. Instead I grabbed some toilet paper, and I gently pressed it down to my private area until the bleed stopped. I felt ashamed.

How could this have happened to me? I felt immense fear. I felt guilty. I felt hurt. I felt angry. I felt hate, and I also felt a mental change in me. Which was my stance on killing. I know that I said that I would never kill, but at that moment I knew.

I knew that I would kill Alexandre Dax. The only question was when, and how I would do it. He had to pay for killing the old me. Max the kind au pair was no more. Max the sweet kid was history. I was no longer the same, and I would never be.

There was no way of removing those horrible memories of what had just happened to me. They were playing like a reel in my head, and probably always would be. How fucken sad. I wanted to cry some more, but I was just too tired. I closed my eyes, and went back to bed.

Chapter 28

THE REVIVAL & THE ALLY

Bring, bring, bring, bring. The alarm cried out. I grabbed Anne's phone and turned off the alarm. It was 7:30 a.m. I had to get up. I had to get the kids dressed and ready, but I felt awful. I felt like every single cell in my body was sore.

Moreover, my mind felt like a hostage in its own body. I was struggling to even get my hands to rub the sleep from my eyes. My brain did not want anything touching my body. I desperately wanted to just stay in bed.

Why, oh why did this happen to me? It is crazy how we humans are. I felt mad at myself for feeling pity for myself. I should be able to feel pity, but my mind told me to cut it off. I had to get up.

I had to go upstairs and get the kids dressed. I had to look at that monster's face today without losing it. I had to be brave for everyone counting on me, so with all the strength I could muster I moved my body.

I yanked the blankets off of me, and I did my bed. Somehow I made it to the restroom and took a quick shower. Then I don't even know how, but I was up upstairs with the kids before I even knew what I was doing. Things were moving so fast. Kind of like when you press fast forward on a movie.

One second I was helping the kids get ready, and the next we were having breakfast. Everything felt like one big blur. I was not in my right mind. I felt like a walking zombie. "Max, did you not like our star and tree?" Huh? What? Did someone ask me a question? I felt a tug on my jacket. It was Roman and Mylene.

They had asked me if I liked their star and tree. I knew I was outside for the big Christmas tree star reveal, but I couldn't think straight. Still with all the mental power that I could find, I forced a smile, and said, "Yes, that tree and star is beautiful." I smiled at both of them, and they smiled back. One simple smile was enough to make kids feel validated, and conversely their smiles helped me start to regain control of my mind again.

Though it was not enough since I still just felt dead inside. "Are you not going to eat this amazing Christmas dinner?" Confusion all around, dinner already? Who had asked me a question? I tried to adjust my blurred vision. It was the demon. It was Alexandre who had asked me a question.

Sorry, I am not very hungry. "You haven't eaten anything all day, Max." "You should eat something." "Try the chocolate log cake." I turned to stare at Roman. All day? I glanced at the clock that hung over the dining room table. It was 8:00 p.m. Where had the day gone? Who knows? I was a lost soul in a used body.

I was a walking vessel, and I do not know how but in the blink of an eye the kids were opening presents. Wrapping paper was all over the floor. A giant blue motorbike was being assembled in the living room. Barbies all around the floor. Stuffed animals and piles and piles of clothing. I shook my head and I went back into my room.

I grabbed Anne's phone and it was 12:45 a.m. It was Christmas Day. How had I forgotten? *Thump, thump, thump,* footsteps near the door, *knock, knock, knock* the door went. My body tensed up. The adrenaline in my body made me want to puke. The door started to open and he came in. It was Alexandre with another creepy smirk on his face.

I felt the blood rush to my head, causing me to feel dizzy. "Max, I need to talk to you." "The kids and I are going away on a trip starting tomorrow up until January third." "I know we had plenty of fun yesterday, but you cannot join us."

"It is in Switzerland, and only the best and most fanciest of people can go." "I hope you understand." He was smiling overly dramatic. Grinning ear to ear. He felt my absence and was happy to see my death, but I did my best to show him that what he had done to me had not destroyed me.

Uhh, huh, uhh, huh, I cleared my voice and in a normal and composed voice, I asked him at what time they would be back, and what time they would be leaving. "We will be gone by 9:00 a.m. tomorrow, and coming back I am not quite sure yet." "There are

200 euros under the piano's leg." "Make sure you use your money wisely."

He then stood up and came straight to my face and began to make a thrusting movement. It was disgusting. "You have the day off tomorrow, Merry Christmas." "Hahahaaha." He left the au pair room.

I was once again left with my thoughts, but this time I felt more at peace. Ten days without the Daxes was going to be freeing for my soul. I felt a tiny spark of myself coming back, and with that I laid in bed and went to bed.

The next day I awoke with less pain in my downstairs area. I was able to move more, and the bleeding had entirely stopped. That said, I still felt beyond tired, and even though it was actual Christmas day I would not do anything special.

Regrettably, I spent my entire day rotting away in bed. In fact, I did not even eat until 8:00 p.m. My mind was still out of it. I felt worthless, but thankfully towards the end of the evening I started to gain my faith back when I received a text from Anne.

"Hey Max, this is Anne." "I'm free tomorrow at 9:30 a.m for a call." "Does that work for you?" I nervously texted back, "That sounds great." She responded by saying, "Talk to you tomorrow."

Finally something was going my way. I closed my eyes, and once again I fell asleep. Unfortunately, this time the nightmares came. Everything that I had suppressed started to play back in my mind. The feels.

The gropes. The slaps. The pain. The laughter and the humiliation. I saw it all playing live in my mind. I woke up at 4:00 a.m. and I was drenched in sweat. I rushed to the restroom and I splashed cold water on my face.

Max, you have to accept this. You have to accept that you were a victim and that it is not your fault. Only that way can you start healing. Beatrice's voice played in my mind. She was right! I repeated her words out loud. It felt liberating.

I was a victim, but this victim will come out victorious. Not only will I get justice, I will also get revenge. He will die for what he did to me and countless others! Now, feeling more confident I headed back to bed.

This time the nightmares did not come, and naturally I woke up at 8:30 a.m. Nonsurprisignly, I woke up feeling quite hungry. I had not really eaten much in two days, so I hastily headed down to the kitchen.

As I made my way over to the cuisine it felt nice to see that the house was empty. The only person who was on the property that I could see was the gardener, and unlike Mathieu he kept to himself. He only did his work and did not talk to anyone. Not even a hello. I guess he knew the type of people he was working for. He was smart to stay quiet.

Buzz, buzz, buzz, my alarm went off. I must have set the alarm for 9:00 a.m last night. I turned it off as I entered the kitchen. I was ready to eat anything, and the first thing that caught my eye was a buttery croissant. I quickly gobbled it up, and I followed it with a cup of orange juice.

I felt reborn. *Bring, bring, bring,* Anne's phone went. She was calling. "Hello." Hello, Anne. "Are you alone?" Yes. "Okay good, so please Max, please let me know what you think of my husband?" "I am pleading with you." Anne's voice sounded sad and scared. I took a deep breath. I was just about to ruin this woman's life.

Anne, I believe your husband is the one who killed Kaoly. "What about Alexandre?" I think he helped put the blame on me, but quite frankly my intuition tells me it was your husband. "Why?" She gasped.

He used and abused her, and she was pregnant with his child. This means he also killed his own unborn child. I heard another gasp. I waited for Anne to speak, but she didn't. Anne, are you there? I heard a whispered "yes." Shall I continue? "Yes."

He also indirectly groped Blessie, but I am sure you knew that. Anne, you are living with a sexual predator, an abuser, "a murderer." She managed to say. "You want to know something?" What? "I have suspected this for two years now."

"I never had any real concrete proof, but I have seen the way he acted." "I have overheard him in conversations, but never tangible evidence." "When Kaoly was murdered he acted real nervous around me." "He kept talking about her." "I found it all strange, and even though I had no evidence that he was involved in her murder; I still knew in my heart!"

"I mean he talked about her everyday, Max!" Anne, I don't know what to say. "Don't worry, Max, because I do, but it is best if I explain in person." "I know the Daxes are gone, so can I send my driver to come get you?"

I thought about that for a moment. Would it be safe if someone saw me getting into Anne's car from the Daxes' property? No, I had to go somewhere that wasn't close to their property. Hmmm, but where?

I thought for a while, and then I remembered a small bakery about thirty minutes away from here by foot. Anne, you may pick me up, but can you driver pick me up by the bakery in *Montigny*? I can be there in thirty minutes. "You got it." "My driver will be there in half an hour." "See you then."

This was getting real. I hung the phone up and washed my dishes. I then ran back to the au pair room and grabbed my large winter jacket that Mathieu had given me. Within two minutes of having ended the call I was out the front door, and not surprisingly I was greeted with cold arctic air slapping my unprotected face.

However, I did not mind it. In fact I welcomed the freezing wind. It helped clear my mind. Which in turn helped me enjoy my walk through the forest because I was now aware of my surroundings, and boy was everything magical.

The trees had all lost all their leaves, and there was a sense of peace. The air smelled so fresh and the shrubs around the trees had frost. I felt like I was walking through a winter wonderland.

It was all so mesmerizing that I completely lost track, *Honk, honk, honk,* FAITES-ATTENTION!" Crap. Fuck. A car swivered away, barely missing me by a few inches. I had been so distracted and in my own mind that I did not realize that I had arrived into the tiny town.

Desole! I shouted back to the driver. I felt my ears burning. That happens when I get embarrassed. Oh well, at least I made it to the town in one piece. I jokingly said as I headed to the front of the bakery where I was greeted by the wonderful smell of baked goods.

Baguettes, croissants, pain au chocolat, it all smelled wonderful and sugary. I desperately wanted something. Maybe I should go inside and, "Are you Monsieur Max?" Ah! I turned around startled. A woman dressed in fancy clothing stared at me.

Who are you? I asked. "I am Anne's driver." "I am sorry for having frightened you." "Are you ready to go?" I nodded yes, and followed the driver to the *Peugeot* car parked at the side of the bakery.

I was kind of embarrassed. I guess I didn't think it would be a woman driver. Stupid of me, but that just means I have to become more open minded than what I thought I already was, and that was okay with me.

"You may get in sir." I smiled at the driver and got in the car. I felt a little nervous going inside because the windows were super tinted, so I could not see much. On top of that the carpet, seats and interior of the vehicle were pitch dark, so my visibility was nearly at a zero.

I had to feel around for the seatbelt. Thankfully I managed to buckle myself in right as the car started to move, and then out of nowhere the lights in the back of the car turned on. Woah, I said. "Don't be alarmed, this vehicle was designed for privacy."

"It is impossible to see inside it without a light, but thankfully the light allows you to see the outside." Ah I get it, I told the driver. She smiled at me, and I turned my head towards the window.

We were heading back into the forest, but to the east of where the Daxes lived. We drove in silence for about ten minutes and then we came upon a gated compound that had a very similar layout to the Daxes' countryside home.

In fact, it almost looked identical to their property. It was probably designed by the same person. "We are here," the driver said. She slowly pulled up to the large mansion and parked the car. She then quickly got out and opened my door.

I felt bad, but I did not want to interrupt or change her duties. Thank you for opening my door, I told her. "De rien," she responded as I saw Anne coming my way. "Max, it is my pleasure that you are here."

"Come right this way." She gestured for me to follow her back into her home, so I followed her on her green lushful pathway. "Welcome to my place." She opened the door to her house, and as I entered her mansion I immediately noticed that it felt joyful. It did not feel strange or off putting like the Daxes' home.

Here the walls were a colorful light green. There were flowers in every corner. There weren't any frames, and as we walked into the living room I could see how bright the furniture was. It made me feel at ease. "Please take a seat, Max." "Would you care for anything to eat?"

I nodded my head no. "Okay, so let's get started." "Tell me once more, but in detail everything you know about my husband Jacque." Are you sure you want all the details, Anne? "Yes." Okay, but please, I ask for you to not tell anyone that it is me who is telling you. "I promise."

I looked her straight in the eyes, and I told her everything. I told her how Jacque used and abused Kaoly. I told her why I thought he killed her, and shockingly enough as I was telling her all of this she never once flinched.

She kept a straight face. She had a determined look on her mug, and when I was done with it all, she said one sentence that sent shivers down my spine. "I am going to kill him tonight."

Chapter 29
THE URN

I looked at her, and I surprised myself. I didn't try to talk her out of it. I just stared at her and said, "okay." "He has been doing this for quite some time Max." "It is one thing to cheat on me viciously, but to take someone's life?" "To kill someone so innocent, and to kill their own child is diabolic."

"That is unforgivable, and he must be stopped." "He fooled me enough with his kindness, but he is like Alexandre." "Filled with power and a need for control." I did not even bother to ask her how she knew that about Alexandre. It was obvious. He was an obnoxious man.

"Max, I was a fool to ever trust him." "He knew exactly what to say to make me feel good, but you know what?" What, Anne? "He never saw me as an equal." "I was always the poor little girl he helped save." "That is what he liked about me." "He liked the fact that he saved me from a life of hardship."

I was hearing Anne speak, but her shaking hands and quivering lips were making it hard to keep focus. She was visibly hurt. "Did you know that I grew up dirt poor?" I shook my head no. I was surprised

I assumed that she was born into a rich family. "I grew up kind of like you." "I worked hard and got into *La Sorbonne University* here in Paris." "I met Jacque there."

"He was one of the administrators of a scholarship to help the poor that I got." "He became interested in my life, but now I see it was all a lie." "He wanted to be seen as the hero who saved the poor dumb girl, but in reality it was I who gave him a lot of his business ideas."

"Of course I was never credited." "He always told me, "Oh this idea won't be taken seriously because of where you come from, so let me say that it was mine." "It hurt at first but I trusted him so much, but now I see how wrong I had been."

"My veil has been completely lifted." "I see the manipulator, user, stealer, cheater, murderer that he is." "I want to personally stop him." "If I don't, I know I will be an accomplice to every wrong he has done to women."

"Seeing what he did to Kaoly, and how he helped destroy your life, has struck a chord with me." "Enough is enough, and there is only one way out." "He has to be killed." "That is the only way to stop him because with all the power he has he will keep buying himself out of trouble."

I looked at Anne, she had a serious stare. She was right. The only way that these monsters could be stopped was by killing them. They would always invade the law. "It is good that you have your evidence because that will help clear your name, Max, but that won't stop them from not getting in trouble."

"Do you understand what I mean?" Yes, Anne, I understand, and you want to know something? "What?" I will not judge you. If you do this, you are saving the lives of countless women. Anne stood up and came to me. She hugged me.

"Thank you, Max." "Having this conversation with you has reaffirmed my decision." "Unfortunately, this is the only way." How will you do it, Anne? I shocked myself at how easy I was talking about someone being murdered. I guess seeing so much darkness changes a person.

"Simple, with poison." "Jacque is in awful shape." "I have something that will cause a heart attack and that cannot be traced in autopsies." "I am sure no one will suspect anything." More tears rolled down her cheeks. I felt awful for her.

Anne, why do you trust me? I mean you don't even know me, so why? "I was once you, Max." "I come from a poor immigrant family." "My parents are from a small village in Uruguay." What, really, so you speak Spanish? "Si." I couldn't believe it. Anne was Latina! "I came to France to study, and I never left."

"I help my family as much as I can." "I was the different one like you, Max." "I may not know you, but I see myself in you, so that is enough proof for me to trust you." I felt my eyes get teary. She was reminding me of Beatrice.

"What is wrong?" The Daxes also killed their own neighbor in Paris, and their new au pair. Anne looked at me with sympathetic eyes, and then she reached for her purse. She pulled out a black cellphone. It was some sort of android phone.

"This is going to be your new phone." "The other one won't work anymore." I handed her the original phone back. "Thank you." "Now with this new phone you'll be able to calmly browse the net and reach me with just a call."

She handed me the phone, and looked straight into my eyes. "I will get you out of here one way or another." "Do not worry." "Also, it is not your fault that I will kill my husband." "It is something that I must do." "He will never get the punishment he deserves if I do not do it myself."

I really didn't know what to say, but I bowed my head slightly and said, "Yes, you are right." "Max, I will send you a text to this new phone when it is finished." "I will more than likely not text you until I have him cremated." My body got chills throughout itself.

We were talking about taking the life of someone. This wasn't table talk. This was real life. Killing someone, and ending who they are and what they are is dark. It is scary. It is the thing that nightmares are made from, yet I was looking forward to it. "I estimate that I will reach out to you within two to three days." I will be waiting.

"Lastly, if it wasn't clear already, I want you to know that I will get you out of here, and you will see your family again." "Trust me." I trust you, Anne. "Okay, now that we have that out of the way, what if we eat something?" Yes, please. "What would you like?" How about a grilled cheese sandwich?

"You got it." Anne called the cook in her house and ordered us a grilled cheese sandwich. I ended up eating two of them with a giant cup of chocolate milk, and for dessert I had a big chunky chocolate chip cookie.

My stomach was happy, so I was happy. "We will stay in touch." "See you soon, Max." I hugged Anne and her driver took me back to the bakery where I was picked up.

On my way back to the Daxes' home I walked slower through the forest. I needed to distract my mind from all the talk of murders, so instead I decided to focus on the life around me.

From the way the tree branches moved in the cold winter air to seeing squirrels carry their acorns in their mouth.

It was all beautiful. Sadly I could not truly enjoy it, and I would never truly enjoy the wonders of life until I was free. That much I knew, but there was one thing that I could rejoice in at that moment, and that was being lazy.

The Daxes weren't home, so there was no stopping me from doing just that. In fact, wasting no more time, I went straight to the au pair room, and I spent the entire day lounging around doing nothing.

It was blissful, and I actually fell asleep that night rather relaxed. However, I was awoken at the crack of dawn by a call from Alexandre. He wanted me to mop all of the floors in the house. He also wanted me to fold all of the kids' laundry. He even asked me to mow the lawn.

"I let the gardener have a week of vacation because I want to keep you busy." "I hope that isn't a bad thing?" Of course not, Monsieur Alexandre. I responded, barely containing my rage.

"Thank you Max, and when I come back we will also need to talk about the kids' new school schedule for the new semester." Okay, that sounds perfect. Anything else, Monsieur Alexandre?

"Yes." "The night that I come back we will have another special night." "So make sure you are freshly showered." "Bye." He hung up the call. I dropped to my knees and just cried again.

He wanted to use me like he had before. The first time had nearly broken me. I could not let it happen again, but what choice did I have? It was either that or have my family killed, and quite possibly have myself thrown in jail.

What do I do now? I yelled in frustration. I felt like I was wallowing in a black hole once more, but then I heard her voice. *Keep your mind strong*. Beatrice's voice filled my mind, and it brought me peace.

I knew it was probably my own mind making up her voice, but it was enough to get me out of my black hole. Hearing her so confident in me gave me the strength to stand up and start my chores. Which weirdly enough helped distract my mind, and before I knew it another day had passed again.

Which unfortunately meant, a day closer to the Daxes returning from Switzerland. A day closer to my hell. Fuck man. The tears started once more, and I ended up crying myself to sleep again. Woefully, the nightmares came strong that night, and when I woke up the next day my heart was racing.

Calm down, Max. I told myself as I reached for Anne's phone to check the time. *Two missed calls*. Oh shit! Anne had called me. My heart started to race even more. I felt the adrenaline begin to pump through my body.

I had to call her back. I nervously hit redial. I patiently waited for six rings. I was about to hang up, but then she answered. "Max, go to the bakery now, and wait for me there." Anne hung up the call.

I hastily brushed my teeth and got dressed. I was out of the house and in the forest walking within five minutes of the call, and this time I did not sight see. Instead I practically ran all the way to the bakery. Which was probably a good thing because Anne's driver was already waiting for me.

I smiled at her, and she signaled me to get into the car. I got in the car and we drove off immediately without her acknowledging my presence. Uh oh, something definitely was up. I started to get extremely nervous, and when we went straight onto the highway instead of east to the forest I knew that I needed answers now.

What's going on? I asked the driver. Why are we heading this way? The driver simply said, "I am not sure, sir." "I was simply given the instructions to drive to this area." Shit, had Anne been caught? Was I being taken away to get killed in the middle of nowhere?

No, it couldn't be. I had to relax, so I tried to distract my mind with the scenery that we were passing. Regrettably, we passed nothing but empty fields for what felt like such a long time. Nonetheless, it did help distract my mind, and finally after seeing nothing but open road for over half an hour, we exited the freeway. We then entered into a forested area.

This forested area had trees that naturally formed a canopy, so it was dark. The driver turned the lights on, and I could barely make out the dirt paved road. I felt like I was going through a haunted forest like in the movies.

My body was trembling. Should I get out and just run? I thought to myself. No, it will be okay. This had to be just some secret hideout. Graciously, as soon as that thought came into my mind the driver confirmed it. "Anne is in the cabin." "She just texted me." What cabin? "The one right over there."

I turned my head and saw the small wooden cabin. It looked like the perfect place to keep someone that was being held hostage. It had no windows, and it had a massive wooden door. I got chills all through my body as the driver parked the car.

"We are here," she said. The driver got out and opened my door, and just as she was doing that Anne stepped out. She was dressed in black. She wore a long dress and had a veil over her face. She had done it. I knew it.

Without her even telling me, I knew it. She had killed Jacque. My knees felt wobbly. Jacque deserved everything that Anne did to him, but at the end of the day he was a human being. Oh well I thought, as I shakingly walked over to Anne.

She came over and wrapped her arm around my waist. We carefully walked back to her cabin. She then gestured to her driver, and the driver got in the car and drove off.

Once the driver was gone Anne closed the door and removed her veil. Her eyes were swollen from tears. Her face looked puffy, but there was a peace in her that was radiating. She looked rested. She looked at ease.

"Sorry, for bringing you here, but this is my secret safe haven." "I needed to be alone because of what I did to Jacque, Max." Anne, "Don't say anything, Max." "I don't want to talk about that now."

Then what do you want to talk about? "You," me? "Yes." "Max, I got your family released." Are you serious, Anne? "Oui." I couldn't believe it. My hands started trembling, and I dropped to my knees from happiness.

How did you do it, Anne? "I sent someone over to bribe Alexandre's people of course, and to top things off I have people protecting your family now." Anne, you truly are an angel, and I know that you said that you didn't want to talk about Jacque, but I have to say something since you're visibly feeling guilt.

"What do you want to tell me then?" None of this is your fault. You are a brave woman, and you did what you had to do in order to protect other innocent women and men. You are a hero. Tears started to run down her eyes. She began to breathe heavily, and then she started to sob uncontrollably. I reached out and hugged her close to me.

I hugged her until she calmed down. "Thank you, Max, but I still have to tell you more about your loved ones." Please go on. "Your family is being moved, and you do not have to worry about Alexandre finding them anymore." Are you sure Anne? "Yes, I hired the best of the best." Does that mean that I can finally leave and report that wicked Dax?

"Unfortunately, no." "Firstly the charges against your name have not been dropped." "Secondly, I have found out that Alexandre has been bribing quite a few major immigration officers and police officers within the *European Union*." "If you step anywhere to seek asylum you will be arrested." "Your passport is flagged."

Why, why does this never end? I yelled in frustration. I felt my face getting flushed. "Here is the good thing, Max." This time next week you will have a new passport out of here." How? "I have contacted a person to get you a passport, but they need at least a week's time."

"It will all be okay." Are you sure, Anne? "Yes." "Plus, once you are back home you can present your evidence to the authorities, and I will help you." "Alexandre is much less powerful over there."

Without even thinking I ran over to Anne and I gave her another hug. Thank you, Anne. "No, thank you." "Also, do you want to speak to your family?" "They have a special phone they can use for at least the next week." "Do you want me to call them?" Yes, please.

Anne pulled her phone out and dialed a number. The phone began to ring. It then switched to the international ringing. Ten seconds later my sister answered. "Hello?" Anne turned the camera around to me I suppose because the next thing I heard was my sister screaming in joy. "Brother, we thought you were dead!" "I miss you so much brother."

"We heard so many awful things about you." I started to sob. It felt good talking to my family. "Let me get our mom on the phone, Max." "Son, you are alive." "My baby is alive." My mom was ecstatic, and so was I, but even with my excitement I had to warn them all again.

Mom, you must make sure you all are hiding! He is still going to come after all of you. "Do not worry hijo, we are on our way to a special hideout." "We don't even know where it is yet, but just know Anne has everything taken care of." "We will be safe." "Focus on getting yourself back home."

Mom I will, and hopefully I will be back in no more than a week or two. The connection broke. "They must be entering a secluded zone now." I gave Anne her phone back. Thank you again for everything you have done for me. "It is my pleasure."

No, I am serious, Anne. You are my savior, and I want you to be real with me. How are you really doing? You do not have to hold anything in from me. Please, I truly want to know what you are feeling.

Anne stared at me for an entire minute without saying anything, and then she broke down again. She started to cry hysterically. "I killed him, Max." "I told him that I would make him a special dinner, and I mixed in the poison with his favorite chocolate cake." "He died one hour after I made it for him." What happened next, Anne?

"I called the ambulance and they tried to revive him but they couldn't." "They figured it was a heart attack, so they did not pursue it any further." "I had him cremated the next day, and today was the service."

"His urn is over there." I glanced at where she was pointing to. I grabbed her arm and we walked toward the urn. I handed her the urn, and I opened the front door. We both stepped out of the cabin and walked straight into the dark forest.

"I will let him go here." Anne opened the urn and in the cool winter breeze she let Jacque go. She stopped crying. "I'm free, Max." Yes you are, Anne, but what will you do with the urn? "This," she tossed the urn against a tree. It broke into a thousand pieces.

Chapter 30
THE LAST STRAW

"**I** feel liberated, Max." "Thank you for helping me let him go." No problem. We silently walked back to the cabin and sat at the kitchen table. "Max, there is also something else I wanted to tell you." What is it Anne?

"I am afraid that Alexandre Dax will be coming home early from vacation." "He had a multimillion dollar deal with my husband, and he must take care of it now that Jacque is gone." Are the kids coming with him? "No, I believe they are staying with their aunt Sophie." My insides turned, and I simply nodded "okay" to Anne.

"Max, I know he is a terrible man, but is there more to this?" "Has he done something to you physically?" I did not know what to say. I felt embarrassed. I felt stupid. I felt ashamed. Anne was staring at me with worrisome eyes.

I nodded yes. Anne's face got pale, but she did not say anything. She knew that if she did I would have lost it. Instead she simply nodded her head slowly. We both stayed quiet for a minute and then she spoke up.

"You know Max, you have something special in you." What do you mean, Anne? "I mean you light up a room with your presence." "You have something that makes others stare at you."

I knew what Anne was doing. She was trying to make me feel better, and to be frank she was. I needed the compliments. When you have been degraded to the size of a penny for the last few months compliments help you regain your confidence.

Thank you Anne, I really appreciate that, and I needed it. She smiled. "Look at this." She gestured to me to follow her into another room. I did, and I was surprised. The room was filled with candy and chocolates from all around the world.

"I have a major sweet tooth, and I love collecting candy and chocolate when I travel." "Help yourself out." I grabbed some *Milka chocolate*, and some *Kinder bars*. It was all delicious. My sweet tooth was happy.

"Let's go out back." I followed her, and I was surprised when I saw the large heated pool in her backyard. A heated pool in the middle of a forest. That was amazing. Can I get in Anne? "Go right ahead." "I'll be inside watching a movie." Without thinking twice I removed my clothes and dove into the warm pool in just my underwear.

I swam until I couldn't feel myself anymore. I swam until I could not remember who I was, or where I was. I swam until my entire body looked like a raisin. At last, I swam until Anne came over to get me out.

Apparently I had been swimming for over four hours. She came with a set of fresh warm clothes for me, and a towel. "I have talked to

Alexandre, and he is coming back tomorrow evening." "Would you like to stay the night here?"

That would be amazing, Anne! I truly have had such a relaxing time with you today, that a full night would be the cherry on the top. Anne's eyes got bright. I could tell she felt happy to be needed. Truth is, she probably thought I agreed to stay with her to keep her company, but the reality was, I needed her more than she needed me.

"Well, come have some dinner, but first go rinse off please," she said jokingly. Okay, okay. I told her with a smile. I quickly took a nice warm shower, and then I put on the fuzzy warm sweat suit that Anne had gotten me. I felt so warm and cozy.

"I ordered pizza." "I hope that is alright with you." It is more than alright I said, while drooling at the freshly baked pizza. I felt like I was momentarily in heaven. Anne, you are such an angel. You shouldn't have gone to all this trouble for me.

"Nonsense." "It is my pleasure." "Plus if I am being honest, helping you has eased my mind from what I went through with Jacque." I slowly nodded my head in understandment. "Well, anyway, did you enjoy your time here?" Yes, Anne, and I only have you to thank. "I am glad." "Also, Max." Yes? "I have some good news." What is it? I nervously asked.

"Your passport will be ready by tomorrow morning." Does that mean I will be able to go home soon? "That is exactly what it means, Max." "In fact, we can decide tomorrow when and how you'll leave." Anne, you are truly fantastic, I told her as tears of joy ran down my cheeks. "You are welcome, Max." "Now go get some rest." "You have a big day tomorrow."

I walked over to the guest room, and went to bed. The next day I was awakened by Anne. She was standing over me with a blue American Passport. "Here you go." With trembling hands I took the blue passport.

I carefully opened it up. There was a picture of me with blond hair. It had to be AI generated because I never took a picture with this hair color, but gosh it looked so real. How were they able to get it so accurate I pondered as I scanned my passport some more.

My name on it read, Francisco. "Well, Francisco, here is your passport," Anne said while giggling. Will this really work, Anne? "Just like any real passport." "Don't think about it being fake, it is as real as they get." I trust you, Anne. "Good." "Also, Max, I want you to take this duffle bag with you.

I stared at the little black sports bag that Anne was handing me. "Do not open it until tonight, okay?" Okay, I responded skeptically as I took the heavy bag. I was suspicious about what it contained. Moreover, I was curious as to why Anne didn't want me to open it until tonight, but I would respect her wishes and not open it until the evening.

"Max, sorry to rush you, but we must go now, so I can drop you off." "I'll give you a few minutes to change." Anne left the room, and I hastily changed. We were both out of the door and in her car within five minutes. Shortly after we were back in front of the bakery.

"Max, starting tomorrow you can call me at any time and I will book your flight out of here." "Try to stay strong for one more day, okay?" "The passport man said it will take a full 24 hours to be in the system, so if at this time tomorrow you want to call me to book your flight I will."

I gave Anne a tight hug, and then I exited her car. She waved goodbye, and with my black duffle in hand I headed back to the Daxes' property. It was 1:00 p.m, by the time I reached my au pair room.

I felt relieved that Alexandre was not home yet. Maybe this was the perfect time to check what the bag contained. I know Anne told me to not look inside it until it was night time, but curiosity got the best of me. I gently unzipped the bag, and I stuck my hand inside. I felt around it, and there was mainly clothes.

Two pairs of sweaters, and two pairs of jeans. A few pairs of underwear and some socks, but right at the bottom of the clothes was a small bottle. It looked like the shampoo bottles that you buy in travel kits. The difference was that this bottle was made of glass. Moreover, it contained a clear liquid inside.

I cautiously picked up the bottle, and inspected it. Right at the bottom of it was a picture of a skeleton. Oh my gosh. My body got goosebumps all around. I knew exactly what this was. This was poison.

Anne had packed poison for me, but why? I did not tell her to give me any. Why would she do that? I pondered, but then it hit me. In this bottle was the poison that I could use to kill Alexandre Dax.

I instinctively tossed the bottle onto the bed. It freaked me out. I did not want to become a murderer. I know that Anne had done it with a good intention, but I could not do that. No, not me. Take a deep breath, I told myself. Calm down. Just put the venomous bottle away. I grabbed it, and slipped it underneath my bed.

Instantly I started to feel better, but that was short lived when the door of my au pair room was opened. "Oh hi Max." "Just the person that I was looking for." Fuck. My fucken luck! "I feel like I haven't seen you in weeks." Alexandre was smiling from ear to ear. I was not. "How are you?"

"What are you up to?" I was just about to get something to eat. I nervously responded. "Oh we can have lunch together, but first I need you to do something for me." I felt like I would vomit right then and there. He looked me up and down and got a demonic look on his face.

My body tensed up. Please, please do not let it happen again, I prayed. "Why don't you go ahead and shower to get relaxed." My legs became cement. This could not be happening again. It just couldn't. Anything, but this!

"Max, did you hear me?" Ugh, yeah I did, but how about we just have lunch now? I quietly responded. "Let's not play any games, Max." "Go shower now, or else." I quietly nodded, and with all the strength that I could muster I made my way to the restroom. I closed the door behind me, and I hopped in the shower.

I don't even remember if I got in with clothes or not, but everything that happened next was a blur. I awoke in the middle of the restroom. I felt warm blood on my legs. I was naked, lying on my stomach. Everything was hurting again, but I slowly managed to get up.

I carefully walked to the mirror. I stared at my reflection, but there was a monster staring back at me instead. I cringed at the image, and out of pure instinct I punched the mirror. It shattered, and my hand bled. I didn't care. I robotically went back to the shower to wash my blood away.

However, this time around I didn't even scrub myself. I simply let the boiling water burn my wounds away. I was completely defeated, and all I could do now was head to bed. Which is what I did.

I awoke up the next day at 4 a.m. feeling completely disconnected with my body. I couldn't live like this anymore. It had to be done. I grabbed the poison from underneath my bed, and I walked over to the kitchen. I took the bottle of venom out and poured it into the espresso machine water, and I waited. I waited for three more hours and then he came.

"Good morning Max." "Are you waiting to have breakfast with me?" "Hahaha." "Sorry to tell you, but I do not have time." "I have to get on the road again." "I figured everything out with Jacque, so I can go back to vacation."

I watched him as he poured his espresso into the mug. I watched as he drank not one, but two cups of espresso. I glared at him as he took his car out of the compound, and then as fast as I could I grabbed Anne's phone and told her it was time.

"I'll be there in forty-five minutes." I quickly went up stairs and dumped all my evidence that I had acquired into the black duffle that Anne had given me. I then slowly made my way to the small bakery. Anne was waiting for me by the time I got there. Her driver had not come this time.

"When did you give it to him?" Wait, how did you know? Anne gave me a look, so I told her. Exactly an hour ago. "Okay, we have at least a good fifteen minutes before the effects go in." "This isn't your fault by the way." "You did what you had to do to survive, and prevent others from suffering the same fate." I nodded my head at Anne.

"Do you have your passport with you?" I pulled my fake passport from my pocket, and opened it. Francisco Mendez. My birth year was off by two years. They had aged me up. My address was a small town in Utah. "Perfect."

"Say bye to your hell hole Max." I turned my head around and stared at the disappearing forest. We were on our way to the airport. I was going to be flying out of *Orly International Airport*.

How much do I owe you for the ticket? "Nothing." "This ticket is a gift from me to you." Anne, I have to pay you back. "No, this is my parting gift to you." Thank you Anne. I truly mean it.

"You are welcome." It's been over an hour and a half." "He is gone." "Do not worry about him anymore." "Your nightmare is over." "Once you get home we will figure out the proper way to clear your name." Anne, I don't know what to say.

"Don't say anything, but promise me that when your name is clear you will come back to Paris to visit me." I promise one thousand times. She smiled at me, and I shut up my eyes.

"Look right at me!" "Get on your knees." "Cry all you want." "You belong to me!" Please, stop it hurts. It really hurts. "I'll show you what real pain is."

I felt his massive hand shove my head on the floor. The pressure was unbearable. "Open your legs." I felt bruises all over myself. I felt spit hit my body. Help! I yelled. "Max, Max!" "Wake up, you are having a nightmare!" I glanced over at panicking Anne. She was still driving. I must have fallen asleep.

I am sorry Anne. "Don't." "You have suffered a lot." "Just try to relax now. Okay, I replied as I looked at my wrists. They were bruised from the back. Big purple bruises. I wondered how many more bruises I had over my body. I caught Anne staring at them.

She changed the subject. "What is the first thing that you'll eat when you get back home, Max?" Was this really happening? Was I finally going home? It seemed so unreal. "Max, did you hear me?" Yes, I am so sorry, Anne. I am very emotional.

Anne reached her hand and rubbed my shoulder. "Don't apologize." "I am here for you, and will always be." "Now what is the first thing you'll have when you get home?" You promise to not laugh? "Of course." I want to have a glass of chocolate milk with a homemade chocolate chip cookie, but a giant cookie.

I looked at Anne, she was doing her best not to laugh. "Well, don't they have that in France?" "They do, Anne, but French milk is not the same as in America. She lost control and started laughing. "Hmmm, well I guess I never knew that." I started laughing with her, but then she got serious.

"We are only five minutes away from the airport, and you are already checked in." Do I need to check in my duffle? "No, that is a carry-on, so you can go with it." Okay, good. "Oh, and before I forget, here you go."

She handed me my boarding pass, and one thousand euros. Anne, I can't take this money. I did not work for it. "Oh, Max, this money is from the account that Jacque and Alexandre had together." "Don't think I am giving you free money." "You earned this money as an au pair, and more." I smiled at Anne.

She was right. This was my money. It felt good to actually be paid for everything that I had done. "We are here." Anne took the exit to *Orly International* and entered the departure section.

I am so nervous! "It is good to be nervous, but you will be fine." She said, as she parked on the side of the parking space for five minute drop offs. "I wish I could go in with you, but I don't want anyone to see me go in." "I hope that is okay."

Don't worry Anne. I will text you once I get through customs, and of course once I board and land. She looked at me with teary eyes, and gave me a tight hug. "Bye, Max." "Be careful, and congratulations on getting your life back."

Chapter 31

THE FIRST CLASS TICKET TO THE DAMAGED MIND

I got out of the car, and waved goodbye to Anne. She left the departure area and I waited until I could not see her car anymore. I then slowly walked to the airport. It was a bittersweet moment. I was happy to be going home, but I felt numb and depressed.

I had come to France filled with hope and curiosity, but I was leaving France depressed, used, and as a murderer. How sad I thought, but I had to keep going, and with that I wiped a tear from my eye and I entered the airport.

It was time to get my life back, but where do I go now? I looked at the boarding pass that Anne had given me. I had to make it to *gate 45*. Which was going to be a challenge because the airport was packed with people traveling for the holidays. Well here goes nothing.

I followed the signs for the gates, and after fifteen minutes of bumping into people I eventually found them. But shit, I had forgotten that in order to even access the gates I had to go through customs.

My heart started to beat like a hummingbird's wings, so I took a deep breath and made my way to the queue. After waiting in line nervously for thirty minutes it was my turn. *Passport please.*

I shakingly handed my passport to the border agent. The man skimmed through the passport and compared my picture to me. He then looked at the boarding pass. My heart was thumping so loud I thought he would surely be able to hear it. He took another look at me and then handed back my passport. *Have a nice flight sir.*

I grabbed my passport and let out a sigh of relief as I discreetly wiped the sweat from my forehead. I was actually going home! I was so happy that I skipped all the way to my gate. Once I was there I moved away from the crowd of people, and I quickly texted Anne that my passport had worked. She responded within seconds. "I knew it would!"

Boarding all families with small children, people with disabilities and any veterans. I checked my ticket to see what zone I was in. *Zone 1*, written in bright red letters. Wait, what? *Zone 1*, first class? This has to be a mistake.

I rapidly texted Anne. "Anne, did you get me a first class ticket?" I stared at my phone until she texted back. "Yes, I got you a first class seat." "I don't want to hear any complaining on how you don't deserve this."

"Please enjoy it, Max." Once again I was emotional, and I texted her, "From the bottom of my heart thank you, Anne, and see you in eleven hours."

Boarding zone 1. I made my way to the agent. She scanned my ticket and motioned me to the plane. I walked down the aisle till I reached it. *Bonjour monsieur, what is your seat number?* I handed my boarding pass to the flight attendant. *Oh right this way monsieur.*

He led me down to first class. *Here is your seat, monsieur. Anything you need you can press this button and we will come right away to help you.* Excuse me sir, but is this entire seat for me? The flight attendant looked at me and giggled.

First time flying first class? Yes, I said. *Yes, monsieur, this is all for you. You even have these privacy curtains that you can close, but only once we are in the air.* I could not believe it. Anne must have spent a fortune on this! I felt bad, but also amazing at the same time.

First class was everything that I had dreamed of. The seat was so spacious and it reclined all the way back into a bed. I even had my own flat screen 20 inch TV. Plus, I could order all the food I wanted.

Wow. What a break. I was smiling from ear to ear that I didn't even notice that the plane was in the air until the flight attendants came by offering drinks. *What would you like to drink, monsieur?*

Do you have chocolate milk? *We have Nesquik, is that okay?* I smiled at the flight attendant, and said, that is more than okay. He handed me the milk, and I turned my screen on and searched for a movie.

There was so much to choose from, and I was so into my search that I had not noticed the person who was standing behind me until they placed their hand on my shoulder.

I don't know how, but I knew. I knew that touch. My body froze. My heart stopped. My stomach dropped to the floor. I turned my head, and standing behind me was Alexandre Dax.

My face felt hot as all the blood rushed to it. The adrenaline flowing through my body made it almost impossible to stay seated. "Well, look who we have here?" "Is it possible that we are both taking a short vacation to California?"

He began laughing. "What no hello?" "Are you wondering, how I am not dead, Max?" I felt light headed. I tried to fight it as I felt my head hit the TV screen. Dark it all went dark.

Monsieur, monsieur, are you okay? Wake up, monsieur. My eyes flickered open. Alexandre! I yelled. *Who is that, monsieur?* The flight attendant looked at me with confusion. Huh? Wasn't there a man just standing behind me? *There are only six people in first class today, and you are the only man.*

My body went cold. What was going on with me? The flight attendant looked at me with concerned eyes, so I just made an excuse that I had had a nightmare. Thankfully, he believed me and left, but I was left terrified.

Had I really hallucinated Alexandre? I had to find out. I unbuckled my seat belt and I went down the airplane. I looked through every restroom on the plane, and I stared at every person on the plane, and there was no Alexandre.

Wow, I really had. I was probably more damaged than I could imagine, but at least he wasn't on this flight. Feeling a tad better I headed back to my seat and for the next few hours I watched a few movies while taking small cat naps here and there.

Eventually we landed, and the next couple of days were almost a complete blur for me. All I know is that I had to stay on my own in an *Airbnb* that Anne had rented until she was finally able to secure a driver to take me to my family's hiding place.

Graciously, that happened to be on New Year's day. The driver picked me up early in the morning, and after a long seven hour car ride I reached my family's hiding place. I thanked the driver as I quietly stepped out of the car. I could barely contain my happiness.

I eagerly walked down the path to the front door of the house where my family was staying. I could hear the Spanish music being played. The lights were on. There was definitely a New Year's Day party going on. I couldn't help but smile, and I opened the door.

Blood, all over the floor. My parents had open bullet wounds to their chest. My sister and brother were covered in blood. "Help us, Max," they cried. "He is here." Who? I yelled. "Alexandre," they both said. *Bam, bam, bam* they were both shot in the back of the head. They dropped down like statues.

"I was wondering when you would get here, Max." A victorious grin was plastered all over his ugly face. This can't be happening! "Oh, but it can." "I told you on the plane that we would have a California vacation." "Now, if you don't want your nephew shot in the face you will come with me."

I threw up and I fell to my knees. "Maxi, Maxi." I stared at my mother, she had a look of horror on her face. On her clean face. There was no blood. In fact she was elegantly dressed like she always does on New Year's Day.

Oh shit. I had hallucinated again. "What's going on, Maxi?" My mother asked again. My entire family came over to see what was going on. I quickly got up. I couldn't let them know how damaged I was because not even I knew, so instead I played it off.

I'm so sorry guys. I have had food poisoning since yesterday. Where is the restroom so I can clean up? My mom led me into the restroom. "Are you sure you're okay, Maxi?" Yes, mom. I faked a smile for her.

"Alright, but don't worry about coming back out until you feel better, okay?" "I'll clean up the mess too." Are you sure, mom? "Yes, Maxi." "Now wash up." I will. I entered the restroom and once more I stared at myself in the mirror.

My brown roots were showing from my dyed blond hair. I was still an unhealthy pale, but I was me again, except for one thing. The shine in my eyes was gone. The shine that Mathieu had said the Daxes wanted from me, but couldn't take. Unfortunately, he had been wrong.

Not only had it been stolen from me, but I was broken, deeply broken. I couldn't hide the truth from myself anymore. I needed help to heal the scars that the Daxes had cut into me. *The first step in healing is admitting that you need the help.* I felt Beatrice's and Mathieu's voices flow through me.

They were right, and I was up for the difficult journey that lay ahead.